BREAKAWAY

MICHELLE DIENER

ECLIPSE

ISBN: 978-0-6483135-4-0

❀ Created with Vellum

CHAPTER 1

LEO GAUDIER WALKED A DANGEROUS PATH.

Sofie didn't pretend that wasn't part of what attracted her to him in the first place. She was all for sticking it to the Core Corporations. All for it with bells on.

And it didn't hurt that she really liked the look of him.

There'd been a little catch in her heart, a little hitch in her breath. A trembling, like fear or excitement. She'd never been affected like that before.

And it didn't hurt that he'd been interested right back.

Well, generally they all seemed interested, all did a little chasing, but she wasn't into hooking up with some guy in an Upper Reaches bar.

That wasn't in her plan. She was just there to eavesdrop on loose-lipped Cores employees.

Until Leo.

Leo Gaudier was the first one she hadn't actively run from too fast for him to catch her.

She'd run a little, but it was more out of habit.

He'd been just tenacious enough, but not obnoxious with it.

If she'd said no, it would have been no.

No matter how fast he made her heart beat, she'd never have taken the next step with him if it had been any other way.

Now she sat watching him on their third dinner out together with almost embarrassing stars in her eyes, even though the dangerous stuff he was into had just reared its head and interrupted their evening.

Because it was part of the package, and she'd already acknowledged she liked everything she saw when it came to Leo, she didn't show so much as a flicker of displeasure when his comm sounded and he'd stood and excused himself from the table.

It wasn't as if she was all that unencumbered herself. He just didn't know it yet.

They were halfway through an excellent dinner at the best restaurant in Felicitos, the ground-tethered way station on the planet Garmen, otherwise known as Breakaway 1.

The views were spectacular.

From where she sat, up against the window, Sofie could see the curve of Garmen below, the blue of the ocean glimmering far in the distance as the last of the evening light touched it.

Higher up, in the levels of Felicitos that edged out beyond Garmen's atmosphere, it was harder to see the details of the green, blue and rose planet.

Prices and rents went up the lower you got, and you couldn't get any lower than The High Flyer.

She seldom saw this view. She couldn't afford it. But sometimes, like now, when she did see the aching beauty of the curve of the planet, the breath-stealing vistas, she grudgingly conceded her father's work did mean something.

Not everything--she'd never give him that. But it wasn't for nothing, either.

Sofie turned away from the sights and looked over at Leo again.

He stood at ease, hands in pockets, his back to her, talking into his comm a little distance from the other diners, in a small alcove designed specifically for privacy.

He had removed his jacket--it was hanging over the back of the chair opposite her--and he stood in a perfectly fitted shirt and trousers, quite delectable from his dark, slightly wavy hair, broad shoulders and down over long, lean legs.

Sofie lifted her glass of truly excellent wine, turning the glass this way and that to admire the almost luminous lavender hue of it, put it to her lips and took a sip. She shifted in her chair and caught the very last of the setting sun on the planet below her.

A movement caught her eye, a reflection in the glass of the window, and she tilted her head to better see what it was.

A man stepped out of the service entrance, which wasn't strange--waiters had been coming and going since they'd arrived--but there was something in the way he moved.

Years of survival, of assuming danger was all around her, snapped her spine straight.

It took an effort of will to force herself out of the fear, out of the frozen helplessness that descended for the split second it took for the man to walk from the service door to halfway across the restaurant floor.

She was getting complacent. She had things cushier now than she ever had, and it was dulling her edge, she realized. A lapse like that, a victim's paralysis, would have seen her with her throat slit and her body lying in an alleyway faster than she could snap her fingers in the old days.

But she was back to her old self now, the shock of an attack in this cocooned pocket of luxury over with.

She almost smiled at herself. Nowhere was truly safe, and she'd been lying to herself if she thought otherwise.

She moved her head a fraction, looked at the man under the sweep of her eyelashes.

He was making for Leo.

There was no rush about him, nothing to indicate he meant harm, but she never ignored her intuition.

Never.

Leo's bodyguard, who was sitting three tables away, had his eyes on his boss, not on the waiter, and Sofie knew calling out to warn Leo wouldn't work.

The assassin would just shoot that much faster.

Instead, she knocked the nearly empty bottle of lavender wine into Leo's almost full glass, then exclaimed loudly and jumped to her feet, brushing at her clothes, although she'd made sure not a drop of it landed on her pale gold evening dress.

Damned if she would ruin it.

She bent, one hand on the table for balance, as she slipped off her high-heeled gold sandal, and saw Leo had started to turn.

The assassin had, too; eyeing her for a second before dismissing her outright, and focusing back on Leo.

Leo's bodyguard, Zan, flicked his gaze in her direction, and something in the way his eyes jumped over the assassin had her radar screaming high alert.

Inside job.

No doubt about it.

She lifted her shoe and threw, aiming for the assassin's hand as it came out of his pocket with a tiny laz.

The sharp heel tip caught his fingers, and he dropped the slim weapon with a cry more of surprise than pain.

Leo was looking at her by now, eyes wide, and they widened even more when she picked up the fallen bottle of wine and threw it at his bodyguard.

By the time it had smacked Zan in the chest, Sofie saw Leo had pulled a laz of his own.

The assassin dived for his weapon and Leo shot him.

It happened fast, but Zan was still in play--she saw his arm rising up, laz in hand, aimed not at the downed assassin but at Leo.

She'd already tugged off her other shoe and she ran at the bulky guard, screaming to distract him.

He started, flinching as she came at him, shoe raised over her head, and although he got a shot off at Leo, it wasn't the head shot he'd clearly been aiming for.

Leo went down, but his hand went to his chest.

Sofie threw the shoe, then scooped up the fallen bottle of wine while Zan stood, arms raised for another shot at Leo, and swung it at his head.

Hard.

He crumpled.

For the first time, she became aware of the other diners.

Couples were looking at her with eyes wide, mouths open.

She turned away from them, picked up her shoes, which had conveniently landed near each other, and hopped into them one at a time as she headed for Leo.

"Can you stand?" She kept her voice low.

"Just about." His words were strained and his breath labored.

"You're wearing an anti-laz layer?"

He shook his head.

"Ouch." She put an arm around him and hauled him up with his cooperation.

When he got to his feet and could stand without her, she looked quickly around, picked up his comm unit which lay on the floor near the window, and then scooped up his jacket from the back of the chair and her own little bag.

A faint whine and the whiff of ozone had her turning in fright, but it was Leo, laz in hand, pointed in Zan's direction.

She didn't know if he'd killed the bodyguard or just made sure he stayed unconscious.

She didn't want to know.

The restaurant staff had disappeared the moment trouble started, something she was sure wasn't lost on a number of the patrons, but now a wild-eyed manager stumbled out of the same door as the assassin.

Sofie didn't know if he were trying to extract payment or let them know the meal had been on the house--she didn't give him a chance to say anything.

With all their belongings under one arm, she slid her other under Leo's shoulder and half-dragged, half-supported him to the door.

The manager made a sound at the back of his throat, and she sent him a hard glare, shutting him down, and then staggered out with her burdens through the lavender frosted doors.

CHAPTER 2

SOFIE ERDO WAS NOT who he thought she was.

Leo leaned against the wall of the lift, breathing through the pain, and watched her as she bent over her screen, face fierce with concentration.

He belatedly remembered this was the Lower Reaches, and she would need a code to operate the private lifts, but she obviously had one. He didn't have the energy to ask her how.

"Do you have ports?" she suddenly asked, looking up at him.

He nodded, slid a shaking hand into his pocket and handed the portable money credits over to her. She took them without a word and went back to her screen.

He tried to work out exactly what had happened back in The High Flyer.

His thoughts kept catching on her elegantly leaning over the table, one foot in the air behind her, as she reached back and took off a delicate golden shoe.

Then she'd thrown it, and all notions of delicacy had disappeared. Lethal seemed the best description to replace it.

She'd looked lethal.

The thug the Cores had sent after him hadn't expected to be hit by the sharp heel of a shoe, and Leo had almost lost the advantage she'd given him because he hadn't expected it, either.

And then there was Zan.

The bastard had been with him nearly a year.

He wondered what they'd done to get to him, but depressingly, they'd probably just offered him money.

That was the way of things on the Breakaways.

The sole reason for the two planets' existence.

Zan had been part of his security team when they foiled the last attempt to get him two weeks ago. It was why Leo trusted him to work solo tonight, but the Cores were obviously getting desperate enough to part with large amounts of money to end this stalemate.

They'd already killed two of his people this month.

Leo wondered what they'd managed to get out of them before they died.

The bodies had been dumped outside his warehouse, just to make sure he understood how much they'd suffered before they'd been murdered.

And as a warning to his other staff.

Resist talking, and you won't go easy.

He felt a sudden lightness, as if he could float upward, and wondered if it was the laz hit, or if he really was almost weightless as the lift plummeted down. It decelerated suddenly, and the lift door pivoted open.

Sofie stepped close to him, put an arm around him and took his weight.

She drew him out of the enclosed space as fast as she could without hurting him more, and that, more than anything else, quelled the tiny voice in his head that said this might be a set-up, that she might be part of the Cores' plot.

He'd tried to entice her into revealing her stance on the Cores before, and she'd kept her opinions bland and disinterested.

The woman who'd foiled an assassination attempt with two sandals and an empty bottle of wine didn't have a bland bone in her very lovely body.

He wondered how she planned to get them out.

While Leo knew the powerful owners of the Cores had originally mandated a single entry and exit point when they built their tethered way station, that had proved so impractical, they'd had to create several.

What they had planned to be a tightly controlled structure was in fact a leaky sieve. Still, if they were behind this attempt to murder him then they'd be watching all of the ways out.

Sofie gently pushed him up against a cold stone wall and then tap tap tapped away on her heels, taking her warmth and the truly lovely scent he couldn't get enough of with her.

The stone told him they'd gone deep. Underground deep.

Every part of the way station that sat above the ground was tough, rigid and as light as the engineers could get it. It was only the underground levels that would include stone.

He'd never come down this far.

He didn't even realize the lifts reached this low and that anyone other than authorized personnel would have the codes to get to it.

One thing he was sure about, Sofie Erdo was not authorized personnel.

There was a faint squeak of rubber wheels on a smooth surface, and then Sofie was back.

He forced eyes he hadn't realized were closed back open, and saw she'd gone to fetch a tiny electro-magnetic cart.

"In you go." She got an arm around him, and he staggered toward it. As she lowered him down, she lost her grip on him, and he fell awkwardly into the passenger seat.

Pain overwhelmed him.

When he struggled back to consciousness, he guessed only a moment or two had passed because they were still in the same spot, but Sofie was stroking his face.

There were tears on her cheeks, which made him frown. She gave an exclamation of relief when she saw he was back, and ran around to the other seat with the tap tap tap of her shoes, and eased the EM off into the darkness.

"Where . . . going?" he mumbled. He didn't hear her answer.

Panic gripped him, spiking his adrenaline and bringing him a little more into consciousness.

"It's all right." Sofie glanced at him. "I'm getting us out of here."

Her words shouldn't have calmed him--he'd just come to the conclusion he didn't know her at all--but they did. He leaned back in his seat, and let the darkness around them swallow him up.

———

Leo was a big man.

Sofie looked down at him and considered her options.

Picking him up was way beyond her. She guessed his weight was nearly double her own, and while she wasn't short by any means, he was a good head and shoulders taller than her.

She didn't want a repeat of what happened near the lifts. She'd seen him go white with pain as he hit the center console between the seats of the EM with his injured side and then pass out.

It had shaken her, and she'd try just about anything to make sure it didn't happen again.

She'd have to engage brain power here, rather than muscles.

She looked around her at what she had to work with.

The EM track ended in front of what appeared to be a solid wall in a narrow passageway. On one side, an air pump hummed quietly, and lightweight metal boxes lined the opposite wall, labeled with the names of spare parts.

The wall wasn't a dead end, though.

She went to the air pump and typed a code into the keypad on its lock mechanism.

There was a faint click, and the end wall popped open, swinging outward on its hinges.

The EM wouldn't work beyond this point, though, an oversight so egregious she felt like chasing down a few of the construction workers who'd created it and yelling at them.

Of course, they'd built it in secret, risking their lives to create hidden ways into the tethered way station the Cores didn't know about. And this wasn't the only one they'd built.

But still.

You needed to be able to walk out for it to be useful. And Leo wasn't walking anywhere right now.

She opened the door wider, peering down the tunnel to see if anyone had left anything useful inside for her.

There was a hand-pulled hover cart.

She stepped in and walked over to it. To her relief, when she switched it on it started smoothly and lifted up on its cushion of air. It looked big enough to take Leo from head to waist, but nothing else.

The cart suggested someone was using the tunnel to bring goods out or in, but whatever it was, they weren't taking or delivering large quantities.

She wondered who it was. She'd have to thank them, because the cart was a lifesaver.

Stretchy ropes with hooks lay beside it, to secure whatever was piled onto the cart's tray. She sighed. This wasn't going to be fun, for either of them.

Sometimes, she knew, life wasn't fun. It only made the times that were all the more enjoyable.

She turned back to the EM cart and Leo. He looked vulnerable, so unlike she'd seen him before, when he was all cool control.

Tonight had not gone as planned, for either of them.

She wondered with a little spike of worry if there had been anyone in the restaurant who could identify her.

There were scanners watching what happened in Felicitos, but she'd heard a rumor that that wasn't true of the exclusive restaurants frequented by the top echelon of the Cores. They didn't live in a do unto others spirit. With luck, no one would want to admit to seeing anything, either.

It was the safest way to go on Garmen.

She shrugged the worry off. Nothing she could do about it right now, and she had bigger problems on her hands.

She took a deep breath, straightened her shoulders and leaned in to the cart, getting an arm around Leo, bracing herself, and levering him up.

He came up a little way, and fell back down.

His eyes fluttered open.

"You have to help me, Leo." She was panting with effort. "Come on, up you get. Just a few steps, I promise."

He seemed to hear her, struggled up, and it was enough to get him on his feet, leaning heavily on her.

Once they were both upright, she was seriously worried he would take them both down.

"While I like all the muscles, believe me, they are very problematic right now." She couldn't move more than a few shuffles at a time.

By the time they'd reached the hand cart, she was sweating, and close to collapse.

She felt a deep sense of dismay when she tried to work out how to lower him down without hurting him.

Eventually she threw his jacket on the cart where she thought his head would land, and bent, then knelt, grabbing at him as he slid down. He hit the cart, but not as hard as he could have, lying across it at an angle.

It was the best she could do.

She stood, catching her breath and stretching out the kinks in her back, then pulled the wall closed behind her.

She could have sent the EM cart off, but if the system was working, it would go where it was needed as soon as someone on this level hailed one, and if it were discovered in this strange place, the location would be put down to the bugs in the system.

From everything she'd heard, there were a lot of bugs in the system.

She gave a wicked grin, then turned back to the cart and Leo, and steeled herself for some hard work.

She maneuvered him, pulling his legs around to get him straight, and used the stretchy ropes to create a sling over her neck and shoulders to hold his legs off the ground on either side of her body.

The cart moved better if she was in front, pulling it, and she'd gotten about halfway down the tunnel when she heard him make a sound. She turned to look at him over her shoulder.

He was blinking up at her, bemused.

"Am I dreaming this?"

She shook her head. "I'm afraid not."

"How embarrassing," he murmured and then closed his eyes again.

She smiled. Turned back and carried on pulling the cart.

It seemed like he would live.

CHAPTER 3

LEO CAME awake to the sound of rain on a window.

He was in a comfortable bed, and it smelled like Sofie. He was warm, and the bedding he lay on was soft and smooth.

He vaguely recalled Sofie's voice, coaxing him into standing, remembered her hair just under his nose as they staggered into a lift, along passageways.

The only time he'd struggled against the pain and lethargy was when they'd climbed into a hover-for-hire. Sofie had spoken to the driver with a light, joking tone, but Leo had been aware of the danger they were in.

He thought the driver had helped her get him into another lift, and he remembered the faint click of ports as Sofie had handed the ones he'd given her over to the man.

He shifted in agitation, and realized his side was better. The laz must have been on a relatively low setting. Maybe Zan hadn't wanted to kill him, after all. Maybe they'd planned on knocking him out and taking him for questioning.

Like they had questioned Sunar and Petro.

That made more sense than a straightforward elimination. He had secrets they wanted to pry out of him.

Secrets that were causing them a lot of trouble.

He heard a creak from another room, as if someone shifted in their chair, but he didn't feel any sense of alarm. He wasn't in any immediate danger here.

Whatever unconscious evaluations he'd made up until this point, he knew he was safe.

He looked up to find a ceiling with a water stain in one corner and a pretty ceiling fixture in the middle.

When he rose up on his elbows he found he was still dressed, although he wasn't wearing his shoes or jacket, and he was clearly in Sofie's bedroom.

The room was small, and the window faced another building, close enough that he could see the stones in its wall. Despite the cramped quarters and lack of view, Sofie had furnished it in a way that made it seem like the inside of a beautiful box. It was nicer than his own massive space.

Light filtered in, but because of the rain, and the proximity to another structure, he couldn't work out what the time was.

Day time, anyway. He'd slept through the night.

He reluctantly swung his legs over the side of the bed, got out of the comfort and warmth, and took a few steps to the door.

The room beyond was an open plan living area and kitchen.

A deep couch was set against the far window, and Sofie lay on it, a blanket tight around her, her face almost buried in it. Her arm was curled tight against her chest, and he saw she was wearing the same pretty crystal charm bracelet she always wore.

She was curled in on herself and her eyes were closed.

She must have sensed his gaze on her, or heard him move, though, because they flickered open.

Her expression at the sight of him was one of instant relief and delight.

It jolted him.

Had anyone ever been so happy to see him?

She threw off the blanket, and he saw she had changed out of the gold dress and into tight stretchy leggings and a loose shirt.

Her hair was out of the smooth, sophisticated knot at her nape and lay on her shoulders, a rich, dark brown with hints of gold.

He stood still. This unaccustomed hesitancy, of feeling a little untethered, must be down to having been shot.

"You look better." Her voice was husky, and she took a few steps toward him, and then stopped, almost as if she were suddenly shy. "I sat with you for a while, but your breathing sounded strong, and your color came back, so I crashed myself."

He cleared his throat. "How did you get me here?" He looked around the room, found it the same mix of warmth and comfort he'd found in the bedroom.

She laughed, suddenly back to the sophisticated, amused woman who'd captivated him. "With difficulty."

She moved to the kitchen, her manner confident and assured, as if she'd pulled strength around her like a blanket. There were still dark smudges under her eyes, though, and the gray of them was almost silver in the muted light coming through the window.

She switched on what looked like--thank the Stars--a jah machine.

She whirled pods and set the cups beneath it, and then reached into her cooler for a tiny jug of sweet syrup and poured a little dollop into the cup she then handed to him.

"How did you know--?"

She looked surprised. "That's how you took it when we went out to dinner that first time."

He covered his confusion with a deep sip of the dark, fragrant brew.

Could he remember how she'd had her jah?

All he could recall from the evening was how riveting she was.

Then again, this was a woman who'd realized he was about to be attacked before he was. She obviously paid attention to the world around her.

He thought he did, too, but Sofie Erdo was in another league.

Either that, or she'd been watching him a lot longer than the time they'd spent together so far.

At that suspicious thought, he looked up, found her watching him over the rim of her cup.

"Care to tell me why your bodyguard and some fake waiter tried to kill you?" she asked.

He grinned. It was a good ploy, turning the tables and questioning him, but really the more interesting questions he had were all about her.

"Care to tell me where you learned to take out assassins with your sandals?"

She raised her mug in a toast, as if saluting him. "You *are* feeling better."

A buzz of sound caught his attention and he looked over at the dining table. Something on it seemed to shake around in a tightly wrapped bundle. He tilted his head as he tried to work out what it was.

"It's your comm unit," Sofie said. "It's been chirping and burbling all night, and as I wasn't going to answer it, and you were in no state to do so, I tried to muffle the sound. I couldn't find out where to turn the thing off."

He set down his jah and pulled it out, saw he'd missed nearly fifty calls.

He put it down, and sat heavily on one of the green chairs set around the table, suddenly feeling not as well as he had a moment ago.

Sofie started pulling food and pans out of drawers.

He took a long sip of jah. "You're going to feed me?"

"Why not?" The question seemed to startle her. "You're in my apartment, and I know you must be hungry."

He closed his eyes at that, adrift in a confusion of mistrust, gratitude and lust. He struggled to find a way out of it. "You never answered my question. Where did you learn to move that way?" As far as he knew, she worked for one of the Cores' export businesses in an Upper Reaches office. Exporting was his profession, too, at least officially. It had been the reason for their initial conversation.

"A woman needs to know how to defend herself on a Breakaway. Garmen is hardly a planet in the Verdant String."

That was true enough. And because of it, he wanted to burn the whole place down.

Was trying right now to do just that. And the Cores weren't happy about it.

"You didn't answer my question." Sofie tossed something in the pan and he realized she was making something from scratch, not heating a ready. The scent of it was tantalizing.

He shook his head, stretched out his legs.

"Better you don't know."

She lifted her gaze to meet his at that, and he saw disappointment in her expression.

He wouldn't let it deter him, because it was the truth. She was probably in danger because of him already, but the more she knew, the worse it would be.

The bodies of Sunar and Petro haunted him. Just as they were meant to.

He should probably never have pursued her in the first place. He'd been targeted once already this month, but that was at the warehouse where he'd been meeting with his team, and he'd thought it was more a chance attack.

Given the latest attempt, and the deaths of two trusted staff members, that seemed unlikely now.

He had been fiddling with his comm unit, but now he got

Sofie's address from her and tapped it in to his security chief. He had the depressing thought that he hoped at least Finkle was unbribable.

He would have said they all were until Zan tried to shoot him in the head.

"Here you go." Sofie slid a plate in front of him, handed him cutlery, then sat herself.

She was too much of a mystery now to be a safe, easy companion, but he tried never to lie to himself, and he knew he'd never seen her as either, even in the beginning when he'd first come across her sitting quietly at one of the cheaper bars in the Upper Reaches.

She was too intriguing to be either safe or easy.

None of them had said it, but his lieutenants hadn't liked his obvious attraction to her. They thought she was a distraction, just when things were getting serious.

His lips quirked. Except, he knew now, he'd be dead without her.

He forked up some of the omelette she'd put in front of him and then raised startled eyes to hers.

"It's good."

She laughed. Shook her head and started eating herself.

He opened his mouth to explain himself, then closed it. When had he turned into such an ass? And when last had he been so clumsy with a woman?

It had to be a side effect of his injury. He just wasn't at his best.

Usually he took women out to dinner, spent nights with them at one of the top hotels in Felicitos, and kept things exclusive until the zing faded, on either side. Everyone walked away happy.

So far, the relationship with Sofie hadn't progressed to a hotel yet, and he realized that for her own safety, it never would.

"Something wrong?"

He lifted his gaze back to hers, saw she was watching him with a little frown creasing her forehead.

"Just working through what to do about Zan," he lied.

She nodded, her eyes softening. "Betrayal is always a punch in the gut."

His comm unit buzzed and danced on the table again.

He ignored it, savoring the breakfast and finishing his jah.

It danced again, almost falling off the table.

He sighed. Picked it up. It was Finkle.

He knew it would be.

"The world of crime never stops." She was looking at him with a level gaze.

He let his breath out, slow and easy. "Crime?"

"Leo, I know you're smuggling things out under the Cores' noses. That you're sticking it to them is fine with me." She leaned back. "I guess the attack on you means someone in upper management got tired of you ripping them off. Or you're seriously cutting into their bottom line."

"What happened to the woman who wouldn't give a straight answer about her feelings for the Cores? The one who played the charming export administrator?"

Sofie lifted her shoulders. "A bit pointless now I've saved your life. The charming export administrator probably couldn't have done that."

Silence settled between them.

"I don't know what to make of you," Leo said, quietly. He waved his hand to encompass the room, the breakfast, the bedroom beyond where he'd safely slept through the night. "How do you know about my operation?"

She quirked her lips. "In certain circles, it's well known."

That was true. He knew it was, but he hadn't thought she belonged in those circles.

He'd obviously been wrong.

One thing he wasn't wrong about though, was the danger to

her after last night's excitement. "It's not safe to be anywhere near me right now."

She tipped back her head as he stood up, her expression neutral.

"Which means?"

"Which means good bye."

He walked into the bedroom, pulled on his shoes, and grabbed his jacket. His comm buzzed again.

Finkle was waiting downstairs.

When he walked back into the living room, she was still seated, cup of jah in hand.

She was a mystery. A mystery he wanted to solve.

He fought every selfish inclination within him that told him he could somehow still see her and keep her safe.

But that was bullshit, and from what Finkle said, things were already ramping up now that whoever ordered him abducted realized the plan hadn't been successful.

Someone had tried to break into the warehouse.

He didn't have time to explore the secrets of the delightful Sofie Erdo.

He stopped at her front door, turned back to look at her.

"Thank you."

She crossed her arms under her breasts. Inclined her head.

It seemed as if she was going to say something, but she changed her mind with a quick shake of her head.

"Keep safe," she said as he opened the door, her voice husky.

He gave her a nod and forced himself to walk away.

He'd get Finkle to post watchers on her apartment and on her.

At least for a while.

Sofie Erdo was not going to be caught in the crossfire if he could help it.

And if it meant he'd get daily updates on her, that would be the sweetest torture.

CHAPTER 4

SHE DIDN'T KNOW how long she stared at the door after it closed behind Leo.

Her first reaction when he'd stood up and gone to collect his things was outrage, but she could tell he was sincere in his belief that she was in danger.

He was trying to protect her.

If he knew who she really was, and where her loyalties lay, he'd understand she was in far more trouble than she could possibly be as a crime lord's . . .

She frowned, annoyed she couldn't come up with the exact description of her relationship with Leo.

Lover didn't fit, not yet. Although if someone hadn't tried to kill him, they'd have gotten there soon enough.

She shrugged.

She hadn't been happy to see him leave.

It had been a long time since she felt attracted to a man, and the breathless, heady feeling she got around Leo was precious to her.

She didn't want to let that go.

She wouldn't fight his leaving, though.

She'd learned long ago that someone either wanted you or they didn't. You couldn't force it, and if you tried, you were the one who ended up damaged.

Years of her and Rach trying to get their father to give even half a damn about them had taught her that.

Leo would come back around, or he wouldn't.

But in the meanwhile, she had better let Zyr know what was going on.

It had to be significant, the Cores trying to take out one of the biggest crime lords on Garmen.

Zyr might get a little testy with her for seeing Leo, but that was no one's business but her own.

She had drawn that line in the sand when Rach had died, and no one was stupid enough to try and cross it.

Well, Veld had been. But that hadn't worked out so well for him, and now that Zyr was in charge, everyone knew the score.

She stood up and cleared away the dishes, a smile playing over her lips as she thought of Leo's surprise at her knowing his preferences with jah. It had thrown him.

He'd almost been more suspicious of that than anything else.

Her mouth stretched into a full-out grin. She liked keeping him off-balance.

It's how she felt around him, so it was only fair.

She got ready to go out, pulling on warm, loose trousers and a waterproof jacket.

The rain seemed to have intensified since Leo left, the drops hitting the window like tiny, tapping fingers.

She pulled her jacket hood up as she closed her front door, and ran down the narrow stairwell and out into the rain-darkened street.

She lived in one of the better areas of Tether Town, although nothing like the glitter and shine of the Felicitos apartments.

Even so, everything was run down.

The Cores didn't care how the buildings around Felicitos were built or what they looked like, as long as they didn't pose a danger to the tethered way station.

It showed in the general derelict appearance of everything.

The only places of any interest to the Cores were the warehouses where they stored their goods. Goods they sold to the traders who flew in from all over the galaxy to the massive landing deck at the top of Felicitos, where it poked its flat silver head out into space.

The warehouses were large, well-kept, and set on wide roads that led straight to the way station, but everywhere else, they let the flotsam and jetsam of Garmen fight it out amongst themselves.

Even if you had the money for an apartment inside Felicitos, which she was sure Leo did, unless you worked for the Cores you wouldn't get in.

A few people walked the street with her, heads down, scurrying along, headed for the way station.

She headed toward the way station herself, the procedure ingrained in her to make it look like Felicitos was her final destination before she ducked down a quiet street or alley and worked her way east to Zyr's apartment.

Even though the lake was to the north of the way station, the stink of lake weed, sulfurous and pungent, blew in on the icy breeze and she wrinkled her nose in disgust. Even the rain couldn't dampen the stench.

The waters of Lake Felicitos, lying below the tethered way station like a long, thin footprint, had been necessary for the building of the station, but the Cores had used it and then left it to rot, poisoned by the metals and solvents used in the building process, and unsafe to drink or swim in.

Lucky for everyone it rained a lot here. Almost every building had a water tank, or they'd all be sick.

She'd heard someone was working on a solution to the lake, but she'd dismissed it as wishful thinking. Gossip at its most optimistic.

A gust of cold rain pelted her, lifting the hood of her jacket and blowing it back so icy needles hit her face.

She turned her back to the wind to pull the hood up and her hands trembled a little as she spun back to face forward, hands gripping the hood to keep it in place.

Someone was following her.

She'd caught the quick dart of movement, the impression of a man, tall and in dark rain gear.

She cursed herself for a few steps, blind to anything but the acceleration of her heart.

She moved with the same purpose she had before, but she couldn't go to Zyr now, even though talking to him was even more urgent than it had been.

If they'd started watching her building since last night when she'd brought Leo back, then Leo was being followed too.

Did she send him a message? She fingered her comm set in her jacket pocket.

The Cores had their fingers everywhere. She wouldn't be surprised if her very ordinary comm unit had been hacked. And surely, with his security, Leo would have picked up a watcher far faster than she had?

Up ahead, with the way station a looming silver column in the background, she saw the warm lights of In the Shadows Cafe and angled toward it.

Two hovers came racing down the street toward her, weaving through the pedestrian traffic, and she used the fact that they flicked up rain water as they passed her as an excuse to turn and look after them in irritation.

Her watcher was still there.

She shook her head, as if annoyed, and then crossed the road and entered the cafe.

If her watcher came in, he'd have to order something and sit, and she'd have plenty of opportunity to watch him right back. It was why she'd chosen to enter a public place.

As she stepped inside, the light and scents broke over her in a warm tropical wave, with the sweet and spicy smell of fruni, the crisp pastries filled with pureéd fruit mixed with a hot chilli powder, tickling her nose.

After the chill and the gray of the street, it was a haven of warmth.

She rubbed her hands together, and got a smile from the woman behind the counter.

"It's like winter's come three month's early," the woman said.

Sofie nodded and concentrated on the display case rather than whether someone was coming through the door behind her.

The cafe was almost full, with the gentle buzz of conversation that made her feel as if Garmen had a chance as a society. It wasn't always violence in the streets and being ripped off by the Cores.

She'd heard in the Verdant String you sat at your cafe table and ordered from the electronic menu embedded in the table surface.

Here on Garmen, things were done a little more primitively.

She wasn't hungry, she'd just had breakfast, but she chose a small, sweet biscuit, and a cup of jah, and turned to look for a table.

The watcher was still outside.

She paused, as if debating her choice of seat, and flicked a glance out of the small, metal-framed window as more rain threw itself at the glass.

She could sit down and pretend to have a cup of jah, and then walk home, having accomplished nothing, or she could step back on the resistance carousel she'd stepped off of after Rach died.

She'd been out of the game for a year, but she knew what to do, and choking down a cup of jah she didn't want seemed excruciating to her all of a sudden.

She turned on her heel.

"Problem, sweetie?" the woman asked.

"Just some creep who followed me here, hanging around outside." She waved her mug. "Do you mind if I get this in a takeaway and leave out of the kitchen?"

The server's gaze flickered over her shoulder, and her lips pursed. "I see him. He looks like he's trying to decide whether to come in or not." While she spoke, she took the mug, poured the jah into one of the thin paper cups stacked by the till and snapped on an equally thin paper lid. "Head on back."

Sofie gave a grateful nod, and walked briskly through the tiny kitchen, smiling politely at the thin, nervous-looking girl standing beside a stove, and out into the rain again.

She moved fast, turning right as soon as she stepped into the narrow alley that ran the length of the block.

She made it to the corner, but before she could dart around it and get out of sight, she heard the sound of running feet behind her.

The sensation of being hunted wasn't new to her, but she hadn't felt it in a long time.

She hadn't missed it.

She ran, making no effort to hide the fact that she was trying to get away.

She dived into a narrow alley between two wooden buildings, the timber laid bare where the waterproof coating had peeled off.

She came out the other end of the narrow lane, and stepped into a street that stretched from the way station down through Tether Town in a straight line.

There were more people here and she tried to merge with a group of laughing teenagers, then drifted into a small, loose group of workers to reach the next alley. She ducked down it.

It was darker than back on the street here, the high buildings and rain-washed sky blocking most of the light. She hesitated for a moment, but the sound of footsteps in the street behind her spurred her forward at a run.

It was a mistake.

A small huddle of men standing beneath a broken awning which spanned the alleyway broke up and spread out as she ran toward them, and she slowed and then stopped, her heart feeling like it was trying to leap out of her chest.

She glanced behind her, but there was no one there. It looked like she'd managed to evade her watcher.

Out of one mess, into another.

She started backing away, eyes on the men as they braved the rain, coming out from under the awning toward her.

There were three of them, all wearing thin shirts which stuck to their skin in moments under the onslaught of the weather. One was seriously muscular, his arms and abs defined as the fabric of his shirt clung to him, his face a mean, hard-set sneer. The other two were not in as good shape, the one more pot-bellied than the other.

They advanced in a feral pack.

Sofie pushed back her hood so she could see better, and kept up her steady retreat.

Only a few steps until she was back on the main street.

One of the men lunged, hand out to grab her.

She threw her paper cup full of hot jah at him, and when he flinched back, arm raised, she kicked, high and hard, and heard the satisfying sound of a crack as her boot hit his forearm.

He didn't make a sound, he simply dropped to his knees, cradling his arm.

It seemed to spur his two friends on, rather than discourage them.

They moved together, in a way that told her they'd done this before.

And she couldn't fight both of them at once.

There was a whine and snap near her ear, and the attacker to her left collapsed.

The other one's gaze jumped over her, to focus on someone behind her, and Sofie didn't stop to see who he was looking at.

She jumped over the slumped body and raced past the third man just as a second snap sizzled in the wet air.

She smelled the ozone as he fell, and it made her run even faster.

She hoped, beyond anything, there was no one else in the alley, tensing as she ran beneath the awning the men had been standing under, and then heaving in a huge breath as she made it to the street beyond.

She wasn't safe yet, though.

She glanced behind her, and saw a grim figure in black drag one of the men out of the way and start down the alley after her.

She hadn't managed to shake him off, and she couldn't risk leading him to Zyr.

She headed home.

She didn't know of a single place that was safe enough if it was really the Cores who were after her.

At least there were dry clothes and hot water at her apartment.

If the Cores were coming for her, there was nowhere she could hide, so she might as well make herself comfortable while she waited.

They owned Garmen. And they would find her.

CHAPTER 5

"HOW'S THE SIDE?"

Leo turned in surprise as Finkle stepped into the room, and realized he'd been rubbing the place where Zan's laz had hit him.

He shrugged. "They didn't want me dead, so it's already nearly healed."

The solid night's sleep he'd had at Sofie's was mostly the reason for that.

"Just heard from Carver."

Leo's attention snapped to Finkle and his eyes narrowed. "Trouble?"

He suddenly saw the massive hole in the plan he'd had to keep watch on Sofie. If the Cores came for her, there was nothing a single watcher could do but let it happen.

Why hadn't he persuaded her to come home with him?

"She went out," Finkle said, and he was watching Leo right back, as if studying his reactions.

"And?" Leo could hear the snap in his voice, and didn't care.

"And she somehow caught on to the fact that Carver was following her. Led him on a bit of a chase."

Leo took a step forward. "Chase?"

"He couldn't watch her if he couldn't see her." Finkle lifted both hands in a fatalistic way that had Leo's temper rising.

He swallowed it back down. "No. But he could have pulled back, made her think she'd lost him."

"If he'd done that, he might not have been there to save her from the attack."

Leo closed his eyes for a beat, opened them. "Attack?" He kept his voice careful.

"Don't think it was the Cores," Finkle allowed. "She was trying to lose Carver, ran down an alley, and had the bad luck of running into a group of oppos."

Oppos were one of the reasons why Leo wanted to burn Garmen to the ground and rebuild it. Opportunists who took advantage whenever they could to rape, steal, and hurt.

The oppos used the lack of any consequence for crimes on Garmen to make life unsafe for everyone.

"Carver says she brought one of them down, some sort of kick, then he used his laz on all three of them."

"Dead?" If they weren't, he'd go do it himself.

"Dead," Finkle confirmed.

It was part of what Leo's organization did.

Leo had long made peace with being judge, jury and executioner in Tether Town. Someone had to take on the responsibility, and the Cores certainly weren't going to.

He tried to keep an emotional distance usually, but in this case ... he knew he'd be acting in anger.

He realized with a jolt he was perfectly fine with that.

"And Sofie?" He tried to keep his voice steady.

"She went home. Carver doesn't know if she meant to go to the cafe all along, but got spooked when she saw him, or whether she was going somewhere else and then decided it was too dangerous and gave up on her journey."

Leo thought it through. Had to lift his shoulders. He didn't know nearly enough about the woman who occupied too much time in his head.

"Put a second watcher on her. Carver obviously needs backup."

Finkle looked like he was going to argue at the waste of resources, but he closed his mouth and gave a nod.

As he walked out, Leo turned and looked out of the big living room window that gave him a view of the far hills.

The tethered way station was on a flat escarpment, but there were foothills and then mountains in the distance.

He'd built his house at the edge of Tether Town, facing away from Felicitos. He didn't want it in his view, and he'd positioned the house so that it did not fall in the shadow of the way station, either.

If he brought Sofie here, there would be no way the stain of association with him could be rubbed off.

Right now, she was just a woman he'd been seen with socially.

He'd never installed a lover in his house before.

She would be seen as his weak spot, and that would be right.

She already was his weak spot.

Now he had to work out how to put that aside, and hope neither Sofie, nor the Cores, ever discovered his secret.

———

Sofie stepped out of her building and looked around.

She made no effort to hide the fact she was looking for watchers--that notion had pinched out to the black yesterday.

She'd seen no one from her windows, but that didn't mean

much when her two views were the side of one building and the back of another.

Things looked normal. Just the usual people headed for work and the high, bright sound of children going in their walking bus to school.

The same two women shepherded them every day, and one of them nodded to her as they passed.

The children looked cold and too thin, but that didn't seem to dampen their spirits.

Above their heads, high on the wall they walked along, was a graffiti image of a shadow prowler.

Everyone in the street had breathed a little easier the morning they'd woken to find it there, six months ago.

It meant protection, which was ironic, given the shadow prowler was a relentless, vicious predator. But the group behind the sign was relentless only with the oppos--the opportunist criminals who took and even killed when it suited them--dishing out consequences for criminal behavior where the Cores never would.

In the Verdant String, Sofie gathered there were whole units devoted to keeping the citizens safe. In Tether Town, it was a shadowy, illegal organization who dealt death with no judge or jury.

And most were happy to have them.

She knew some of the hardcore resistance members resented whoever had taken on the job of dealing justice.

Whoever it was was winning hearts and loyalties. Diverting focus from the cause.

And there was probably some resentment because the shadow prowler was good imagery.

More exciting than the clenched fist symbol of the resistance, anyway.

She looked away from the stylized image of the lethal black beast and back to the children. Some of them were skipping, others walked slower, as if they didn't have the energy to spare.

It was wrong.

Wrong that they were going without, scraping a bare bones education here, through no fault of their own, when they could be on a Verdant String planet, cared for and educated to the highest level.

The life she and Rach could have had, if her father hadn't been seduced by the idea of Felicitos. Of a lasting legacy in his name.

She gave a bitter smile. That hadn't worked out so well. For him, or her and Rach.

Rach had had access to the interplanetary comms in her job, just a few times, but enough for her to have gotten the idea that the Verdant String would do something if they knew the children of Garmen's workers didn't have the right to leave, that they were bound by their parents' work agreements.

Rach had wanted to escape and get the word out.

Sofie fiddled with the bracelet around her wrist. The Verdant String had to know about the exit rules already. They'd have spies here, for sure.

Since Rach had died, she still harbored the dream of escaping, but not with the aim of prodding the Verdant String to see if it had a conscience. She just wanted to get away.

She drew in a deep breath, caught the smell of rotting lake weed at the back of her throat and coughed. It motivated her to start walking to the way station.

Some of the children's parents might be like her, brought here as children themselves, with no choice in the matter. It had been fifteen years since she and Rach arrived with their parents, after all. Some of her contemporaries would have children of their own.

But some of these children's parents had come recently as adults. They knew what they were doing, knew the Cores would let you in but would never let you leave, and even so, still had brought their children into the hellhole that was Tether Town.

She had nothing but contempt for them.

And this anger wasn't helping her get in the zone.

Ugh!

She shook her shoulders out, started going through the mental exercises she did every morning as she made her way to Felicitos.

To get in the mood, she shook her arm to hear the crystal charms on her bracelet tinkle against each other.

She thought about time spent with Rach, running up and down the scaffolding of Felicitos as it was being built. The thrill and fear as they ran across the thin metal walkways over the open core of the growing column. The times they'd run out onto the escarpment, picking the tiny purple flowers that grew everywhere, and then splashing in the stream that fed Lake Felicitos.

They helped her find peace, so she had the reserves to deal with security at the entrance, the push and shove onto the hovers that ran up and down the center of the way station's core, the aura of entitlement that seemed to surround the top Cores employees.

The only reason she could do this at all was the knowledge that she was tearing them down from the inside. But for the visualization, she'd have given herself away by now. Would have snapped.

A year could feel like forever.

The stream of people coming toward her suddenly swelled to a flood, as the night shift came off duty.

The road, which the Cores only bothered to seal because it was a main route in for trade goods, was so much better than the muddy lanes everywhere else, that most people kept on it as long as they could before they had to turn off to their homes.

She caught the eye of someone she knew from her street, gave a friendly nod, then reared back as the woman grabbed her arm, gripping just below her bracelet and causing the two of them to be jostled and bumped as commuters tried to get around them.

"Got some ports?" The woman pulled her closer, eyes a little wild. "I'll pay you back." The woman, she didn't even know her name, tightened her grip, her voice husky.

Sofie stared, momentarily at a loss for words.

She pulled her arm up and back, charms tinkling, and as she did, out of the corner of her eye, she saw a man jerk forward, as if he planned to intervene.

She ripped her arm back with even more force, and the woman let go, mouth slack.

Before she carried on her way, Sofie pulled the one port she had left in her coat pocket from the handful Leo had given her and held it out.

The woman took it, more subdued than she'd been before, and stammered a thank you as Sofie turned away, head down, and stepped back into the stream of workers, all headed for the way station.

The rain started up again as she neared the main entrance, a light, steady fall. She pulled up her hood.

So, they were still following her.

Whoever they were.

She was starting to doubt it was the Cores. For one, they were being more discrete than she thought the Cores were capable of. Secondly, they also seemed interested in her well being.

The oppos who'd attacked her yesterday had been taken down. And they'd thought her neighbor was a threat for a moment there, and shown their hand.

So it was either someone from the resistance, or it was Leo.

She didn't know what to think of either of those options.

If it was Zyr, he might have found out about her relationship with Leo, and decided to watch her, see if he could still trust her. If it was Leo . . .

Well, he had said he was concerned for her safety.

Either way, things had gotten out of hand.

She would have to track both men down. Find out what was going on.

She realized, as she stepped up to the two guards at the entrance and raised her arms to shoulder level for the security check, that life had suddenly become a lot more interesting.

She knew getting involved with Leo would change things, but she was only just realizing it was going to change things irrevocably.

CHAPTER 6

AS THE LINE for the exec hovers moved forward, and Leo stepped closer to the front of the boarding platform, he nodded to a few of the high-flyers, either Cores or independents like himself.

To his right, on a different platform altogether, the gen-pop queue shuffled and ground its way forward, too.

The third platform, which only had two stops, ground level and the Deck, was for the transport hovers, and they had priority over everyone.

Even if the hovers used for the executive option were as filthy, poorly maintained, and crowded as the gen-pop ones--and they were not--he'd still pay the hefty monthly fee to use them.

The line for gen-pop snaked back to the entrance in a tightly-wound skein, and anyone getting in line at the back was looking at an hour's wait, at least.

Water fell down the hoverway in glittering droplets, vented from the hovers' outlet pipes. It mirrored the rainfall outside, and he caught the whiff of liquid ammonia, the liquid fuel for the hydrogen fuel cells that powered the hovers.

It was ancient tech.

And yet, by going old school and cheap, by luck more than design, the Cores had solved two problems in one.

They didn't need to vent exhaust fumes from the hoverway because hydrogen fuel cells didn't emit dangerous gases, they produced water; and they didn't need to bring in water--it fell from the hovers down into the massive water tank that sat just below the first floor platforms, and was then drawn back up through filtration systems, to be delivered to the apartments, restaurants and businesses in the way station in a pure, drinkable state.

It was a good thing, too, given they'd polluted the lake.

An executive hover rose up in front of the platform. He'd seen it going down on the other side of the hoverway earlier. It would have docked below, been given a quick interior clean, and then would have crossed over into the upstream.

It was an efficient system, except at rush hour, like now, where there were too many people coming in for the hovers to handle.

The gen-pop hovers didn't get a clean. They simply crossed from downside to upside, waited their turn if an executive hover was just in front or behind them, and then trembled and shuddered their way up to load up to the max, and sometimes over the max, if the pushing was vicious enough.

He didn't miss those days.

A concierge stepped out of the exec hover and held up a massive umbrella for him so he didn't get wet.

He nodded his thanks, stepping inside with Finkle and Dee flanking him.

The deal in exec was there were never more than five VIPs plus their entourage of two at any one time.

This being rush hour, the full five execs stepped in.

No one spoke to each other. Everyone went to a point as far from the others as they could, and Leo was no exception.

"Sofie's just entered Felicitos," Finkle said quietly.

Leo couldn't help turning to the door, but it had closed already, and they were rising up.

He wouldn't be able to see her, anyway, not if she was joining the back of the line.

He would throw Finkle or Dee off in a heartbeat to get her in with him, save her the push and shove of gen-pop, but that would defeat the whole purpose of staying away.

Nothing would come to the Core's attention faster.

"Any problems? Carver notice anyone watching her?"

Finkle shook his head, and Leo forced himself to drop the topic, pulling out his screen and firing off a list of instructions to his office manager.

"You sure you want to be here?" Finkle asked.

He raised his head. "If we don't make money, we get kicked out of Felicitos. We get kicked out of Felicitos, we die."

He shrugged as he spoke.

Finkle knew the rules. They all did.

Money made Garmen go around. If you didn't make a certain level of profit, you were out. The upside was the Cores couldn't touch you, by their own rules, as long as the tax you paid on that profit was over a certain amount.

The reason some took their chances here, gambled with their future on Garmen or Lassa, the other Breakaway, was because that tax was minute compared to the tax a company paid on the Verdant String. But unlike a Verdant String Coalition planet, not a cent of it went toward education, housing, defense or law and order. It landed directly into the pockets of the Core Companies who'd claimed Garmen.

Independent companies who operated with the Cores' permission made more profit, but they lived with a lot more uncertainty.

And Leo knew the time of reckoning was coming. The lack of a stable, healthy, well-educated workforce who didn't live in fear of crime and violence was beginning to take its toll.

The lack of good roads and good infrastructure was also a sticking point.

Fifteen years after Garmen had been settled, the utter lack of social structure was starting to be felt.

He knew how bad it was out beyond the escarpment, at the mine sites, as well. That's where he'd made his start. Where most of his wealth still came from.

There were problems everywhere on Garmen, and Felicitos was just as dangerous as shadow prowler infested mountains, but as long as he paid his money to the Cores, they couldn't touch him openly.

Covertly, of course, they had tried to kill him a number of times.

They had to be getting desperate, because the attack in The High Flyer was in Felicitos itself. They'd never been so bold before. And they had to know they risked breaking the understanding everyone doing business in Felicitos lived by.

If you made money, you were safe.

Blaming his death on the wild crime on the streets was one thing, trying to assassinate him in the tethered way station had stepped over a line.

"If they thought they could get away with it once inside Felicitos, there's nothing stopping them thinking they can get away with it again." Finkle couldn't let it go.

"I can't let them scare me away from the business. Then they've won anyway."

Finkle inclined his head, acknowledging the truth of that.

The hover stopped at the first platform on the Upper Reaches, where most of the businesses on Garmen had their offices.

Two execs got out, one a woman he recognized as one of the few corporate heads who sponsored a school in Tether Town. The hover slid up again, in cocooned silence.

Two stories later, they stepped out, and he took a moment to enjoy the hush and the scent of well-made jah in the air.

His office manager, Eunice, was behind her desk, and given the queues for gen-pop below, he could only imagine how early she'd had to come in to be settled in already.

He regarded her for a moment, gray-streaked head bent over her screen, and wondered if she, too, had been bribed like Zan.

He had to wonder that about everyone, now.

"Leo." She looked up and smiled. "Call just came in from that Core Company you were trying to do a deal with last month. They're finally ready to talk."

He exchanged a look with Finkle.

It was true, the Core Company he'd approached had said they needed a few weeks to consider his offer. That they were reaching out now, two days after what he was sure was a Core-sponsored kidnap attempt, might or might not be significant.

He shrugged. Business was business. He would go.

Finkle was shaking his head. "It could be a trap."

"It could be a test to see if I'm too scared to go out and about." Leo kept his gaze level.

Finkle hesitated, then agreed with a nod. "We take a contingent. Meet in the open."

They both looked at Eunice, who was eyeing them with interest.

"They want to meet outside the hover platform on this floor at the end of the day. Then go to an Upper Reaches bar for drinks."

That was standard. No alarm bells rang.

Leo nodded. "You can confirm."

His screen buzzed in his hand, his comm set buzzed in his pocket, and Eunice's comm set on her desk tinkled a little tune.

Looked like they didn't need to worry about making a profit this month, at any rate.

CHAPTER 7

SOFIE HAD BEEN jumpy all day.

She'd kept her head down, worked hard in her cubicle, and made sure she was one step ahead on every problem, every request, so there was no need for face time with her manager or anyone else.

No one seemed to notice her lack of engagement, and it left her profoundly relieved.

She had convinced herself the Cores weren't the ones following her, but she still had room for a tiny sliver of doubt.

She worked for Firnam Metals Trading, one of the biggest of the Core Companies, after all. Stepping inside this morning had felt a little like delivering herself into the hands of her enemies.

The picture she was slowly building of the deals Firnam was doing, not just with the other Breakaway planet, Lassa, but also the planet Caruso, was starting to worry her.

It had taken time for the full scope to become clear.

Her job in Firnam was mid-level now, but she'd started at the bottom. In just a year, she'd worked her way up as those above her had either been promoted, fallen ill or been killed or maimed in street violence. There was a lot of turnover in a place where there was no deterrent to crime.

Now she had a better salary, and a cubicle to herself, running on-planet logistics. Getting the ore from the mines to the furnaces, the metal from the furnaces to the way station.

She only caught glimpses, now and then, of where the metal was going after it was traded on the Deck.

That was usually the province of her manager, but he liked to drink a little too much on his night off, and was starting to make a habit of dragging his ass in late the next day.

Twice he'd had to give her one-time codes to access his documents from her screen, and she'd been careful to write down what she'd seen in the only untraceable way there was. With pencil and paper.

The information was sitting in plain sight on her desk, rolled up inside the printed list of company rules every employee received, tied with a silver bow that matched the company's logo.

She studied it as she cleared her desk of paperwork and slid her screen into a drawer and locked it away.

No one with any sense took their screen home if they lived in Tether Town.

It *would* be stolen, and the Cores did not take kindly to their employees losing company equipment.

If she were lucky, they'd dock her for the screen. Most likely, she'd lose her job.

She reached out and picked up the tightly rolled paper tube.

She needed to speak to Zyr.

She should have contacted him with what she'd learned earlier, especially regarding Firnam's dealings with Caruso; the dark, vicious planet ruled by a dictator and his thugs that had the Verdant String and all other sentient life in the galaxy worried.

The secretive race that inhabited Caruso were its planet's

natural inhabitants, unlike the people of the Verdant String, who were interlopers who'd traveled to the eight planets--seven, now that Halatia was uninhabitable--from some mysterious other place.

They hadn't taken their planets from other indigenous occupiers though. The planets they'd settled hadn't yet produced intelligent life. And by the time the other sentient races had encountered the Verdant String, the eight planets had already found each other again after centuries apart, and had formed a coalition based on their shared common heritage, even if the alliance sometimes had its ups and downs.

They were a force to be reckoned with, though. One every other intelligent being who'd come across them had decided to leave alone.

Well, except the rebels of the Faldine War. But they had learned their lesson.

The Breakaways were another story.

Although they were populated by former Verdant String citizens, they couldn't rely on the VSC to have their backs. Not when they'd turned *their* backs on the VSC.

The greed planets, the Breakaways were called.

Unlike the Verdant String, with its economic equality, its insistence on everyone taking a turn at public office in some form, no exceptions, and its citizen's dividend, the two Breakaways were all about profit only for those who could control the means of making it. Where might was right and only those who could pay could play.

And the Cores made sure very few were paid enough to play.

The Verdant String didn't like the formation of the Breakaways. They thought everything about the two planets was an affront, but they'd been unwilling to fight a war over the matter, so they'd reluctantly let them be.

If they knew Garmen, at least, was getting into bed with

Caruso . . . Sofie didn't think that hands-off state of affairs would continue.

Caruso was too aggressive. Too dangerous.

Forget the trampled rights of the children of those who'd moved to Garmen that Rach had been focused on, Sofie bet the VSC would act if they thought Garmen and its fellow breakaway, Lassa, were taking a military turn.

She pushed the roll of paper down into her inner jacket pocket, made sure everything else on her desk was secure, and walked out.

She needed to find Zyr, but if she hurried, she might just be in time to catch Leo first.

She knew he worked at home most nights, that he kept normal shift hours in Felicitos.

She should be able to find him before he left.

As she stepped out into the general walkway, she checked the queues for the hover--not as bad as the morning run, but still significant--and made her way to the stairwell.

The stairs were the only alternative to hovers in the Upper Reaches. There were no lifts.

The Lower Reaches lift she'd used the night she'd saved Leo at The High Flyer only went as high as the Lower Reaches' top floor.

It was considered too much of a security risk to allow lifts up to the Upper Reaches.

You used the hovers, or you used the stairs, and the stairs only covered five floors.

The stairs were only available at all because they made things quicker for office grunts running packages or information between Core Companies, rather than waiting for the hovers. They helped make money, so they were allowed.

Sofie ran lightly down the one flight she needed to to get to Leo's floor, and as she exited the door, her gaze went to the exec hover platform, to make sure he wasn't already waiting to take one down.

And there he was.

She stopped short.

She wished she didn't feel a zing when she saw him. It was too dangerous. Gave him too much power.

And yet, she was so glad she was able to feel this much at all since Rach died.

She realized, belatedly, that he wasn't alone.

He stood facing a group of people who she immediately pegged as Cores upper management.

There were two men and a woman, and they had four beefy bodyguards standing behind them.

Leo had two guards of his own, a man Sofie recognized as Finkle, his head of security, and a woman who'd been Leo's bodyguard on their first date, Dee.

Leo and the three Cores execs were talking to each other, but their body language made them look like they were walking across Lake Felicitos after an ice snap. Cautious and afraid the ground would give way at any moment.

They were obviously planning to take an exec hover, standing as they were between the up and down hover platforms.

She realized with dismay that she couldn't approach Leo now. He was obviously doing a deal.

A gen-pop hover had come down while she was taking the stairs, and the last of the gen-pop line disappeared inside it. It dropped away, and she noticed an exec hover coming down after it.

As its roof came into view, Sofie blinked.

There was a man crouched on the flat silver surface, a laz in his hand.

She made a sound, some kind of shout perhaps, because

Finkle and Dee both glanced at her, then in the direction of her pointed finger.

But it was too late.

The assassin on the roof took his first shot, and then pandemonium broke out.

The four Core guards snapped up their weapons, aiming them at Leo, and Dee and Finkle countered. Finkle also jumped in front of Leo, blocking the assassin's angle, and a Core guard countered his move by edging around to get a better aim at him.

If the Core guard shot, Finkle was going down, and all of Leo's defenses would go with him.

Sofie had started running for the platform as soon as she saw the assassin on the roof, and now she put everything she had into it.

A hover was rising up from below, one of the over-large gen-pop models that took up almost exactly half the circumference of the hoverway. She knew what she had to do--she'd spent her childhood running across the hoverway while Felicitos rose up around her, had seriously talked about hover hopping as a wild teenager-- but even so, her heart felt like it was trying to fight itself out of her chest in panic.

She reached the up platform just as the roof of the gen-pop hover came in line with it and she jumped onto the roof. She took three running leaps across the shortest part of its roof, feeling her shoes slide a bit in the glistening wet, and then used the height it gave her as it lifted up to dock at the platform to fling herself onto the roof of the exec hover that was now stationary, holding itself in place to give the assassin on its roof a good angle to take a shot at Leo.

The shooter had been concentrating on Leo, trying to find an opening, and she wondered if he'd even noticed her at all.

He turned at the sound of her landing beside him, laz still pointed in Leo's direction, and his eyes went wide.

She slid across the roof straight at him, her shoes giving her no grip at all, and she put her hands out and shoved.

He made a short, sharp sound of surprise and flew off the edge.

She skittered back, using the push she'd given him as a counterweight to stop herself following him over, then she crouched in the middle of the roof, her hair and clothes sticking to her as they were soaked with falling water, her legs and hands shaking with aftershock.

Would the shooter be lucky and hit another hover roof on his way down which would break his fall?

It was a hundred thou from the top of the tethered way station to the ground, but most likely he'd hit a hover before he reached the water tank at the bottom.

A shout from the platform penetrated her thoughts and she looked across to see what was happening to Leo.

Everyone at the platform was staring at her.

Her gaze went to Leo, and he took a step toward her, face slack with surprise.

At that moment the hover started to move downward, and she didn't know why, but she refused to crouch any more, as if she was afraid.

She stood and lifted her hand to him in a jaunty salute as she dropped like a stone.

CHAPTER 8

LEO HAD a lot to say to Muli Vanasta, the head Core manager involved in this little meeting.

Like whether he knew what was going to happen, and whether his guards had been instructed to make the shooter's job as easy as possible by trying to take down Leo's own people.

Good thing they'd all been wearing anti-laz layers. Finkle had insisted. He'd felt the first shot the assassin had got off, but it was a glancing blow.

He didn't have time for questions, though, because Sofie was on the assassin's hover, dropping down into the depths of the hoverway with no weapon, no help.

He raced to the platform, looking down, and caught a glimpse of her crouched in the middle of the roof, head turned toward the platforms to her right, as if waiting for a chance to jump off.

It was a long, long way down.

An imagination-stumping distance.

His gaze caught on a small maintenance hover just under the lip of the platform, and he sat on the edge, gripped it with both hands, and swung himself down. He scissored his legs, hooked the tiny hover with an ankle, and pulled it toward himself, and dropped in.

He blinked to get the water out of his eyes, and then switched it on, turned it, and sent it dropping down after Sofie.

He heard Finkle shout to him from above, but he couldn't risk looking back up.

He moved around and past a hover stopped at the platform on the floor below, missing it by a hair's breadth, and then hunched over the simple controls, trying to keep track of Sofie and her hover.

It was dropping fast. Faster than was allowed.

Twice it slid across into the up stream, also strictly forbidden, and then back into the down steam when it had passed whatever was in its way.

Leo did the same, but it was easier for him, the maintenance hover was small enough to squeeze between hovers going in both directions.

Finally, he saw it get stuck.

Massive gen-pop hovers were docked both in the up and down streams, taking up every available inch, and Sofie's hover slowed to a stop.

He caught a glimpse of her stepping off the roof's edge onto the rungs of a maintenance ladder fixed to the wall of the hover-way. She pulled herself up cautiously.

He wondered why she was being so careful, then saw her foot slip on a rung. The falling water was making the going treacherous.

He was making progress, dropping fast, but she hadn't seen him, her concentration was on the ladder, and the tunnel opening above her head.

She pulled herself in, and disappeared.

He'd moved to the outer edge of the hoverway when he saw

her grab the ladder, and now he moved as fast as he could to reach the opening.

A sign on the wall announced the entrance as a maintenance tunnel, and his hover fitted through it comfortably, something he hadn't expected. He rode in a little way until a barrier of metal bars forced him to stop.

He powered down, stepped out, and saw the door set in the grid was open.

He could hear the patter of water from the hoverway behind him and the noise of the hovers and people at the platforms, but they were almost drowned out by the roar of sound that came from up ahead.

He pushed through the door and then started after the woman who'd saved his life.

Again.

The tunnel was covered in pipes, in places there were so many bracketed to the wall that there was only room for one person to fit through.

It intersected with other tunnels, and at set intervals there were doors to rooms filled with machinery. Pumps hummed and pipes hammered.

At every junction, Leo paused, having to make a choice on whether to keep going straight or turn.

He had a strange feeling of panic, as if he'd get to the end and Sofie would be nowhere to be found, vanished into thin air, a little like his handle on her.

He reached out again and again, sure he had her measure, only to find his hand empty.

At the third intersection he heard the sound of footsteps to his right and started down the tunnel cautiously.

He had seen more than one automaton in the machine rooms, pinchers ready to loosen or tighten valves, but some human intervention would be required.

He warned himself this might not be Sofie he was following.

But as he walked around the curve of the tunnel, he caught a glimpse of her just up ahead.

Then he heard her call out, and his own call of greeting died in his throat.

He pressed himself up against the wall and edged around and caught sight of Sofie as she threw herself into the arms of a massive man in a maintenance uniform.

"Sofie-girl." The man's dark skin gleamed under the harsh tunnel lights as he lifted her up and swung her around. When he set her down, he ran a hand over her wet hair. "How'd you get here?"

She tipped her head back and laughed. "I flew across the hoverway."

He looked at her, waiting, Leo thought, for her to explain the joke, and then he frowned. "What the hell's going on, Sofe?"

"It's complicated, and I never expected to find you here. When I climbed in the tunnel, I thought the best I would do is find one of the others to pass a message on to you, but finding you in person . . ." She paused a moment, then flung her arms around him again.

Leo felt a sick lurch in his stomach.

She let go, stepped back, and pulled something from inside her jacket. "I've been planning on giving this to you for awhile, but things have gotten a little hot. Best you have it now, just in case."

"In case what?" The big man folded his arms across a massive chest and stared down at her.

"In case they get me." She spoke lightly.

"And why would they do that, when you cut ties with us a whole year ago?"

She snorted. "Like that would matter." She continued to hold whatever was in her hand out to him, and he finally took it, slid it into a pocket without looking at it.

"This explosive?" He patted the pocket.

She shrugged. "It's something. Not sure if it's explosive."

"And why would they be after you, Sofe? You get sloppy getting this information? Because I can tell you, it doesn't sound worth your life."

"I got most of it more than three weeks ago, so no, I don't think I'm in any danger over it."

"Then what?" He was still frowning down at her, and then his gaze shifted behind her, hit Leo, and then traveled behind him.

Leo froze, then felt the cool press of a laz against his neck.

"What have we here?" The man directly behind him asked conversationally.

Sofie turned at the sound of his voice, and he watched her eyes widen at the sight of him.

Then she smiled. It was the same warm welcome she'd given him when he'd come through from her bedroom just two days before.

"You're okay."

He was pushed forward, and rather than look behind him to see who was prodding him, he kept his gaze on her.

"Thanks to you."

The big man she'd been speaking to put a hand on her shoulder. "Sounds like you've got a little explaining to do, Sofe."

She angled her head to look back at him, and Leo saw her eyes narrow. "I don't have to explain anything anymore, Zyr. You know that."

Zyr frowned back. "You do when you bring strangers into my tunnels."

"She didn't bring me, I followed her." Leo moved toward her, still ignoring the laz at his neck.

"That's true." The man behind him with the laz spoke reluctantly. "I was checking up on Sofie like you asked me too. I saw the whole thing. Saw this guy following her."

"And who might you be?" Zyr asked Leo, his green eyes shockingly light in his dark face.

Leo didn't recognize him, but he knew the name Sofie had called him. Zyr was someone he'd wanted to talk to for a long time.

"This is Leo Gaudier." Sofie stepped forward, her eyes searching his face as if looking for signs of injury.

"Oh, hell. Sofie-girl, you've decided to play with the devil?" Zyr's voice was soft. "You *want* to put a target on your back?"

She shrugged. "Hi, Sunny." She gave a little wave, Leo assumed to the man holding a weapon on him. Then she turned to Zyr. "There's a target on his back, not mine. I just keep getting caught up in it."

"And instead of walking away, you got involved?" Zyr's voice dripped with annoyance.

Again she shrugged. "I get to pick my own causes these days. You know that."

"Leo Gaudier isn't a cause."

Leo lifted his gaze to meet Zyr's. Finally, something they could agree on.

"She saved lover-boy's life here by jumping across the hoverway." Sunny's voice took on a strange pitch. "She rode the roofs, man."

Zyr went still, shot Sofie a quick look. "That's why you were laughing?" He sounded outraged. "You literally rode the hovers?"

"We talked about doing it, once. Do you remember?" Her question was soft, ignoring the fear and anger in his tone.

"We were playing what-if. It was a game." Zyr's voice softened as well.

"Well, it wasn't as fun as we thought it would be," she said. "Or maybe I'm just a more responsible adult now."

Her words seemed to snap something in Zyr. He straightened up. "Let's get lover-boy and you somewhere nice and quiet, and we can discuss this without worrying about who's going to come along."

She nodded, flicked Leo another glance, as if to check that he was okay with the plan--not that he had any choice, with Sunny's laz pressing into his neck.

But none of that seemed to matter, because Sunny had called him her lover-boy, and then so had Zyr, and she hadn't once contradicted them.

Leo followed Sofie as she turned and walked beside Zyr, and decided it was best no one knew how easily he was pleased.

CHAPTER 9

THE ROOM ZYR led them to was like those Leo had passed on the way down the tunnel, full of machinery and an automaton.

This one, though, had a desk with a few drawers, and an old chair that looked like the castoff of a Cores exec.

If he were to guess, this was Zyr's unofficial office.

Zyr had been murmuring into his headset since he'd ordered them to follow him, and no sooner had they stepped into the room than a woman in a maintenance overall arrived.

She glanced at Leo with a degree of hostility, and then flung her arms around Sofie, as if she hadn't seen her in a long time.

A year, Leo remembered from her conversation with Zyr. She hadn't been part of the resistance for a year.

It niggled, though.

She'd known who he was when he'd approached her. So why had she gotten involved with him?

It seemed she was at least still friendly with the members of the resistance, and she may have thought she'd pick up something of interest from him.

"I don't like the look you're giving my girl, Gaudier." Zyr's hand came down on his shoulder.

"What look is that?" Leo shrugged off the hand and turned to face the elusive leader of Tether Town's resistance.

"Like you're wondering if she got involved with you to pass information to me." He sent Leo a quick grin. "Not that I'd be sad if she did, but I didn't even know she was seeing you, and the last time she passed me information was four months ago. Even then, it was a favor. She walked away and hasn't been back."

"And why is that?"

"That's hers to tell. I'm assuming from your surprise that you didn't know she used to be one of us."

Leo shook his head. "I started to suspect she was more than just an office worker a few nights ago, when she saved my life. I knew it for sure this evening when she saved it again."

Zyr whistled. "You don't have good security, do you? I'm surprised."

"The first time, my security was bought out by the Cores. Tonight, we were simply overpowered." At least he had the comfort of knowing Finkle had been prepared to put his life on the line for Leo. He wouldn't have to deal with another betrayal.

"And you're sure you didn't know who she was? Because I'm betting you chased my girl, not the other way around."

"Would you do me a favor?" Leo tried not to snarl. "Would you stop calling her your girl."

Zyr grinned again, a quick, joyful flash that reminded Leo of Sofie's own reactions. "She *is* my girl, because we grew up together. Her sister, Rach, and I, we were a thing, and even when that didn't work out, we were tight. We were family." Then his expression hardened. "And I don't like the thought of someone trying to use my girl to get to me. So, straight up, did you know who she was?"

Leo gave him a cool look. "No. But you're right, I have been trying to get in touch with you. How many times have you ignored my messages?"

Zyr looked down on him. The man was at least three inches taller than Leo, and Leo knew he was well above average.

"Why would I trust a message from you? You could have been a Cores operative, trying to get me to break cover."

Leo nodded. He had guessed why Zyr hadn't come out of the shadows. Still . . . "I communicated with Veld when he was the leader. He strung me along for a while, until I eventually worked out he was playing me, that he never intended to meet. But I tried to reach out again when I heard he'd been . . . deposed."

"Veld and Garde, his second-in-command, both," Zyr agreed. He said nothing more, but Leo had long wondered what had happened. A falling out was obvious, but if Zyr hadn't killed the former leader and his second-in-command, it was a mystery as to where they were.

The Cores didn't let anyone off Garmen, and while Tether Town ran to at least a million people, Veld couldn't have disappeared that completely into the shanties.

Not with Leo actively looking for him.

"Well, now you're here, right in front of me, what do you have to say?" Zyr asked, and a hush seemed to fall over the small group.

Leo had kept watch on who had entered the room while he was speaking to Zyr.

Sunny stood to one side of him, still on some sort of guard duty, but aside from the woman who'd come in, a man has also joined them. The two newcomers stood beside Sofie, and now they turned toward him and Zyr.

Leo shook his head. "Before I say anything that would get me into a lot of trouble with the Cores, who are these people?"

Zyr nodded in respect. "Raym and Fallia are my deputies. You already know Sunny, who was checking up on Sofie while she was in Felicitos."

At that, Sofie lifted her head, eyes wide.

Zyr shrugged. "Sorry, Sofe, but things are complicated."

"Explain complicated." She was shocked, Leo could see, but she kept her tone even.

Zyr looked over at him. "That's not something I'm going to say in front of a stranger."

This is where they had their sticking point.

Neither of them trusted the other enough. And Leo knew that was probably how it should be. This was a high-stakes game, and he wasn't prepared to throw it away by trusting someone he shouldn't.

Even if they obviously cared for Sofie.

"Let me guess--Veld and Garde switched sides to work for the Cores, but none of you realized it." Leo had guessed that was the reason the old leader and his deputy had vanished just under a year ago. "And now you're afraid that Veld told the Cores Sofie was one of you."

There was absolute silence for a moment.

"Tell me what you know." Zyr's voice had deepened. His hand reached out, as if to grab Leo's arm, but he managed to control the instinct and dropped it.

"I don't know anything for sure." Leo kept his gaze on Sofie, who seemed to be even more stunned than the others. They knew this, she obviously didn't. "But when the head of an organization and his second disappear so completely, it's either because there's been a coup, and someone wants to take the organization in a different direction, or they are suspected or discovered to be traitors." He finally glanced at Zyr. "But the resistance hasn't changed direction; in fact, I'd say you've been more successful against the Cores in the last year than you were in all the years before that. So my inference was that Veld was undermining you from within, and taking payment from the Cores to do so."

Zyr seemed to deflate. "Fucker was probably working for them from the start."

"Keep your friends close, and your enemies closer." Sofie spoke for the first time. "That's what Veld used to say. Every time he said it, he must have been laughing to himself."

Zyr's light green eyes flashed in fury. "You and I were always alike, Sofe. Of everything, thinking back on it now, that little saying of his is what pisses me off the most."

"So what happened to Veld and his deputy?" Leo asked.

Zyr lifted his shoulders. "I wish I knew. He and Garde worked the transport hovers up on the landing deck, loading and unloading goods from the big transport ships to the warehouses. It's hard to get up there without the proper authorization, but I managed it once, spied on them for a little while. There's a big warehouse there where they were always working, but I couldn't see any obvious signs of collusion. Unlike what you think, I didn't work out Veld and Garde were traitors and kick them out until after they left. I was working on it, Veld knew I was suspicious, but they disappeared before I could confront him. One day they were here, then they headed for work, and no one saw them again."

"And after they left?" Sofie asked him.

"When I got into that office of Veld's, and had Fallia work her decrypt magic, we found deals going back years with the Cores. I don't know if he was independent, and sabotaging us when they chose to pay him, or whether he was a mole they'd put in at the beginning who'd always been on their payroll. Everything was compromised."

"Rach." Sofie said the name as if she was lost. "I knew he was responsible for Rach's death. I just thought he'd sent her in somewhere without enough protection."

Zyr rubbed a hand over his mouth. "From what Fallia found in the files, it seems Rach had worked out Veld's secret. I don't think the Cores killed her like we thought, Sofe. I think either Veld or Garde did it themselves."

Sofie sucked in a breath. "And he's still out there somewhere?"

"Not on-planet." Zyr shook his head. "He's gone. Garde with him. I paid a lot of what we had in the war chest to someone who worked with them on the Deck for information. They told me both of them got off Garmen. Got a Cores job elsewhere."

"The Cores don't operate elsewhere," Sofie said.

"If you believe that," Leo said, "I have a tethered way station to sell you."

CHAPTER 10

SHE'D HATED Veld for so long.

Hated the way he'd manipulated Rach, had sucked her in and then spit her out, sending her--she'd thought--to her death.

But it had been more direct than that. Less complicated.

Veld had killed her himself.

And then stood beside Sofie and tried to tell her that sacrifices had to be made sometimes. That it was a dangerous world, and belonging to the resistance was risky. A risk everyone accepted.

Rach had died getting information, he'd told her. Her death was an honorable one.

She *had* died getting information, it seemed.

Only, it wasn't information about the Cores exec Veld had pushed Rach to get involved with. It had been information about him.

"Do you think Veld got paid for Rach sleeping with that exec? That he got pimp money?" she asked. "After all, he sent her to him."

The room fell dead silent.

"I never even thought about that," Raym said. "But knowing what I know now about him, I wouldn't be surprised."

"We don't do that anymore, Sofe. I agreed with you from the start there was no need for any of us to compromise ourselves like that, and since I took control, it's off the table as a strategy." Zyr took a step toward her, but there was a lot he'd kept from her in the last year, and she gave a quick shake of her head to back him off.

"And you think he sold us all out? That the Cores know I'm a previous operative?" A wave of cold fear flowed over her just thinking about how she'd delivered herself into their hands day after day.

"I don't know. A few members have gone missing since he left. Just disappeared." Zyr shrugged. "I think some went with him, to whatever dirty job the Cores had for him. But others have died nasty deaths on the street. Some of it may just be T-Town being T-Town, but there's a little too many for coincidence."

"And you didn't think to tell me?" Sofie didn't know what to do with her hands. She gripped them together, let them go. Gripped them again.

"I didn't want to admit to you I hadn't seen it." Zyr was watching her with those beautiful green eyes, and she could see he was agonized. "And I wanted a better grasp of the situation. I needed to know who was in it with him. Could he have been in bed with the Cores that long and not turned others, or paid them to look the other way?"

"You think the rot goes deeper?" Leo's question made them all remember he was in the room.

Zyr nodded. "Has to. Just . . . has to. So Fallia and I kept things quiet after we read the decrypted files. And we worked through them. Found ourselves a rat or two. And they paid the price." His voice was grim. "But there might be others. We cleared who we could. Raym and Sunny, and probably about twenty others I can absolutely say are clean. But that leaves a lot of others. Most are innocent, but I just need to trust one wrong person, and the Cores will know. I'm waiting for someone to approach me. Someone to offer me money to keep Veld's work up."

"You thought it might be me," Leo murmured. "You thought I might be the one the Cores were sending to offer you the same terms they'd given Veld."

Zyr nodded.

"How do we know it's *not* him?" Raym asked.

"Sofes?" Fallia turned to her.

Sofie lifted her gaze to Leo's. "He's no Cores agent. They've tried to kill him twice in three days."

"That would make it three times this month." Leo's lips quirked at the edges.

"What have you done to rile them up so much?" Zyr asked.

Leo hesitated. "Like you, I have a few trust issues. Suffice to say, I'm hitting them where it hurts them the most."

"Their profit column," Sofie said, and Leo flashed a quick smile at her.

"To what end? Your own enrichment?" Sunny shifted his stance, but Sofie saw he'd dropped his hand, pointing his laz at the ground, rather than at Leo.

Leo turned and gave him a cool look. "Again, that's my business. I don't know you well enough to go into details."

Neither side did, Sofie thought, with a touch of impatience. But given Veld's betrayal, and Leo's recent brushes with assassins, she couldn't blame either group.

And she was stuck in the middle.

"What's your end game?" Leo moved his gaze from her to Zyr. "What's the resistance hoping for."

"We want to overthrow the Cores, but given that that would

take more than a few of us with it, we've settled on doing what you say you are doing, too. We're cutting into their profits."

Leo frowned. "How?"

Fallia and Zyr exchanged a look. Raym looked mutinous, as if he didn't think it was a good idea to talk, but eventually, Zyr's body language changed, relaxed a little.

"Sofie isn't the only person working in a Core Company. We have an army of them. And they pass us what they hear, who's dealing with who, what price X is paying compared to Y. And then we pass the information along to whoever is losing out. It stirs up resentment, it degrades the Top Five's trust in each other, and ultimately, it disrupts their businesses."

Leo whistled. "I wondered why I started making more money about six months ago. That's the accumulated effect of this, isn't it? The Cores would rather go to independents like me, because you've eroded their trust in each other, and it's hurting them. They're starting to get reckless with their off-planet machinations, because they're getting desperate."

"What off-planet machinations?" Raym asked, suddenly fully engaged.

"There's been a few incidents recently . . ." Leo frowned at them, and then realization dawned in his eyes. "You can't get access to interplanetary comms, can you?"

"We aren't Core execs," Zyr reminded him. "I'm assuming you can?"

Leo nodded, and Sofie stared at him. She hadn't realized he had access.

"The heads of independent corporations that make over a certain amount do have access. It's a concession for the level of trading fee we pay them."

"And?" Zyr asked.

They were all suddenly hanging on his every word. Sofie

herself hadn't realized how hungry she was for outside news until now.

"There've been two incidents recently in the Verdant String, one on Cepi, a moon that used to orbit Kalastoni, and another in Var, the capital city of Parn. Both cases involved a ship that looked like stolen Verdant String tech, and had at least some smugglers involved."

"The Verdant String is blaming the Breakaways? Blaming Garmen?" Sofie didn't know whether that was good or bad news.

"Not outright, but it has the Breakaways' fingerprints all over it. It's got to be coming either from Garmen or Lassa, or both working together."

"What happened in the incidents?" Fallia leaned in.

Leo lifted his shoulders. "They tried to steal some tech from Cepi, and when they were caught, they destroyed the evidence by strafing the moon from their warship. And in Var, they blew up a string of buildings. Both times it was made to look like rebels or insurgents causing trouble. They used Halatians as hostages both times, as well."

There was silence for a beat.

Everyone went still.

"What did I say?" Leo's gaze swung around the room, came to rest on her.

"Veld always used to say Halatians would make the perfect hostages." Sofie forced herself to speak. "He used to complain to me and Rach that even though we had a Halatian father, we didn't get the blue hair because our mother was Arkhoran. He used to say if he held a gun to a Halatian's head, he'd get whatever he wanted from the VSC."

"That's exactly what they tried to do." Leo tilted his head. "Maybe that new job Veld got from the Cores involved planning insurgent maneuvers off-planet."

"Did they arrest the insurgents?" Raym asked.

"Some of them," Leo said. "Most of them are dead."

"The VSC killed them?"

Leo shook his head. "Every single one was killed by their own side, the VSC assumes to stop them from talking."

"Now that clinches it." Zyr's voice was a deep rumble. "The Cores are definitely involved."

CHAPTER 11

LEO FELT the itch to be back in his office, accessing the interplanetary comms to find out if there was any mention of Veld or Garde in connection with the Cepi incident, or what had just happened in Var.

But there was something more important he had to do first--he had to work out how to protect Sofie.

"The Cores execs and their guards saw you earlier," he said to her. "When you jumped from hover to hover over the--" His throat closed up. He hadn't realized how much what she'd done had scared him until now. He cleared his throat. "Over the hoverway."

"You think they'll be looking for me?"

His automatic response was yes, but he hesitated. "It's possible they'll assume you're one of my guards."

Zyr nodded. "That's true, and if it is, they won't spend any time on her."

Leo looked over at him. "Unless they want to bribe her. Like they did the guard Sofie saved me from two nights ago."

"All the more likely they'll think I'm your guard, then," Sofie pointed out. "They might decide you were pretending to be out to dinner with me to see if they'd make a move."

Leo realized she was right. "That would be as good an outcome as we can expect."

"I'd rather they didn't take me aside for questioning when I try to leave Felicitos tonight, or when I come in to work tomorrow." Sofie's tone was dry.

"Don't go out the the main doors. Use an alternative exit," Zyr told her.

Leo wondered if the alternative exit was what she'd used two nights ago to get them both out of Felicitos. He would have to ask her to show that to him again, this time when he was conscious.

"I'll find out what I can from Finkle about what happened after I followed you. If you're in any danger from the Cores, I'll make sure you get the message."

Sofie narrowed her eyes at him.

"Would the person who gives me that message be the same person who scared the life out of me the other day?" She turned her narrow-eyed gaze on Zyr. "Or can I thank you for that?"

Leo cleared his throat. "That was my doing."

Sofie's look should have dropped him where he stood.

"I thought it was the Cores," she said, her voice cold. "I nearly got killed running into some oppos because I was trying to get away from your guy."

"I should have told you." He still went cold at the thought of her down a dangerous alley, but it had been replaced in his head with the sight of her leaping across the hoverway. "I wanted to make sure there was no fallout for you after what happened in The High Flyer."

"And was there?" Zyr asked. "Any fallout?"

Sofie shook her head. "I don't think so."

Leo also shook his head. "My team says there's been no moves against her. No followers, no watchers."

"Jumping over the hoverway is a little more high viz," Fallia said. She had dark eyes, and they were full of worry. "You have to be more careful, Sofe. Zyr's right. Go out the alternative route. I'll go with you."

Sofie looked over at him. "And you? They're ramping up their attacks on you."

"And you still haven't told us why," Zyr said.

Leo hesitated. A little information wouldn't hurt. "When Veld was running the resistance, I tried to get in touch, to coordinate my efforts with him, if that was possible, but as I told you, he strung me along, and I gave up. I didn't tell him who I was, something I'm grateful for given what you've told me about his connection to the Cores, although I'm surprised he didn't try to find out more about what I wanted. It would have been in the Cores' interests."

"What Fallia discovered in the files she decrypted shows a pattern of laziness more than anything. He made as much money as he could with as little effort as possible. He wasn't prepared to go the extra mile for the Cores. He wasn't a believer in anything but his own profit."

"How convenient for us." Leo knew the type. Knew he'd rather go up against someone like Veld than a fanatical believer any day.

Zyr inclined his head. "So when Veld brushed you off?"

"I started doing a little resistance of my own." Leo wasn't going to give them anything too specific.

"Like?" Raym scowled.

"That's all I'm prepared to give you." Leo gave him a cold smile. "Suffice to say, what I'm doing interfered with some of the Cores' plans, and they've come to the conclusion it's best if I go away. But my guess is they want to have a little chat with me first."

"Except, tonight they tried to kill you, not grab you," Sofie pointed out.

"Perhaps after The High Flyer, they decided it would be easier to just get rid of me." Not a happy thought.

"Where do we go from here?" Zyr asked him. "We obviously aren't prepared to put everything on the table with each other, but if you're telling the truth, we might be able to coordinate some things."

Leo gave a slow nod. "Sofie can be our intermediary. If something comes up I think you can help with, I'll let you know."

He realized he'd made a mistake when Sofie went very still, and Zyr sent her a quick, nervous look.

"Would that be all right with you, Sofie-girl?"

"It'll be hard for me to be an intermediary as I don't have anything to do with Leo any more." Sofie turned to Leo as she spoke, and Leo winced.

"I said good bye because I wanted you to be safe. I thought if we didn't see each other again . . ." He closed his eyes, tipped back his head and rubbed his forehead. "I'm sorry. What I really want is for you to come live in my house, where no one can get you."

She looked genuinely startled. "And how will I pay my bills? And how will I be an intermediary if I'm not coming and going from Felicitos? Staying with you will trap me in your house. They'll know I'm definitely linked to you after that."

He had sort of hoped her staying with him *would* trap her in his house, where she would be nice and safe, out of the hands of oppos and the Cores. Where she wouldn't be put in a situation where she thought jumping from hover to hover over a chasm that dropped one hundred thou to the planet below from the upper atmosphere was a reasonable response.

He drew a deep breath in through his nose. "What do you suggest?"

"I'll sneak out the hidden tunnel, go home, and wait to hear if you have any news. You can ask your guy to knock on my door like a normal person. And then, if all is well, I'll go into work tomorrow, just like I usually would. I think the more I deviate from my schedule, the more visible I start to become."

"We'll keep a watch on you," Zyr said.

"My people will, too."

Sofie shook her head in frustration. "Be careful you don't bump into each other."

"I'll do you a deal." Zyr looked over at him. "While she's in Felicitos, we'll take care of her. While she's outside in Tether Town, she's all yours."

Leo gave a nod. That worked for him. It seemed the resistance had back doors in the tethered way station he knew nothing about. They'd infiltrated the maintenance crews, and obviously knew the place better than the Cores did.

Whereas when it came to Tether Town, just his name was enough to make the oppos run and hide.

"Ever find the kill switch while you were crawling around in these tunnels?" he asked.

There was a short moment of silence, and everyone shifted uncomfortably.

Everyone except Sofie. She gave him a stony look.

Then Sunny darted a quick, guilty look at Sofie and cleared his throat. "That would be sweet. I've kept my eyes open for it, ever since I heard the story."

"The story is bullshit, Sunny." Sofie's tone brooked no argument.

"Sorry, Sofes, but you weren't there when Fadal died and you didn't hear what that nurse heard."

Zyr sent Sunny a furious look. "No, she wasn't there when he died."

Sunny seemed to realize his mistake, and looked down at his feet.

"What am I missing?" Leo asked.

"Nothing. Except that we all knew Ronald Fadal a little. We

worked the construction crews," Zyr said, his tone dour. "He was a brilliant engineer and architect. Not once did he ever let on he'd built a kill switch into Felicitos's design."

"I heard he did it when he realized the Cores weren't going to stop shielding the smugglers from the Verdant String. They kidnapped his own people after Halatia was destroyed, and the Cores did nothing to stop them taking refuge on Garmen." Leo had followed all the rumors--after all, he wouldn't be the wealthy man he was today without Ronald Fadal.

"It would have been a bit late to add in a kill switch right at the end." Raym shook his head. "They murdered him when it was finished, rather than have him walking around, bitter and with the plans in his head. But he didn't know that's what they'd planned until he fell ill from poisoning, two days before he died."

"The thing is, the Cores execs knew that what the smugglers had done to the Halatians was a hot button for him. They told him they would round the smugglers up and he went on believing their false promises right until the end." Sofie's mouth was turned down in a sneer. "He gave them everything. He would never have put his precious tower in jeopardy with a kill switch."

There was so much more here than he understood. Every instinct in Leo was screaming at him. He turned to Sunny, the weak link among them when it came to this. "What did he say on his deathbed that makes you think there's a kill switch?"

"He said, 'I built it, and I can bring it down'." Sunny's voice held the suppressed excitement of a treasure hunter.

Zyr shook his head. "Then he tried to slit his own wrist with a knife from his dinner tray. The poison had obviously driven him mad."

"Give it up, Sunny." Fallia's mouth formed a hard line of disapproval. "This tethered way station is an engineering marvel. Fadal was proud of what he'd done for its own sake. Did he love the

Cores at the end? No. Did he want to bring down what he'd spent eight years of his life building? No again."

"You got that right." Sofie seemed to have shaken off the fury that had burned in her earlier. Now she exuded calm. "He gave everything to Felicitos, and then died with nothing. But he loved it like he loved nothing else. He would never have wanted it harmed."

"I worked on the crew building this place at the end, and I never saw anything that looked like a kill switch." Zyr's voice was matter-of-fact.

"There still could be one," Sunny said stubbornly. "If he was hiding it, he wouldn't make it obvious. The Cores had to be watching him."

Zyr shook his head, and Sofie said nothing, her face a blank page.

"You need a guide to get you to your floor?" Zyr suddenly asked Leo, and Leo realized this little meeting was over.

He nodded.

"Sofie . . ." He hadn't touched her once since he'd left her apartment two days ago, and he really wanted to, even with the disapproving audience around them. "Will you play intermediary? Please?"

It would at least be a way to keep the connection between them open.

She lifted her gaze to his. "How? Will there be a signal between your watcher and me?"

He didn't want that. Didn't want to hear from her via someone else. He suddenly thought of an amazing solution.

"Come work for me in my office. The Cores already know you've got some link to me. This way, you'll be able to pay your bills, and you won't be sitting in a Cores office, putting yourself in their hands every day."

She angled her head. "Doing what?"

"Whatever it is you do for them would work. Although I'd prefer it if you didn't pass on my company information to Zyr. If you don't mind."

Her lips quirked in a quick smile. "I have to give one day's notice. And it means I won't be able to help Zyr anymore."

"You'll be helping as an intermediary," Zyr pointed out. "And I'd rather you work in a place where you'll be protected, rather than on your own in a Cores office."

She nodded slowly. "All right. I'll see you the day after tomorrow."

It wasn't the relationship Leo'd envisioned when he'd entered the Upper Reaches bar and stumbled at the sight of her. But he'd take anything he could get.

CHAPTER 12

"WHICH EXIT ARE WE USING?" Fallia asked as Sofie bypassed the small pad and swiped her finger through the activated laser lock to open the lift hidden at the back of the maintenance tunnel.

"The bottom one. I used it two days ago." She had only used it once before, nearly a year ago. Now she was using it twice in almost as many days.

Life had most definitely gotten more interesting since she'd met Leo.

"After the first attempt on lover-boy's life?" Fallia asked as she stepped in after her.

Sofie nodded, punched in the code for the level below the water tank, deep underground. "He was hit. I couldn't carry him out, and we needed to leave. It was the best option."

"So he knows where it is?"

Sofie looked across at her sharply, and Fallia lifted her hands, palm up.

"I just need to keep track of who knows, that's all. Basic security."

Sofie considered, gave a nod of acceptance as they hurtled downward. "He was unconscious almost the whole time. I don't think he'd be able to find it again. And he was definitely unconscious when I opened the tunnel door."

"So he knows it's there, but not where to find it?" Fallia tapped her finger to her lip. "What are the chances he'll go looking for it?"

"I'd say pretty high. He now knows first hand what a handy exit it is." Sofie had no illusions about Leo. His relentless focus was one of the most attractive things about him.

"You going to show him?" Fallia leaned back, arms crossed over her chest.

Sofie thought about it. "Depends."

"On?"

"On whether it's to use for his business, or whether it's to help someone."

"He could lie about that." Fallia's lips formed a thin line.

"He could, but I don't think he will. Not to me." She was aware she sounded like a fool when she said that, and wasn't surprised to see Fallia roll her eyes.

"You don't *think* he will?" Fallia didn't hide her sarcasm.

Sofie sighed. "I won't tell him, unless it's life or death. Happy?"

"No," Fallai shot straight back. "But I trust you, even if I don't trust him. He's a parasite, Sofes. Just like the parasites we used to watch when we were kids. Sucking the life and the blood out of this place, getting fat on the gen-pop's hard work."

"I don't think he's the same as those leeches. There's more to him."

"That's what you want to think." Fallia looked at her with pity.

She shrugged. "Maybe. But he makes my heart do double time and I feel a thrill just thinking about him, like I'm hover hopping over the hoverway." She reached out and gently touched Fallia's hand. "It's been a long time since anything touched me. And he does."

"I'm scared for you. Scared it'll end really badly." Fallia's gaze bore into hers. "You're a special case. You could help someone like him a lot with your access to Felicitos. Are you sure he didn't set out to find you?"

Sofie shook her head. She didn't, but she couldn't prove it. Didn't want to try.

The semi-circle that was the lift door pivoted open, and they stepped out, both subdued.

Rach had been the link that bound her and Fallia together, and Sofie wanted that connection to continue. She didn't like feeling Fallia was disappointed in her, but she hadn't done anything wrong.

"He's seen and done some bad, bad things." Fallia wouldn't let it go. "It's in his eyes."

"And your point is?"

"Can't go against the Cores and not get your hands dirty."

Sofie scoffed. "And you're going to tell me that bothers you?"

"No." Fallia drew the word out. "I agree with going against the Cores. But that kind of thing, it leaves a mark on the soul."

"So far, I haven't seen his soul." She shot Fallia a deliberately bawdy look, and despite the tension between them, Fallia let out a laugh.

"And what have you seen?" She was smiling for the first time.

"Never you mind. Just understand that it was all prime." No need to say everything she'd seen had been covered in clothing of some sort--this was definitely helping calm the waters.

"That, I did notice." Fallia fanned her face with her hand.

They looked at each other for a moment, and then burst out laughing.

"It's really good to see you, Sofe." Fallia gave her a one-armed hug as they walked down the long, echoing passageway. "You should have come back to us sooner."

Sofie sighed. "There were too many who did nothing while

Veld pushed his horrible little plans on Rach. I can't be in the same room with them. They didn't say anything, they didn't protest. They had to know it was all kinds of wrong."

Fallia nodded. "Some of them have dropped off. Zyr thinks they may have turned on us, or were with the Cores all along."

"Like who?" Better she knew, in case she saw them. She'd passed many of her old friends on the street or in Felicitos this past year, and the rules about not acknowledging each other in public had worked in her favor.

Fallia named a couple of people, but Sofie couldn't remember seeing them since she left. So maybe Zyr was right, maybe they had gone with Veld, to meddle somewhere else in the name of the Breakaways.

She did not wish them well.

They were approaching the end of the passageway. Sofie could heard the thump of the pump next to the secret tunnel entrance.

"What's your end game in all of this?" Fallia asked. "You still want to leave Garmen?"

Sofie hesitated for the first time in a while. "That was the plan. To leave. To find a way off, and get to Arkhor."

"It's not anymore?"

"I don't know." She hated that things had become so much less clear of late. It was easier in black and white. When Rach had died, there had been no gray. She wanted to be gone with every fiber of her being. "Everything is wrong with this place. It needs to change. If I could leave, would I just be a coward, saving myself, and leaving everyone else to rot?"

Fallia stood back as Sofie tapped the code into the keypad on the pump and then pulled the wall back so they could step through.

"It's hard, caring too much, is it?"

As the wall snicked closed behind them, Sofie nodded in agreement.

It was so much easier not to give a damn.

CHAPTER 13

SHE HAD slid through work the day before like a curn, one of the gilled, snake-like fish from the river, twisting and weaving through the obstacles in her way as she tendered her resignation, kept her head down, and did her full day's work without a word to her colleagues.

Leo's watcher had knocked on her door the night before and told her there was no indication anyone was looking for her, but it didn't hurt to keep her head down and look innocuous.

In her experience, the left hand of the Cores didn't know what the right hand was doing. They made money in spite of themselves, not through sharp management or logical processes, but simply because they controlled everything.

Her resignation was logged without question, and it didn't appear anyone informed her manager. She stayed late, handing off the balance of her workload to him after he'd already gone home.

Then she'd taken a gen-pop hover down, waiting in line like a good worker, giving no one any cause to look at her twice.

Today she'd come in to Felicitos the same way for her first day at work with Leo, blending with the crowd, submitting to the push and shove without question or reaction.

When she reached Leo's floor, she stepped from the hover onto the platform and forced herself not to look down.

She'd had nightmares two nights running where she slid across the hover roof, but instead of shoving the assassin over the edge and crouching down safely, he'd grabbed her and pulled her over with him.

She woke before she hit the bottom, both times.

Finkle stood waiting for her just beyond the platform, and she walked toward him.

"Problem?" she asked when she was close enough.

He shook his head. "Just keeping the boss happy."

"You don't approve?" There was nothing in his tone to suggest it, but she sensed a reticence in him. And Leo's interest in her had to have complicated Finkle's life.

She bet he wished Leo had never laid eyes on her.

He sent her a quick glance as he turned to lead the way to the office. "I have no opinion."

Sofie grinned. Like hell he didn't.

She let it go. Finkle had put himself in front of the assassin to protect Leo. He could disapprove of her if he wanted to.

The passage curved and then ended in an open area with seating and a circular jah bar. A massive window looked out into Garmen's upper atmosphere.

Far below, thick clouds swirled and no doubt rained on Tether Town. Up here, just above the stratosphere, light from the sun was harsher, more intense, and the window was tinted. It cast everything in a lavender glow.

She hadn't been in this part of Felicitos since it had been finished. The independents were on the lower floors of the Upper Reaches, and they'd made their surroundings a lot nicer than the Cores had done for their offices on the floors above.

Those had no lounges, no jah makers, and no windows.

No unnecessary money had been spent.

Finkle swept his arm toward a set of double doors, and held one open for her.

She stepped into an oasis of calm.

A woman with silver-streaked hair looked up from her desk and gave Sofie a thorough once-over.

"Sofie Erdo." Sofie extended her hand.

"Eunice Daly." Eunice took her hand in a firm grasp. "Leo said to send you straight in whenever you arrived."

Sofie nodded and Finkle led her down a corridor and past a series of open doors containing numerous people murmuring into comm sets. He rapped on the door at the end of the corridor, opened it, and stood aside so she could go in first.

He followed her in, which surprised her.

Leo was standing by a big window, looking out at Garmen far below him, talking on his comm set. He turned, his gaze jumping to her face. He seemed to relax.

His tone made clear he was wrapping up conversation, and as he turned away again, Sofie looked around the room.

It was a standard office, not the one room on each floor her father had . . . modified.

The modifications had been a game, in the beginning.

It had started with a lesson on Halatian architecture, on how the Halatians were the most innovative designers in the Verdant String.

Her father had left Halatia to work for the Cores, had married her mother when he was stationed at one of the Core Companies' offices on Arkhor, and had taken them all to Garmen when they'd discovered the Breakaways.

But life was brutal on Garmen, and their Arkhoran mother had died of one of the many diseases that had swept through Tether Town in the early days. And then shortly afterward, Halatia had been destroyed, the tectonic plates on the planet ripped asunder in a massive natural catastrophe that had killed most of the population and caused the rest to flee.

Her father had never gotten over it.

He'd thought he'd have the chance to go home again. Show her and Rach the wonders of Halatia and the beautiful cities built with glorious buildings.

But not only was Halatia destroyed, those who'd managed to escape had been taken hostage for ransom, and it had taken the Verdant String months to get control of the situation.

By the end of it, not only was Halatia gone, so were most of her people.

Her father had found it hard to grasp that he was one of the few Halatians left.

At the start, he'd coped by telling them stories about Halatia, and specifically about the quirks the Halatians liked to build into their homes, the secret rooms and hidden passages, the insistence on beauty as well as function.

They'd encouraged him to put a Halatian stamp on Felicitos with a child's delight in the idea of secret passageways and rooms.

But they'd lost him to it.

He'd become obsessed with dedicating the way station to his destroyed home planet. As a memorial to everyone he'd lost when it had been ripped apart.

As he sunk deeper and deeper into the abyss, she and Rach had to fend for themselves.

She still didn't know where his salary had gone. All she knew was that they barely had enough to feed themselves. When he'd died, she and Rach had gone through his financial affairs, and found he had been paid by the Cores. They weren't cheating him, as they'd suspected at the time.

It was a mystery. Her father had had only one vice, and that was his obsession with Felicitos.

Out of desperation, they'd aligned themselves with the construction crew, playing up and down the ladders and scaffolding as Felicitos was built from the ground up, forging networks and friendships that had kept them safe. Kept them sane.

Her father had coded her and Rach's birthdays into every lock as the tower rose up; more, she was sure, so that they could come and go without him needing to take them home when it was bedtime.

She hadn't met a door on Felicitos she couldn't open.

When her father had realized not only would the Cores never officially dedicate Felicitos to Halatia and its people, nor stop the smugglers who'd ransomed the Halatian survivors from hiding from justice by using Garmen as a safehaven, he'd turned bitter and angry.

And he'd built his secret rooms and passageways with a vengeance.

He made it a tribute to Halatia without the Cores knowledge or approval.

And because he couldn't do it by himself, because he needed the construction teams on his side, he'd fallen in with the resistance, and brought Sofie and Rach with him.

But her father, to her knowledge, had never considered including anything that would damage his precious tower into the design. He'd clung to the hope the Cores would change their minds, name the tethered way station for the Halatian victims, and hunt the smugglers down.

He loved this tower more than he loved either her or Rach.

He'd lived for it. He'd died for it.

"Sofie?"

She had walked to the window herself while Leo finished up his call, leaning against it and looking out over Garmen. She'd been cloud gathering, as her mother used to say.

Leo and Finkle were both looking at her, Leo with concern, Finkle with scrupulous politeness.

"Sorry. What did I miss?"

Leo gave her another careful look, as if she were fragile, and then waved at the screen on his desk. "I did a search yesterday for any mention of Veld or Garde. Nothing came up, but this morning there was a cryptic message waiting for me. Someone in Arkhor is interested in why I'm looking."

"How did they know who you were?" She hadn't had access to interplanetary comms since she was about thirteen, when the Cores cut off gen-pop access, but she thought searches were anonymous.

Leo gave a cynical smile. "I'm guessing the VSC has their ways. Maybe they've set up an electronic trip wire on those search terms." He shrugged. "They know I'm from Garmen, and they want to know how I know the names of two of the insurgents who infiltrated Cepi and tried to steal the alien enviro generator that covered the ruins."

"So Veld and Garde *were* involved. And that means the Cores are, too." Again Sofie didn't know if this was good or bad. If the Verdant String wanted to punish Garmen, they could put sanctions in place, and that would affect everyone, not just the Cores. If they were really serious about stopping the Cores, though, they could take the planet by force . . . and for her, that would be a better outcome.

"Who's the person in Arkhor who's interested?" Finkle asked.

Leo's lips quirked. "They wouldn't say. My guess is someone in Arkhor Special Forces."

"So is Veld in custody? What happened to him?"

Leo shrugged. "So far, all I've got is questions, not answers."

She could only hope Veld and his little side-kick Garde were locked up somewhere. "I'll need to pass this along to Zyr."

Leo nodded. "I agree. Maybe he can speak to that source of his on the Deck again. If he knows what questions to ask, we could find out more."

"Will you tell whoever on Arkhor has contacted you that Garde and Veld were working for the Cores?" Finkle asked.

Leo lifted his shoulders. "I don't know whether it's wise to let Arkhor Special Forces know that just yet. It's something I'll have to think about."

"I'll send a message to Zyr and organize to meet up with him later." Sofie turned toward the door. "Which office am I working from?"

Leo looked a little disconcerted. "I don't know. Eunice arranged that."

She gave him a cool nod. "Well, I'll let you know what I hear back from Zyr."

She stepped to the door, opened it.

"Sofie."

She turned, saw Finkle looking down at his shoes and Leo standing with feet planted apart, as if ready to go to battle.

"Yes?"

Leo was silent for a beat, then sighed and shook his head. "Have a good day."

She nodded politely and closed the door behind her.

He wanted it both ways. He wanted what they'd had before, but he also wanted to stay away from her, to keep her safe.

There was no safe, but he had to come to that realization on his own.

Her days of chasing after love were over. She either had enthusiastic participation, or she had nothing.

No matter how much it hurt.

She let her fingertips rest against the closed door of Leo's office, then straightened and walked away.

CHAPTER 14

THE SECRET CHAMBER on Leo's floor was in one of the bathrooms. There were six of them, and Sofie simply followed the floor tiles to the one on the far left at the end of the day.

Her father had insisted on designing the flooring, and the Cores had given him his way when he'd promised it would cost them no more than if they'd contracted out.

And if you knew how to read them, the floors gave up Felicitos's secrets like a loose-mouthed gossip.

It was, according to her father, very much the Halatian way.

She slipped inside the bathroom and closed the door. She didn't lock it, she just moved quickly, bending down to depress the tiny tile in the corner.

The wall gave a delayed click and then popped open a little way.

It was clearly in need of some maintenance. She would have to bring some oil tomorrow and grease the hinges, because if she was working on this floor, she'd need to use it again--although not too often. In the full year she'd worked upstairs for the Cores, she hadn't used the secret tunnel once. It wasn't in a bathroom up there, it was in a store room, but if she'd been caught, she'd have been killed.

She'd made the decision when she started working there she would only use her escape hatch in a life or death situation.

But things were different now. The Cores had seen her twice interfering with their plans for Leo. Even if they weren't actively looking for her, if the wrong person caught sight of her moving through the public access spaces, they might just follow her.

That wasn't a good idea tonight.

She pulled the wall back, stepped through and it swung shut behind her.

As soon as it clicked shut, the lights flickered on, went dark, and flickered on again.

She was halfway down the passage when they went off permanently.

It wasn't lack of power, the whole of Felicitos was coated in a thin solar film that trapped enough energy to power not only the way station, but most of Tether Town as well.

There had to be a short somewhere, or a loose wire. She wished for once she had her screen with her, it would light the way, but instead she kept a hand on the wall and walked slowly until she came to the stairs, where the lights were on.

She ran down four flights until she came to a lift, and took that down to the floor where she'd met up with Zyr and Fallia after her jump across the hoverway.

The lift was hidden, lying back to back with the maintenance lift, and she stepped out, walked around the tight curve to the right, and then looked out through a wall of one way material, which allowed her to look out as if through a window, but on the other side, it would seem the same as the rest of the passageway.

She waited a beat, but there was no one around, so she pulled the lever to open the door and stepped out into the maintenance tunnel.

She made her way to the room Zyr had taken them to the other day. It was dark inside, and she frowned as she entered, looking left for the light switch.

Even if Zyr had stepped out for a moment, surely he'd have left the light on?

She heard the whine of a laz and then pain exploded through her.

The last thing she remembered before she was swallowed into darkness was the smell of ozone.

———

She woke to someone patting her cheek. The pats started out softly, but then became a little more forceful.

"Careful. We want her to be able to talk, remember?" The man who spoke had a bored voice, and she heard him move just behind the one slapping her, a slide of expensive shoe on the hard floor.

She fluttered her eyes, just to stop the slapping, which had softened after the other man had given his warning.

"There." The man stepped back. "She's awake."

"Semi-conscious, more like it." The bored voice again. "Give her some water."

Because she felt really thirsty, she fumbled for the cup, sipping from it with both hands, her eyes still half-closed.

She wasn't restrained in any way and she was on some kind of couch or large upholstered chair. When she'd finished the water, she lifted her head, and forced her eyes open.

Two men stood in front of her, in the sharp, dark clothes of Cores bodyguards.

That wasn't a surprise.

What was a surprise was the room they'd put her in. It contained the couch she was sprawled on, a small desk with a chair, and nothing else except the murals on the wall.

She studied them.

This was her father's old office.

She half-remembered it. Back in the day, there was a huge desk here, covered in blueprints, and big screens up on the walls, where her father would scribble equations.

They had brought her to the Under Deck, just under the landing pad at the very top of Felicitos. The place her father had moved to when the bare bones structure was complete.

They had had to import so much of the building materials for the way station, it had been easier for him to be close to the top, where the ships were landing, than down below.

How odd they had turned his office into some kind of strange interrogation room.

At least, if they left her alone for even a minute, she had a way out that didn't involve the door.

Her father had of course made sure the secret tunnel on this floor was through his own office.

"She must really be out of it." The man who'd been tapping her frowned, and Sofie realized she had been paying too much attention to the room, not enough to the threat in front of her.

She took her cue from him and groaned, putting a hand to her forehead.

"You probably used too high a setting," the other man said. "She's not exactly large."

"Where am I?" She blinked as she spoke, squinting up at them.

"That doesn't matter. We want you to talk to someone for us."

She didn't know why her first thought was they wanted her to speak to Veld. She went still at the idea. "Who?" She stuttered it.

"Leo Gaudier."

She was so thrown, she looked up at them, dumbfounded, and both men shifted a little uncomfortably.

"You know Leo Gaudier." The man who stood behind the tapper frowned at her, as if she was being difficult. "You're his lover."

She shot him an incredulous look. "Where did you hear that?"

He frowned again. "You saying you're not?"

"Yes, that's what I'm saying. Are you crazy?"

There was a heavy silence as the two men glanced at each other. "You know him, though."

"I work for him, sure. So do plenty of people." She relaxed back into the couch.

"You're going to call him and tell him you're dead if he doesn't come up here, answer a few questions we have."

She was quiet for a moment. When she looked up, there was no need for her to pretend the fear and acceptance on her face. "Then I'm dead." She shrugged, and closed her eyes.

"What?" The tapper shook her shoulder. "Why do you say that?"

"I'm a low-end employee of Leo's. Even if he were my lover, and he's not, you think he'd come racing over to rescue me, knowing your 'questions' are no more than a thinly veiled attempt to grab him on the quiet and kill him?" She actually managed a laugh. "You must be desperate."

That didn't sit well with either of them. She guessed they had their doubts about the enterprise themselves, because they knew the Cores execs would have openly laughed at a threat like the one they were making if it was one of their employees being held captive. Laughed until they cried.

They didn't think Leo would be any different.

She could only assume someone in the resistance had sold her out for money, or because they were a mole for the Cores. Zyr and Sunny had called Leo her lover-boy, and she'd hinted to Fallia that she was sleeping with him. Someone had gotten the message, and thought it worth a shot to see if Leo would bite.

If he didn't, they'd still have messed with his head, and her death wouldn't weigh on anyone's conscience.

"You're going to contact him."

She shrugged again, opened her eyes. "Sure. He's going to be sorry to lose me, sad I've been caught up in this. That's about it."

They exchanged another look.

"Here's your comm set." The tapper held it out to her, and she went cold at the thought of him searching through her pockets for it while she was unconscious.

When she took it from him, her hand trembled. She used her shock, used her revulsion, to project panic. "I'm no one to him. I'm dead." She started to rock. "I'm dead, I'm dead, I'm dead."

"Shit." The tapper turned. "I believe her."

"Whoever sold the execs this story was getting creative with the truth, all right, but we've got our orders. I'm following them." He shouldered the tapper aside, gave Sofie a smack on the cheek of his own. "Pull it together."

She choked back a hysterical laugh. "Pull it together? Why the hell should I?"

They were quiet, because what could they say to that?

He leaned forward, getting into her face. "I'll tell you why. Because right now, you're not in pain, but that could change really fast if you don't cooperate. Contact Gaudier. Now."

She went still and looked straight into his eyes, saw the promise in them. He wouldn't take pleasure in hurting her, but he wouldn't lose any sleep over it, either.

She hunched over her comm set to give a verbal command. "Contact Leo Gaudier."

She lifted her gaze to her two captors as it connected.

"Sofie?" Leo looked up at her from the tiny screen.

The tapper took the set from her. "We have your lover, Gaudier. Either you come get her from us, or we kill her. Just like those other two who worked for you."

Other two?

Leo hadn't mentioned that.

"I've told them we aren't lovers." She knew her tone had to be just right, felt her heart pounding in her chest at the thought of getting it wrong. She made herself sound exhausted. "I've told them there's nothing between us, and that they've got it all wrong."

"Doesn't matter if it's wrong or not. She works for you. You come get her, Gaudier, or her blood is on your hands."

Sofie grabbed her comm set back, hung on to it while the tapper tried to wrestle it from her hands. "I don't expect you to come, Leo. There's no reason for us both to die, because they're not letting me go, either way. Revenge me well." She cut off the link.

The fury in the tapper's eyes flared up, and he finally wrenched the comm set from her. "What do you think you're doing?"

"Being logical," she said. "Just connecting the dots. You going to tell me you'll let me walk out of here?" She let disdain drip from her voice.

The other man pulled the comm set from the tapper's hands. "I'm going to get further advice. And we can call Gaudier ourselves now." He tapped the comm set against his palm, then walked out the room.

The tapper walked after him, then turned to face her at the doorway, pointed a finger at her. "Don't plan on living much longer." He closed the door harder than necessary, and she heard it lock.

She pursed her lips in satisfaction as she stood up, walked over to a particularly ornate mural, studied it for a moment and pressed in a bird flying over a mountain.

The door whispered open on a quiet sigh, and she stepped in and shut it behind her, then leaned back against the wall and closed her eyes, caught her breath for a minute.

She couldn't say her father never did anything for her ever again.

CHAPTER 15

LEO WAS HER NEXT PROBLEM.

She needed to get to him, let him know she was safe, and Tapper and Flunky had her comm.

She was standing in a long, narrow passageway which stretched out to the right and the left.

She tried to remember where her father's office had been in relation to the hoverway.

The Under Deck was the last hover stop before the hovers reached the Deck, the massive open landing pad for the space craft that came to deliver or carry off the goods the Cores bought and sold.

There was no way she could slip onto a hover and get back down without being seen. But with luck, her father had built a hidden staircase or lift that could take her down.

Leo was probably still in his office, huddled with Finkle, working out a plan.

She didn't expect him to come for her, but she knew he would be upset about her abduction. Angry. He would try to think of some way around it, or some retaliation.

She didn't want him doing anything foolish.

The corridor widened a little, and she stopped dead as the passage wall changed from solid metal to the one-way transparent material her father had used to build windows into various offices and passages from his secret corridors.

There was Tapper and his friend, Flunky, standing around a desk, talking seriously to someone on a screen.

She couldn't hear them, but she could see everything--the one way material extended from floor to ceiling along the full length of the office wall.

There was a dial to one side, and she turned it cautiously. The conversation was suddenly audible.

"They're wrong about her being anything to Gaudier. She's not." The bigger man set both hands on the desk. "She doesn't think he'll come for her, and seriously, why would he?"

"It'll weigh on him, and his other staff, if she turns up dead. That's why we left the other bodies outside his warehouse. If you don't think he'll come, then kill her and leave her body near the entrance to Felicitos, in a place where everyone will see it. In the main road, or something." The man who spoke sounded articulate and resigned. A Cores exec. "It may not be what we hoped to get out of it, but it's something."

"I'll do it right now." Tapper turned toward the door.

The bigger man, Flunky, looked up at him, and Sofie thought she caught a glimpse of disgust in his gaze before he turned back to the screen.

"At least give Gaudier a chance to come up." The Cores exec sounded annoyed. "Don't kill her before she stops being useful."

That should be the Cores motto. Keep them alive until they stop being useful.

She couldn't leave Garmen, she realized with spike of anger.

It had been her goal since Rach had died, to leave this terrible place and never look back, but she couldn't brush the dust of it off, even if she was able to.

Not when she knew how they thought. How they would keep behaving.

The children jumping and skipping along to school deserved a lot better than this.

Tapper had paused at the door when the Cores exec told him to wait, and he stalked back, threw himself into one of the office chairs.

"I'll call Gaudier. See what he's going to do." The man leaning over the screen fiddled with her comm set.

"Let me know if you get your hands on Gaudier. Otherwise, put it in a report." The Cores exec cut out.

Flunky lifted his gaze to Tapper. "Let's see what Gaudier has to say."

She waited while they made contact. Leo wasn't coming, but their conversation might give her a clue where to find him.

The comm set connected.

"I can't come get her if you don't tell me where to go," Leo said.

She saw the surprise on Flunky's face.

It was nothing compared to hers. She forced her mouth closed.

"The Under Deck. Take a hover to the highest level of the Upper Reaches and then take the lift."

"You're not even trying to hide that this is a Cores deal." Leo's voice was cynical.

"You would know anything else was a lie."

"True enough. What are the codes?"

No one had access to the Under Deck without punching a one-time code into the lift. Well, except her. But she hadn't been up here since her father died. It had never been worth the risk of getting caught.

Why the hell was Leo coming up?

Her brain couldn't comprehend it. It made no sense.

You would come for him.

She made a face at the thought. It was true, but somehow she didn't think it was the same for him.

He had obligations.

She was beholden to no one but herself.

She'd made sure of that a year ago.

She didn't know whether her father had built a hidden lift on this floor, or gone with stairs. Either way, she had a feeling from the intensity of Leo's tone that she wouldn't have time to find her way down to let him know she was safe before he came up.

Which meant she'd have to save him up here.

She listened as they gave Leo the codes, then watched them get up and walk out the room. She followed them, back down the passage to her father's old office.

The passage wall that was part of the office didn't offer a floor to ceiling view like it did at Flunky's office, because her father hadn't needed to spy on himself, but there was a small window to one side. He would have had to make sure the room was empty before he popped back out of the wall after he'd done his snooping.

She got there before Tapper and Flunky, and so she had the satisfaction of seeing their faces when they swaggered in and found her gone.

Tapper ran around the couch, to check she wasn't hiding there, then he looked over at Flunky and shook his head.

"Where the hell could she have gone?"

"You locked up, right?" Flunky narrowed his eyes.

"Yes, I locked up."

"You were pretty steamed, and I heard you slam the door behind you. Didn't hear you lock up."

"I did." Tapper clenched his fists.

"Well, she's not here, so you couldn't have." Flunky spoke through gritted teeth.

"She has to be on this floor. She can't leave without a code." Tapper's shoulders relaxed a little as he remembered that.

"Then go look for her. I'll wait for Gaudier by the lifts."

Flunky turned and walked out the door, and Tapper stood for a moment, breathing heavily, before he followed his colleague out.

She had better not bump into Tapper again, Sofie thought. If she did, he would not hold back.

She followed the passageway to the left again, past the office where she'd watched them earlier and then the length of two more offices before she got to the foyer. The hidden passageway was narrow here, but like Flunky's office, the view was floor to ceiling.

Her father had thought it would be useful to spy on the Cores execs here and in that office, so perhaps when he'd been alive and the way station was still just a shell, this had been where the execs had gathered to talk.

She could just see the hoverway a little to the left of the lift doors. A massive transport hover rose ponderously up toward the Deck while she waited, slowing to a stop as it waited for permission to rise through the floor onto the open landing pad.

Five minutes later, just as the transport hover disappeared upward, the lift doors pivoted, and Leo stepped out.

He must have started moving the moment they'd made her call him.

She looked behind him, wondering if Finkle was there, wondering what the plan could be.

He must have one. He wouldn't come for her with no escape route.

Flunky didn't quite know what to do now he had Leo.

She found the sound dial, but there wasn't much conversation. Flunky pointed a laz at Leo, and called over his shoulder for someone to hurry up. A moment later Tapper appeared, his face tight with anger.

He patted Leo down, found nothing, and stepped back.

Flunky jerked his head, and Leo gave a nod, began walking down the corridor.

Now she had to hope they took him to her father's office, which had handy access. If not, she'd make a plan.

She walked slowly, got to Flunky's office, waited nervously for a moment, and then moved on to her father's office.

And relaxed.

They were predictable.

The door was opening, and she saw Leo step into the room. "I won't answer any questions until I see Sofie."

"We have other ways to make you talk." Tapper hovered just by the door.

Leo shrugged. It was an insolent 'bring it on'.

The two Cores guards exchanged a look.

Then Flunky stepped into the room and pointed his laz at Leo.

No, no, no, no!

Sofie looked for the lever to open up the wall, but just as she located it, Tapper came back in, carrying a chair with restraints.

Leo stood still, but she could see the tension in his back.

"Move," Flunky ordered, and as soon as he was in the chair, Tapper strapped him in.

Sofie stood, frozen. If she ran in now, she'd do nothing but put herself into the Cores hands, and give them more leverage over Leo.

So she would have to come at them a different way.

Shit, shit, shit.

She ran down the passage to the right, trying to keep calm and stay focused. She didn't even know what she was looking for, specifically. Just something, anything that would help distract Tapper and Flunky.

She passed another floor to ceiling one-way wall into what looked like a conference room. It was empty, but she imagined it would be worth being a silent observer when it wasn't.

She reached a stairway that led upward only, and hesitated. It would go up to the Deck. That would be risky and it would take time.

Time she didn't have.

She ran on, keeping her gaze on the floor patterns to find clues to where else the secret passage opened out.

She found an exit point at the same place she found a box up against the wall.

The lid was loose and she pushed it aside to find general construction tools.

Whoever had built these passages--and she was beginning to think her father had done this floor single-handed--they had left their tools behind.

She pulled out a laser lance, checked the battery level was sufficient, and then peered out of the one-way window into the open passageway beyond.

She wished her father had had the forethought to create a floor plan, but he'd had it all in his head, and probably had never intended anyone else to use this.

She pulled the lever, stepped out, and ran down to the first intersection.

As soon as she reached it, she could hear the hovers coming up the hoverway to her right, and turned that way.

When she passed an open door, and carefully peered in, she recognized it as Flunky's office.

She turned, realizing she'd passed the door to where Leo was being beaten.

She ran back and knocked briskly on it.

Then she stepped to one side and switched on the lance.

"What?" Tapper flung the door open, a scowl on his face, and she tilted the lance straight at his body.

He screamed, falling back with arms raised, and she waited a moment to let her gaze lock with Flunky's. Then she turned and ran, sprinting down the passageway, turning at the intersection and then fumbling for the button to let her into the secret corridor.

As soon as she was through, she ran back toward her father's office, the lance still clutched in her hand.

She was just in time to see Flunky helping Tapper out the room and closing the door behind him.

Leo bowed his head as soon as they were gone, his hands in tight fists along the arms of the restraining chair.

His lip was bloody and his eye was swollen.

She waited for him to make some contact with Finkle, but he did nothing.

Could he have just come for her? Without a plan? Without backup?

She had to take a deep breath.

Then she touched the lever and the secret door swung outward.

"Hey, lover-boy," she whispered. "It's nicer on this side of the wall."

———

Sofie had been in this room. Leo had smelled a faint trace of her scent the moment he'd stepped into it.

Finkle was sure she was either in league with the Cores on this, or she was already dead.

He didn't want to face either possibility, so he sat in his chair, trying to breathe her in.

The bodies of Sunar and Petro kept edging out any other

picture in his head. He could not stomach the idea of Sofie ending up like that.

There was a faint squeak to his left, and then he heard her whisper.

He whipped his head around, saw the wall was now at a strange angle, and then he met the bright, wicked gaze of Sofie Erdo, beckoning him with a crooked finger.

Relief was the biggest emotion that roared through him. Surprise had to take a back seat.

He wriggled his hands in their restraints and she ran in, hit the release catches, and then pulled him out of the chair and behind the wall. She leaned across him to close it.

It left her pressed up against him.

He lifted his arms, winced as his abused muscles protested, and pulled her closer. "I thought you were dead." It was embarrassing that his voice was so unsteady.

"I didn't think you'd hand yourself over to them."

"Really? After you said 'Revenge me well'?" he asked, incredulous.

She tipped up her chin, smiled into his frown. "Well, I wanted you to get the message not to try to save me. I thought you could read the subtext." She went up on tiptoe and kissed his cut lip gently. "I have to say, throwing caution to the wind to rescue me is a very sexy look. Even if it was also really stupid."

Behind them, he heard the sound of the door to the office banging open.

She walked backward, although she didn't try to get out of his hold, and he walked with her, found himself looking through a window made of one-way material. It must be top grade, because he hadn't noticed any hint of it on the other side.

Resen and Mart, the two Cores bodyguards who had been beating him up, slammed into the room. Mart had a new shirt on, and he was moving cautiously.

Sofie had obviously not done a lot of damage, but it must still hurt.

"Fuck." Mart looked around wildly. "That was why she barely aimed at me, it was a distraction. *You* locked the door this time. I'm not taking the heat on this."

"She obviously waited until we left and got him out." Resen pointed a finger. "So it's still on you."

Mart took a step closer to his colleague and Leo thought he was actually going to take a swing.

"This is a big floor," Resen didn't seem to notice Mart's struggle with himself. "She obviously hung around waiting for him to come get her, distracted us to get him out, and now they could be anywhere."

"They still can't get down without a code." Mart took a step back, although his face was still twisted with rage.

"Well, I'd rather not report that we lost them both, so that means we can't ask for assistance. We'll have to make sure we watch the platform, because taking a hover is the only way down without a code."

Mart sneered. "Well, let's hope they aren't jumping on one right now."

Resen's eyes went wide, and he made for the door.

"Wait." Mart rubbed his mouth. "What are we going to do if we don't find them?"

"Tell them Gaudier didn't fall for the bait, and that we killed the girl."

Mart stood still for a moment, then gave a nod. "We'll probably find them, but yeah. That will work."

"I won't forget you fucked up here," Resen said to him, eyes hard. "And I really won't forget if we have to lie."

"I don't forget either, asshole." Mart took a threatening step forward, but Resen was already gone. Mart stood for a beat, rubbing his chest where the laser lance had hit him, and then walked out as well, leaving the door open.

"Well, that certainly didn't sound friendly." Leo looked down at her.

She smiled, wriggled deliciously in his hold as if to underscore how close they were, and in the gloomy light he saw the snap of laughter in her eyes. "Not like us."

They were safe. They had privacy. He'd like to know Sofie Erdo's secrets, but that wasn't important right now.

"No, not at all like us." Leo grinned, bent his head, and took her mouth.

CHAPTER 16

LEO HAD KISSED HER BEFORE.

This time was just as good, but there was something a little desperate about it. And she worried that it was hurting him.

He pulled back and then rested his forehead on hers. "I really thought you might be dead."

Her arms were around his waist, but she lifted a hand and rubbed his back, soothing him.

"What is this place?" He kept his hold on her, almost unconsciously brushing a kiss to the top her head as he looked around.

"Ronald Fadal, the architect and structural engineer who designed Felicitos, was Halatian." She stepped out of his arms. "Halatians like stuff like this. Secret rooms, hidden passageways."

"How did you find it, though? Through the resistance?"

"Ronald Fadal was my father."

Leo's attention was suddenly wholly on her. "Your father?" There was something strange about his sudden focus, his utter shock. It was almost as if he were horrified.

She tried to shrug it off. "Rach and I were neglected children, but we were allowed to hang around him, playing when we were younger, helping the construction crews when we were older. And yes, the resistance knows about most of these passages. They built them for my father in secret, hid them from the Cores. My father was able to run around and spy on the Cores, and the resistance got the same benefit, along with the ability to melt away if there was any trouble."

Leo was silent for a long time. "I wish I'd known who you were sooner."

She shrugged again. This was a secret she had kept for a long time. Only old, close friends like Zyr knew the truth.

When it was obvious she wasn't going to respond, he cleared his throat. "What about Veld? If he was a mole, surely the Cores know about these tunnels."

She nodded. "The revelation that Veld was a Cores spy gave me a few sleepless nights, but even Veld didn't know about them all. No one does. Not even me." She leaned back against the wall. "No one group could build the whole of Felicitos. People came and went, died in Tether Town or on the site, secrets were lost. Only my father would have known it all, and he died seven years ago."

"And the passages don't connect to each other?"

She smiled at his perception. "Some do. I think they all do, but only my father knew how. The passages the resistance uses on the Lower Reaches are connected, so are the passages in the Upper Reaches, but there's no link between the two." She shrugged. "Or, no link anyone knows about."

"If the resistance had access to these tunnels, they should have toppled the Cores by now." She could see he was thinking if he'd known about them, he would have.

She nodded. "We trusted Veld, but he was just stringing us along. My guess is he didn't tell the Cores about the secret passageways. Not if he had some way of profiting from it by keeping it to himself."

Leo gave a slow nod. "That, I'd buy." He reached out a hand, ran a finger down her cheek. "And how did you know about this one? You a regular up here on the Under Deck?"

She lifted her own hand, caught his fingers in a gentle grip. "That's my father's office you were in. I recognized it when I regained consciousness. But even if I hadn't, my father covered Felicitos in clues. If you know how to read them, there's almost nowhere you can't go."

"Regained consciousness? How did they get you?" His hold on her tightened.

"Laz." She shrugged. "Someone in the resistance sold me out. I was supposed to meet up with Zyr, but that message would have been passed on to him through an elaborate system. Anyone along the way could be the traitor. They changed the message, probably, and let the Cores know where I'd be."

"Whoever it was told them we were involved?"

She nodded. "Tapper and Flunky didn't mention the hoverway or The High Flyer to me, so I don't think they recognized me from that, or even knew about it. They only found me useful because whoever gave them the tip told them you would come for me."

"They were right." He bent his head and she felt his lips against the skin of her neck. She shivered.

"Why?" She didn't understand. "What plan could you have come up with to get us out?"

"I didn't have one." He brushed his lips just under her ear. "I didn't dare wait. I believed they'd kill you."

She tightened her hold around his waist, then leaned back so she could look him in the eye. "You could have been killed. It's you they really want."

He shrugged. "What we need to work out is what this means for you. Are you safe in Felicitos and Tether Town now?"

She shook her head. "They won't admit they lost me to their boss, so the Cores execs will think I'm dead. The only worry I'd have is coming in Felicitos's front door. If those two see me, they'll grab me for sure."

Leo turned his head, looked out into the empty room through the one-way window. "If they follow the plan they worked out, they're going to say I never came up at all, so I'm safe." His gaze met hers. "You need to stay with me from now on, Sofie."

She raised her eyebrows. "What happened to keeping your distance." She clenched her fists in his shirt under his jacket. "Not that that's working out so well for you right now."

"It was never what I wanted. It was what I thought you needed to be safe."

"They'll be watching you and your house. If they think we really are involved, they'll try take me again."

"We'll be clever about it. Sneak you in."

She hesitated, then gave a nod, and felt him relax a bit against her, when she hadn't realized he'd tensed up.

"I can use the secret tunnels to get in and out of Felicitos, as well. Just to be sure no one spots me."

"I agree, although you won't have to worry about those two in particular."

She frowned up at him in surprise.

"I know who they are. I can find out where they live," he said simply. "Now, let's get out of here."

———

Sofie led the way.

Leo kept hold of her hand, still a little dizzy at the reality that she was safe. And even more off balance at the news that she was Fadal's daughter.

It was something he pushed away for the moment. Something he didn't want to deal with right now.

Finkle was most likely handing in his resignation at the office. Either that, or waiting to launch an offensive on the Cores.

He fiddled with the tiny comm set pinned to his jacket and tapped it once. "No need for a rescue party, Finkle. We're both safe."

Sofie turned to look at him in surprise, then grinned when she realized he was talking into his lapel.

Unfortunately, in order to pass a Cores scan, the comm set had to be switched off, and needed a tap to reactivate. Something he couldn't do with both hands in restraints. The receiver was hidden behind his ear, and he heard Finkle take a deep breath.

"That's good, sir." It was said through clenched teeth.

"Sofie rescued me. Again." His swollen lip twisted into a lopsided grin. It was a bone of contention between Finkle and himself. Finkle wanted to mistrust her, but couldn't counter the fact that she'd already rescued him twice.

Now it was three times.

"Where are you?" Finkle chose to ignore what he'd said.

"Still on the Under Deck. We're looking for a way down, but we're not in any danger of being caught."

"That sounds like something very difficult to pull off." Skepticism dripped from Finkle's words.

"Not if you're with Ronald Fadal's daughter," Leo told him, and Finkle's silence was thoughtful.

"I didn't know that about her."

"Neither did I. Sofie is just full of surprises."

Finkle gave a grunt that could have been amusement. "We'll see you later then. Let me know if you do actually need rescuing."

"You'll be the first," Leo told him, and cut off the transmission.

"Poor Fink. He just doesn't know what to make of me." Sofie had laughter in her voice.

"I don't, either." Leo squeezed her hand lightly. "But unlike Finkle, I like it."

CHAPTER 17

SOFIE COULDN'T FIND a lift behind the one Leo had come up in. For some reason, her father hadn't modeled this floor on the layout of the ones he'd had built on the Upper and Lower Reaches.

She followed the passage around, Leo's hand in hers, and he slowed in surprise when they walked past the floor to ceiling one-way view into the big conference room she'd seen earlier.

It was still empty.

"I'd give a lot to be standing here during a full Five Cores meeting," Leo murmured. "You're sure your father didn't tell anyone about this? I almost can't believe he went to this effort and then took the secret to his grave."

Sofie thought back to the bitter, sick man her father had been at the end. "He didn't trust anyone. He wanted to control everything, and when he realized that wasn't possible, he turned inward."

And if the secrets on this floor had been his special project, maybe this was where all his money had gone. Could he have paid for this himself, built it himself in the long nights he'd stayed away from home?

She had to admit it was possible.

"Do you think he did make a kill switch?" Leo asked.

She lifted her shoulders. "He loved this building. It was the pinnacle of his career. I just don't think he could have brought himself to harm it in any way."

She stopped when they came to the stairs going up to the Deck.

"Have you been up there?" Leo's hands moved up to rest on her shoulders.

She shook her head. "I've wanted to, but I've heard what happens if they catch you." There was an enviro and grav generator up on the Deck. Verdant String tech that cocooned the landing pad from the emptiness of space around it.

Rumor was that if they found you up there without permission, they simply threw you off.

She put her foot on the first step. "My father had permission to be up there until near the end, but this is part of his secret passage system, so presumably we won't be stepping out into general view."

She looked back at him, to see if he agreed to taking the risk, and he gave a nod.

She started up.

This had been her plan for a long time--more vague while Rach had been alive, but a solid goal for the last year. To get to the Deck. To smuggle herself off Garmen.

To escape.

And now, when she realized she wanted to stay and fight, the opportunity had just been handed to her.

She would laugh, if it wasn't so frustrating.

The stairs spiraled up, rough metal steps that looked like something her father would be able to do himself.

Had probably done himself in those long nights that he hadn't come home.

And then the stairs ended in a gray metal door.

Leo crowded in behind her in the tiny space at the top. "Looks like it needs a code."

She angled her head to look up at him. "That's not a problem, I know the code. The problem is what's on the other side?"

Something sparked in his eyes, and he leaned forward a little and touched his lips to hers, almost as if he couldn't help himself. "We won't know until you try it."

She nodded, squared her shoulders, and felt something flutter in her chest as his arms came tight around her waist, as if he were anchoring her in place.

She punched in the code.

The door opened, and she felt Leo tense at the same moment she did.

Someone was walking directly toward them, a man dressed in the black overalls of a Deck worker. He was carrying a long laser lance in his arms, and she realized a moment later, when she saw his focus was on a spot just above their heads, that he couldn't see them.

"One way wall," she murmured as the man lifted the lance and placed it in a bracket.

Leo dropped his hold and they stepped into the narrow corridor together.

Her father had built it to run the full length of a massive warehouse.

There were pallets and boxes stacked up against it ceiling high in some places. In one area, mechanics were tinkering with the sturdy transport tugs that carried goods to and from the massive container space craft that hovered above the way station, too big to land on the Deck.

It took her a while to see the big ship in one corner of the huge space. It was a matte black, the lines and shape screaming high tech military.

It was only because three of the workers strapped to the outside of the ship were Carusons that it drew her attention at all. She noticed them first, then slowly her eyes adjusted and she realized what looked like a dark mass was in fact a space craft.

She made a sound, and beside her, Leo nodded.

"I see it."

"What *is* it?"

Leo hesitated. "It looks like the ship that was involved in the Cepi incident. I saw some visuals of it blowing up the Cepi ruins on the interplanetary comms."

Sofie touched the one-way wall with her fingertips. "That would make sense if Veld was involved." She stepped right up to the wall, cupping her hands on either side of her face to see better. "Do you think this is Veld's ship?"

She couldn't believe it.

Veld might be a Cores thug, but surely he didn't have the experience to command a ship that looked like this? But if it was his new assignment, then maybe he was here right now. Maybe he'd step out at any moment.

She realized her heart was pounding at the thought. She wanted him punished, not living it up on some secret warship.

Leo shook his head. "If what I read on the interplanetary comms is right, the ship from Cepi was destroyed a month ago. It was being chased by Parnian Special Forces after three of the ship's crew blew up some buildings in Parn's capital city and kidnapped a Halatian woman. Parn Special Forces didn't destroy it, according to their statement. They think there was a self-destruct explosive onboard."

"So this is another one?" And could Veld be dead, then? That was something she really wanted to find out.

"There was mention of a second mysterious ship that appeared in Parn's sovereign space after the first one was destroyed. But this isn't necessarily it."

"Even if it isn't, what's it doing here, sitting openly in a Cores warehouse?"

"I think we can safely say the Cores are in this up to their necks. Especially if Veld and Garde can be traced back to Cepi." Leo looked over at her. "And nothing in this warehouse is open to view. If it's the one I think it is, it's impossible to gain access to this place unless you have high Cores security clearance. This is as good as hidden away as you can get."

Sofie watched the stocky Carusons, with the armored-plated segments on their faces and neck, and two other mechanics, stand back as an automaton lifted what looked like a cannon up. When it was in place, they swarmed around it, fixing it to the outside of the ship.

"They're upgrading the ship's weapons." The worrying trade she'd noticed in her work for the Cores with Caruso clicked into place. That had been payment for this.

The Cores were trading precious ores for expertise and weapons know-how.

"What are they up to?" she whispered. "Are they trying to start a war?"

Leo leaned against the wall, watching with a grim expression as the cannon was attached. "That is a very good question."

Sofie knew that if the Cores were trying to stir up war, there would be no respite for the people of Garmen. They'd be the ones to really suffer. "The Breakaways don't have enough power to win a fight with anyone. Why would they do something so stupid?"

"I don't think they're planning a frontal attack." Leo glanced at her. "The Verdant String has been pulling back from trade with the Breakaways for the last year. I'm lucky that the ore I sell is in high demand, but there's been a noticeable drop-off in Verdant String trade ships to Garmen. The prohibition on interplanetary comms and on anyone leaving Garmen has been noted, and that isn't sitting well with VSC rights protection groups. The Verdant String can't justify trade with the Breakaways to their people, so they've made the decision to limit interaction."

"So the Cores aren't making as much money as they were. How are the sneak attacks on Verdant String targets like Cepi going to change that?"

"My guess is someone has decided a VSC that's dealing with crises will pay less attention to what Garmen is doing."

"They're killing people and blowing up cities as a distraction?" That shouldn't shock her. It was just what the Cores would do. "So what are they planning to do next?" She looked back at the sleek black ship.

"Nothing good." Leo leaned back against the wall, eyes closed, and the sight of his battered, bruised face sparked both tenderness and a rage inside her.

He looked like he had the weight of Felicitos on his shoulders.

She stepped close to him and took his hand.

He opened his eyes, looked sidelong at her with a quirk of his brow.

"Look at us." She grinned at him, then let her head drop onto his shoulder. "And here I thought it'd be all fancy dinners and kisses in dark corners of the Lower Reaches with you."

He didn't laugh as she'd intended him to, so she lifted her head.

He was watching her with steady, serious eyes. "I had even more ambitious ideas."

A taut, electric silence built between them.

"Let's get you down to your office and a med kit," she said at last, tugging at his hand. "And then I'll have to find Zyr without going through the usual channels."

"Not alone." He was still staring at her, but now he was frowning.

She nodded. "Not alone."

But first, she'd have to find a way out of here.

———

It wasn't easy.

She tried to prop Leo up against a wall and walk the whole circumference of the Under Deck while he rested, but he refused.

"There should be more markings on the floor. It's as if he lost interest in doing that up here about halfway through." She curled a fist in frustration, tapped a wall.

"Or he didn't see a need, because he was the only one he ever intended would use this floor, and he built the exit points himself." Leo's voice was a deep murmur in her ear. He was keeping distractingly close, but she couldn't find it in her to complain.

His words from earlier came back to her and she forced down a shiver.

"I think you're right. Which means the way down is probably where I thought it should be, only it isn't marked." They were already more than halfway around the Under Deck, so she kept going.

They had views into a number of offices, some with execs in them, most empty. It was past the end of the day, after all.

"I'm going to spend all day up here tomorrow," Leo said as they glanced into an office and saw an exec packing up for the day. "We'll learn more in one morning than I've got my hands on in months."

When she found the way back to the foyer where Leo had come up in the lift, she made for the section of passageway directly behind it, and studied the wall.

It seemed impenetrable.

There were no murals--it was plain, made from the thin metallic material used for all the inner walls on Felicitos.

But there had to be a way down, and it made sense it was here.

She leaned forward and touched her hand to where she would expect to find a button in the Lower or Upper Reaches.

There was a hum, and she just stopped herself pulling her hand away in surprise as it was scanned.

Electro-film. Invisible to the naked eye. Incredibly expensive.

This was definitely where the money had gone.

There was a sweet click, and the wall popped open on one side.

"Something tells me the only person whose hand could have opened that was yours." Leo was leaning against the far wall, arms crossed over his chest.

She thought about it. Nodded. "He scanned my and Rach's hands often, the last time a couple of weeks before he died. I was eighteen then, so most likely my hand is the same as it was then."

She pulled the wall open and stepped through into the tiny landing at the top of a staircase that led down. She looked back over her shoulder at Leo. "I'm sorry. I think he really did do this all on his own and in secret, which meant he had to install stairs, because putting in a lift would have required help from the construction crews."

Leo joined her, squeezing in and pulling the wall closed behind him. "I grew up working for prospectors and avoiding shadow prowlers out in the plains, Sofie." He tucked a strand of hair behind her ear. "I can walk down some stairs with a few bruises on my face."

She was going to make a snappy comeback, but her gaze hooked on an image that was stenciled on the wall opposite.

She grabbed the hand rail and stepped down to get a closer look.

"What is it?" Leo leaned over her shoulder.

The image wasn't very well defined, but it seemed to be someone holding out an arm, holding a knife in their other hand, posed as if to slice their wrist or inner arm. There seemed to be a pool of water or blood at their feet.

"That is . . . bizarre." She whispered it. "If my father build this himself, it stands to reason he painted this, as well."

"It doesn't mean anything to you?" Leo's hand on her shoulder was comforting; real and steady.

She shook her head. "Nothing. I accused him of being crazy--a few times directly to his face--but I didn't think he really was mad, just obsessed."

She walked down a little way further, but there were no other images. She honestly didn't know what to make of it. "It's what he tried to do on his death bed," she said, suddenly making the connection. "He tried to cut himself, but he was stopped by the medic. This . . ." She looked back up at the image. "This shows he was already thinking about doing it."

A nagging sense of guilt tugged at her. Had he been truly disturbed, and she had not only not noticed, but in fact been angry with him for something he couldn't help?

Leo walked down the steps to stand just above her. "None of this is your doing, Sofie. Let's just go home. It'll all make more sense after a fancy dinner and a few kisses in the dark corners of the Lower Reaches."

"The Lower Reaches?" She gave him a look over her shoulder.

"Well, no. My house," he admitted, and she laughed.

"And then you can show me how ambitious you really are," she said, and enjoyed it when he tripped on the stairs and had to grip the rail.

CHAPTER 18

SHE WAS SAFE. Would not be left, mutilated and dead outside his warehouse as a reminder of who was in charge on Garmen.

Leo kept reminding himself of it as she led them downward.

Every now and then, when they reached a landing, she would open the door and check to see which floor they were on.

But the Under Deck was a long way up from the Upper Reaches.

He didn't mind. It was soothing walking behind her as they spiraled down. Like a respite between madnesses.

And hovering at the front of his thoughts was that he had never even considered looking for Ronald Fadal's daughters. He had taken over Fadal's operation on the mines, profited from it beyond his wildest dreams, and all the while, Fadal's children were working for the resistance, scraping a living in Tether Town. Being murdered.

He didn't know how he would ever explain to Sofie that, while he'd had a vague notion of Fadal having a family, he'd been so focused in the early days, so determined to make the most of the opportunity Fadal's death afforded him, he hadn't given them a second thought.

Had, until she said who she was, forgotten all about them.

How fucking convenient for him.

And now, he was following Fadal's youngest daughter down her secret stairway with lust and desire tugging at him, and protectiveness making him almost a stranger to himself.

He would have to tell her what an asshole he was, but he didn't know how.

"I think we're here."

He looked up, realized the stairway had come to an end.

She hesitated at the door, as if she was worried where they'd step out.

Theoretically, they were in a secret system within a secret system. Ronald Fadal would surely not have risked the door opening into a pubic area.

Sofie pulled it open and peered out.

Her shoulders relaxed and she held the door for him as she stepped out.

"Where's this?" He didn't recognize it.

"It's the top floor of the Upper Reaches." She turned back to stare at the closed door, which had now completely disappeared into the wall, and then ran a hand over it. It glowed when she touched the middle, and he heard the click as the door opened.

She leaned against it, closing it again, and Leo finally let himself look around.

He'd never been to the top floor of the Upper Reaches. He'd had meetings on the floor below, but this was the powerhouse of the Cores.

If the top execs frittered away their time on the Under Deck, their immediate subordinates scurried around here, carrying out the orders that were issued from on high.

He looked through a one-way window into what was a bare,

stark foyer, and shook his head. "They really don't believe in spending a port more than they have to for their staff."

Sofie was standing beside another door, and she smiled cynically as she tapped in a code. "No. It drove my father mad." She stopped short, and he watched her struggle for a moment before she was able to look at him again.

"More stairs, I'm afraid."

She pushed open the door and he followed her inside and down the tight spiral staircase.

"Will you give me that code?" he asked.

She looked back and up at him. "It's my birthday." She rattled off the numbers. "But in case the system won't let two people use the same code if we're in different parts of Felicitos, which is possible given my father's paranoia, rather use the general resistance code. Seven Four Two Five." She turned away. "The year of the Halatian Incident."

She had been counting floors under her breath as they went down, and stopped at the next door and tapped in the code again.

When he joined her on the other side, they were in a pitch dark passageway.

She stepped in without hesitation. "For some reason the lights went out when I came this way earlier. There must be a faulty wire somewhere, but I know the way."

He felt her hand reaching for his, and threaded his fingers through hers. They walked until they came to a one-way view into a bathroom. No one was inside, and the light was off, but lighting from the foyer seeping under the door was just bright enough for him to make out the rough size of the room.

Leo tapped the resistance code Sofie had given him into the small pad beside the wall, and nothing happened. He looked over at her and she frowned. Tapped in the same code herself and the wall gave a faint click as it opened.

"Have you ever gotten the code wrong and it's opened up anyway?" Leo asked.

He couldn't see her expression in the gloom of the darkened bathroom, but he bet she was frowning as she thought about it.

"If I did, I didn't notice it."

"Go back in, close the door, and deliberately do it wrong," he suggested.

She hesitated a moment, then gave a nod and brushed past him, stepped into the hidden passageway and closed the door.

Almost immediately, he heard the click as it opened again.

"And?"

"And I pressed buttons randomly. And it opened." She sounded a little lost.

"I think the code was a ruse for the others around you. I don't think the numbers ever mattered." Leo thought back to the hum of the scanner on the wall of the Under Deck. "I think it's activated by your DNA."

"But some of the secret tunnels are used by the resistance all the time." She pushed the door closed behind her.

"Then there's levels of access. Your father obviously realized he had to give the resistance some access, that's why they were helping him, after all, but other areas are obviously for him and his family alone." He tilted his head toward the secret opening. "Has anyone from the resistance used this entrance before?"

She shrugged. "I hadn't used it myself until today. I found it by reading the patterns on the floor."

Leo looked down, saw nothing more than a pretty, swirling pattern of flowers, leaves and birds set into the flooring.

"So they don't know about it, and even if they figured out it was here by reading the signs, they wouldn't be able to get in." He opened the door of the bathroom and held it for her. "Or, not without you."

She looked down at her fingers, but didn't say anything. Leo wondered if she understood.

She was the key to unlocking the whole of Felicitos.

She lifted her head. "I always wondered why Veld was so relentless about wooing Rach. And never understood how he could go to such lengths to romance her, and then turn around and persuade her to get into a relationship with a Cores exec. How he could stand to push her to do that, when he supposedly loved her so much." She walked through the doorway, and then stood in the gloom of the corridor. "He must have seen her going somewhere he couldn't follow. He worked out he needed her to open doors for him. Literally."

So she did understand, then.

Leo had to hope she also understood he was not Veld. He didn't care if she could open doors or not.

But he had to admit, it was damn useful that she could.

———

Sofie tapped her fingertips against the conference table as Leo debriefed his security team. It made her charms clink together, and she stopped immediately.

The conversation swirled around her, hardly making an impact.

Most of them stared at her surreptitiously every now and then, and Sofie hunched a little under their gaze.

Leo's face was already healing. Finkle turned out to be a medic as well as a thug, and he'd doctored the bruises and cuts.

"What do you think they're going to do with that ship you saw up there?" Dee asked, and Sofie blinked back into the present.

"I'm going to ask Sofie if she'll take someone on the team up there to watch them. We can organize shifts so we can listen in and see what we can pick up." Leo looked over at her, and she sensed a moment of hesitation in him--so unusual, it stood out to her. "Would you do that, Sofie?"

She nodded. "I'm sure the boss will give me time off work."

There was a nervous ripple of laughter at that, but Leo did not look amused.

"Do you want me to do that now?" she asked politely.

Leo stared at her, anger suddenly rolling off him. "I'm not one of the abusive assholes you've had to deal with before," he said, voice cold. "No, obviously not now."

She was so tired of bullshit, she simply stared back at him for a beat, then shrugged. "Of course you're not."

She might have been mistaken, but as he turned away, she thought she saw a flush on his cheeks.

She got to her feet, suddenly done. "Do you want to give me your address?"

Leo looked back at her, frowning. "Why? You're coming with me."

She shook her head. "No. I'm going home first to collect some things I need."

He paused, looking at her, really seeing her for the first time since they'd stepped back into his offices.

It seemed like a cool wall had descended between them the moment they'd been met by his security team; the humor, warmth and flirtation of their time on the Under Deck evaporating away.

Leo inclined his head. "We'll come with you. Then go on to my place."

She thought about it for a moment.

"Please, Sofie. I don't want you out of my sight." His voice was soft, and from the astonished looks on the faces of his security bad asses, she guessed they'd never seen Leo ask so nicely for anything before.

"All right." She stood, straightening her shoulders. "Let's go."

"Do we need to get her out in disguise?" Dee had been leaning against a wall, watching everything with her arms crossed over her chest, but now she straightened. "I'd need to find her something new to wear."

"No. There's another way." Leo looked over at her, and Sofie realized he was waiting for her permission to talk.

She waved her hand for him to continue. The secret was out now. They knew about the passageways on the Under Deck and the Deck. What did a few more matter?

"Sofie has a secret way out of Felicitos. That's how she rescued me when I was attacked at The High Flyer. We can take that route."

Everyone was suddenly intensely interested in her.

"How long have you known about this way out?" Finkle asked.

"Since it was built. I helped build it." There was more than one secret exit, and she hadn't actually helped build the one she'd taken Leo down before, but she might as well preserve some secrets.

"You would've been no more than twelve when Felicitos started going up," Dee said.

She nodded. "And I was sixteen when the tunnel was built."

There was silence as everyone stared at her a little more. She wondered how many of them were latecomers to Tether Town. There were only a small core of original inhabitants, and she knew most of them. These people had most likely all come with the massive wave of immigrants when Felicitos had started taking shape, and everyone began to realize it was probably going to work. Until then, it had been every hand on deck. Children as young as ten had helped built the TWS.

Sofie walked toward the door, and Leo joined her.

Finkle was signaling to others in the room, and by the time they reached the bathroom, Dee, Finkle and two others had fallen in around them.

Out of pure habit, Sofie made sure they were alone, then stepped through into the narrow room.

"This is interesting," Dee murmured.

Sofie ignored them all, even Leo, stepping up to the wall and crouching down to press in the tiny tile in the corner, her body blocking everyone's view.

The wall clicked, and as she pulled it back, she remembered the lights had gone out. "Do you have a light?" she asked Leo. "I forgot they're out in the passageway."

He turned to Finkle, was handed one, and gave it to her. Their fingers brushed, and she looked up at him, let their gazes lock for a moment before Fink cleared his throat.

That damned zing. It got her every time.

The only consolation was that it seemed to get him, too.

CHAPTER 19

HE HAD MESSED UP.

Leo knew it and he didn't know how to fix it.

It didn't help that Finkle, Dee, Sam and Erdia were pretending not to notice that he was not himself.

He walked beside Sofie as she got them down into the depths of the tower, down the tunnel and out into T-Town, then wound her way through the alleyways until she reached the main street.

"I'm sorry," he said.

She tipped her head a little, and then reached out a hand and took his. "Now *that* is how you show me you're not one of the abusive assholes I'm used to dealing with." She squeezed, and a weight seemed to lift off him as he squeezed back.

"Tell me, was I just dreaming it, or is the memory that came back to me as we were walking through that tunnel of you holding me by my feet and pulling me along in a cart true?"

She sent him a grin. "It wasn't elegant, but you do weigh about one and a half times what I do."

"Thank you." He didn't think he appreciated how hard it must have been until now. "Truly."

She gave a nod. "Any time, lover-boy." Her footsteps were quiet on the rough stones that had been tipped onto the ground and then packed with earth to make them level.

The Cores execs never walked anywhere in Tether Town, they only used hovers, so it had been up to the gen-pop to pave the routes through the town.

"You took a hover." Leo suddenly recalled her staggering under his weight, guiding him to the road.

"Yes. You gave me some ports, and I ordered one to meet us using your screen." She fluttered her hands. "I told him you'd had too much to drink."

"You were nervous of him."

She looked sharply at him. "Yes. I'm surprised you picked that up."

He was, too. He'd barely been able to stand on his own. But her nerves had helped to sharpen his focus a little.

She shrugged and then turned down a side road he recognized as her own street. "He was fine, though. He helped me get you to the door."

She pulled the door open, and Leo saw Erdia and Dee split from the group, Dee going around the back of the building, Erdia taking up position in the front.

Finkle and Sam followed them up the stairs.

Sofie gave Finkle a dark look when he brushed past her as she opened her door, but she stayed put when Leo put a hand on her shoulder.

"Let him do his thing."

Her lips thinned, but she nodded.

Finkle's face showed nothing when he eventually gave the all clear signal with his hands.

"Just in case they've bugged you, say nothing," Leo whispered in her ear, and got a jolt himself as she shivered when his lips touched her ear.

She stepped through the door, and he followed her in, taking time to look around in a way he hadn't the first time he'd been here.

She went through to her room, and when he looked through the doorway he saw her carefully folding clothes into a large, soft fabric bag.

"We'll need a hover," he said to Finkle.

"Better not. We're more unpredictable when we're on foot. And no one followed us out of that tunnel." Finkle glanced through at Sofie's packing and winced. "Can she take less?"

Leo shook his head. "She's given up a lot already. She brings whatever she wants."

Finkle sighed. "I suppose knowing about the tunnel alone is worth it."

Leo turned to him. "We get one thing straight. Yes, the tunnel is a massive advantage, so are the passageways up on the Under Deck and the Deck itself. The people we can spy on . . ." He shook his head. "But if she refuses to lift one more finger to help us, it doesn't matter. She's valuable in her own right."

"Besides, now we know about the tunnels. It's not as if she can stop us using them." Finkle's tone was satisfied.

Leo got a grip on his temper. Finkle was thinking like a security chief, not a man in the hold of . . . something else. Not a man wrapped around a certain woman's finger.

"Oh, we can't use them. Or, not all of them." He kept his voice level. "Not without her."

Finkle's eyebrow went up. "Dee and I watched what numbers she punched in the whole way."

Leo shrugged. "They won't work if you go back and try them. But she did give me a code that will get me in wherever the resistance can go, so yes, we could probably use those passageways. But all the really interesting places, like the Under Deck?" He shook his head. "She'll have to take us, or we don't go."

"She won't tell you how to get there?" Finkle sounded like he respected that. It was certainly something everyone on his team would understand--keeping a tactical advantage.

Leo kept his gaze on Sofie as she reached up to get something from her cupboard, and decided he didn't even trust Finkle enough to share her secrets. "Something like that."

———

Sofie looked around her bedroom.

There was so much more she wanted to take, but her bag was already full, and she could sense Finkle's impatience.

To his credit, Leo looked like he was prepared to wait all night for her.

It wasn't as if she wouldn't be back here, she told herself. This was temporary. A precaution in case the Cores came looking for her.

But she couldn't quite believe it.

This was different. This seemed final. Like either they won, they beat the Cores, or they died.

There wasn't any retreat from the course she'd put herself on.

She fiddled with her bracelet, the only thing she had of Rach's, and realized it was all she really needed.

Everything else was replaceable.

The bracelet gave a tinkling chime as the crystal beads knocked together, and Sofie looked down at it.

Most of the crystals were tiny data stores full of interviews Rach did with children and people on the street, talking about their experience on Garmen.

Rach said if the people of the VSC could only see it, it would be like what happened in the Halatian Incident, when the investigative journalist Darline Xan had snuck onboard a smuggler ship and filmed what was happening to the Halatians imprisoned there--most of whom were children.

Captain Drake of Parn's Special Forces had seen the footage, and had led a team onto the ship and taken it from the smugglers, freeing the children, and turning the tide on the smugglers.

Every other Verdant String planet had followed suit.

She'd told Rach the VSC had to know what was happening here, had poured cold water on her sister's optimism time and again, but she touched the beads now, and vowed if she could, she would get them out on the interplanetary comms.

Rach deserved that and so much more.

"Ready?" Leo ran a hand along her shoulder and down her arm, and she realized she'd been standing in the middle of the room staring into space.

She nodded. "I spent a long time making this place a home for myself. It's hard to leave it."

"It'll still be here," Leo told her, and she nodded again, but she didn't believe him.

Sam came in and picked up her bag, and even though it must have been heavy, he lifted it onto his shoulder and walked out as if it weighed nothing.

"If you've forgotten something, we can come back," Leo told her when she hesitated in the doorway.

Again, she nodded. She hoped he was right.

"Time to go." Finkle tried to keep the impatience out of his tone.

And so she followed Leo Gaudier's henchmen out into the night.

There was no doubt about it, she was about to lie down with the devil.

CHAPTER 20

THEY WERE HALFWAY to Leo's house when she remembered Zyr.

"We need to let him know he has a mole."

Leo's grip on her hand tightened. "He has to know it. And what if he's the one who sold you out?"

"No." That, she could never believe. "Zyr's been a friend since before Tether Town was even Tether Town."

"Where's his family from?" Leo asked.

"Parn. His mother worked for the Cores in mineral exploration. When she was killed in a mining accident, he ended up on the streets. There is no way he'd sell me out."

Leo said nothing, and she stopped dead.

"I'm not asking permission, Leo. I'm going to tell him. He needs to know."

Leo turned, and she sensed the tension in the team around her as they all came to a halt.

"I'm not trying to be difficult." She resented that she even had to say it. "But you don't have a say over what I do, either. It's inconvenient, I know everyone would rather be going home, but someone sold me out tonight, tried to have me killed, and that person works for Zyr. He's vulnerable, because whoever handed me to the Cores could hand him over at any time, too."

Leo inclined his head in acknowledgment. "What do you suggest?"

"I can't send him a note. All the systems are suspect, now. I have to go to him in person. And if whoever betrayed me to the Cores knows I'm not dead, that I'm running around and can start shouting traitor, maybe they'll panic and try to kill the one person who will definitely be coming after them, no matter what."

Finkle made a sound that she suspected was a grunt of annoyance.

"You're welcome to go home to bed, Fink," she said sweetly into the darkness, because she couldn't see him properly where he was standing in the shadows.

"How will you contact him?" Leo ignored the byplay.

"Go to his house." She rubbed at her eyes. "I'm tired too, but if something happened to him . . ." She cleared her throat. "It won't take long. I just want him on his guard."

"Zyr strikes me as a man who is seldom off his guard," Leo said, but he didn't sound as if he was trying to persuade her against it.

She turned to the left, and glanced over as Leo joined her. She didn't bother checking where Finkle, Dee and the others were. She assumed they were sliding through shadows all around them.

She knew she'd assumed correctly when she saw a dark shape dart from an alleyway as if to attack, and then suddenly fly backward with a cry that was quickly cut off.

"They're handy to have around," she murmured to Leo. "I should ask Fink who the person was who dealt with those oppos for me the other day and thank them."

"My understanding is you wouldn't have had to deal with the

oppos if Fink's watcher had stayed out of sight to begin with." There was something implacable in his voice.

"Yes, but whoever it was probably didn't know at the time I worked for the resistance and could spot a tail. He thought I was a clerical worker."

Leo gave a grunt. "So did I. But you have a point."

She slowed as she came to the narrow alleyway that led to Zyr's apartment, looking up to see if the secret sign he put up to let others know he was in was displayed. When she saw it, she crouched beside the ally entrance and moved a piece of wood to one side to expose an open pipe, bent down and put her lips almost against it. "It's Sofie," she whispered.

She stepped back into the street to wait.

No one said anything for a long time, and just when she was sure Fink was going to complain, Zyr stepped out of the darkness.

"You brought a whole team, Sofie-girl?"

"I wouldn't let her come alone," Leo said. "Tether Town was where I was to watch her, remember?"

Zyr shifted. "I remember. What's going on?"

"I set up a meet with you after work today." Sofie stepped close to him, lowering her voice so just she, Leo and Zyr could hear.

Zyr angled his head toward her. "I didn't get the message."

"I hope not." Leo's voice was cold. "Two Cores guards were waiting for her in your office. They used a laz on her, and took her up to the Under Deck."

Zyr went still. "This true?" he asked her.

She nodded. "Someone told them where I'd be, and that I was Leo's lover. That he'd come for me if they used me as bait."

"So what I want to know," Leo kept his voice low, too, "is who you had watching Sofie in Felicitos, and who in your system took that message and sold Sofie out?"

"Not me." Zyr vibrated like Felicitos in a hurricane.

"I know it wasn't you." Sofie sent a quick, angry look to Leo. "Who could it have been?"

"I'll have to check the roster. Have to check everyone." Zyr lifted a hand and ran it down his face in a way that spoke of pure exhaustion.

"I wanted you to know there was someone actively working against us. I don't want you taken unawares." Sofie touched his arm.

He sent her a smile. "I'd say that's unlikely, but I would never have thought someone would have done this to you."

"How long is the list of people on the roster?" Leo asked him.

"Long enough." Zyr stared him down. "I'll clean my own house, Gaudier."

"See that you do." Leo stepped back, held his hand out to Sofie.

She sighed. Leaned forward and kissed Zyr's cheek. "Watch out for yourself."

"You, too." He drew her in for a tight hug, and the scent of him, spicy, familiar, had her hugging him back even tighter. When he stepped back, he flicked a look at Leo and then vanished back into the shadows.

Sofie slid her arm through Leo's, but as they started down the road she dropped it and slid her arm along his waist and fitted her head on his shoulder.

He hesitated for a moment, and then with a hum of contentment, drew her in close.

———

Leo's house was a surprise.

It faced away from Felicitos, over the flat plains that surrounded the tower, and toward the high mountains of the escarpment in the distance.

Everything was hard and sharp, as if he refused to give himself any comfort.

"Not as welcoming as yours," he said, as if he could read her mind.

She looked at him in surprise as he hung his jacket and hers on a rack that looked like a work of art. "You liked my place?"

He simply gave a nod.

Her bag sat between them, dropped there by Finkle, and they were alone at last, in the part of the house that was clearly Leo's private domain.

"So." He reached down and picked it up. "Come through."

She followed him from the lounge, with its massive picture window, into a bedroom that was a little more textured, a little softer, than the rest of the house.

The bed covers where light gray and looked smooth to the touch.

"I don't even need to clear space for you, I have more than I need." He set the bag down inside a walk in closet, and Sofie stepped up right next to him, so the small space became crowded.

"Thank you." She murmured it, letting her breath warm his ear.

He turned to look at her, his body brushing hers. "Sofie, if you want me to sleep on the couch--"

She angled her head.

What was it that was weighing on him, making him retreat now, when he'd been all in with her, enthusiastically all in, up until now?

She lifted up on her toes and nuzzled his neck. "That would be pretty silly of me, since I've been looking forward to this moment since about the second time I went out with you."

She felt the tension leave him, his whole body relaxing as he pulled her close, and she caught a glimpse of a smile on his lips. "Is that so?"

"It is." She gasped as he lifted her up and took the few steps to get them to the bed.

"Well, I can do one better. I've been looking forward to this since we met."

"I know." She grinned up at him.

"Oh, do you?" He slowly lifted her shirt up her body and then tugged it over her head.

She nodded, her hands going to his own shirt, pushing it up and reveling in the feel of his hot skin under her palms.

He looked down at her, his gaze burning wherever it touched her. He reached forward, undoing the delicate hooks at the front of her bra and then pushing the garment off her shoulders.

She pushed his shirt off the same way. "I knew you were trouble the moment I saw you. I knew getting involved with you was going to change things for me. And I also knew if things between us were going to be the way I thought they would, it would be worth it."

He drew her forward, so her breasts pressed against his bare chest.

She closed her eyes and tipped back her head, and he brushed a kiss along the top of her shoulder.

"You had an unfair advantage." His lips followed a path downward. "I didn't know who I was getting involved with."

She caught his chin and tilted it up so he could look her in the eye. "Would you have run the other way, if you knew?"

He looked straight at her, and there was something lurking at the back of his eyes; something she couldn't interpret. "No." He feathered a kiss on her forehead. "No. I'd have had more arguments with Finkle, but nothing else would have changed."

"What's wrong?" She reached up and cupped his cheek with her hand.

"There are things I have to tell you--" He shook his head, "but my mind isn't working so well right now."

She felt a spike of desire as he bent his head to suck the tip of her breast into his mouth.

Then he lowered her down and stood over her, bare-chested, his body blocking out everything behind him.

"Maybe we can leave the questions and answers until later."

"I can do that." His voice was hoarse.

He put a knee on the bed and leaned forward, caging her between his arms.

Then proceeded to show her just how ambitious he could be.

CHAPTER 21

FINKLE, obviously showing some deference to the new situation, contacted Leo on his comm set, rather than knocking on his bedroom door, as he would usually do.

Leo heard it, but with Sofie nestled up against him, he was loath to turn and pick it up.

The comm set chimed again.

Leo sighed.

"I think Fink is trying to tell you something."

He looked down, saw Sofie staring up at him with the warm, laughing spark in her eyes that had drawn him in from the start and fascinated him so much.

"Finkle is used to my full attention."

"I don't think he's the type to interrupt for no good reason." Sofie strained up a little, kissed his chin, and then rolled away from him, off the bed, and disappeared into the bathroom, the slim line of her naked back and the curve of her buttocks a pleasure to watch.

Leo rubbed his chest, a bone deep satisfaction that he didn't think he'd ever felt before settling over him.

The comm set chimed again.

"Yes?"

"We need to talk. There's trouble at the mines."

Mention of the mines sent a prickle of adrenaline racing through him as he listened to the water fall in the bathroom.

He would have to tell Sofie today about what he'd done with her father's legacy. The thought made him curl his fists.

"Sir?"

Leo rolled out of bed, pulled on his pants and walked out to the lounge.

The view of the mountains was obscured today, the clouds low and gray, and rain fell soft and steady against the window.

Finkle stood at the kitchen bench, two mugs of jah in his hand, and Leo took one with a nod, then walked past his security chief to start making another cup.

It took Finkle a moment to work out what he was doing, and Leo saw him blink when he realized who the third cup was for.

"I can do it," Finkle said.

Leo shook his head. "You said there's news from the mines?"

"The scales have reset."

Leo froze, looking up at Finkle as the jah machine merrily ground the pods. "When, exactly?"

"Nearly two days ago. That's how long it's taken them to get the word to us. Someone rode here from Phansi on a small hover almost without a break when they realized."

The jah machine shut off, and there was silence for a moment.

"The Cores will get a daily transmission, but they may not notice the anomaly right away." Leo took a sip of jah, and saw Finkle was shaking his head.

"The daily transmission isn't happening. The tower suffered an inexplicable breakdown." Finkle's tone was dry.

Leo grinned. "Of course it did. The Cores will notice they

didn't get their numbers, will try a few times to see if it's just atmospheric interference." He set his mug down suddenly. "If we leave in the next few hours, we might be able to beat them there."

"And do what?" Finkle asked. "Unless you can put the scales back the way they were?"

Leo shook his head. "But I need to go. It'll be seen as a betrayal if I don't. That's why someone raced here to let us know." He also wondered, if he took Sofie with him, would she see something that none of them could? See some way to take back the advantage?

Until she'd drawn him into the secret passageways of the Under Deck, he'd believed what Ronald Fadal had done at the mines was the biggest coup the architect had pulled off against the Cores.

"Trouble?"

He turned, saw Sofie standing just inside the room. There was something shy about the way she stood, all dewy from her shower, her hair damp, with tendrils curling around her face.

Something squeezed his chest, hard. He wanted this every day. He wanted *her* every day.

He held out the jah he'd made her to tempt her closer.

"Thanks." Her smile as she moved forward to take it made him feel a little giddy, like he'd given her something infinitely more valuable.

Then he remembered what she didn't know about him, about the mines, and he wondered if he'd get that kind of smile again.

Finkle cleared his throat. "When do you want to leave?"

"Leave?" She curved both hands around the mug, as if to warm them.

Leo fought his irritation. Finkle was behaving as usual. It was him who'd changed. "I have to go to Phansi."

She paused, mug halfway to her mouth, and flicked her gaze between him and Finkle. "Neither of you seem happy about it."

"Finkle doesn't want me to go, and neither do I, but I have to. I want you to come with me."

"Come with you? To the mines?" She said it slowly.

"It's dangerous, as I've said, and it'll take at least two days if we stop to rest, but I have to go and I don't want to leave you here without me."

She took a sip of jah. Swallowed. "I've never even been to the mines. How could I help?"

"Because your father built those mines, before he started on Felicitos, and he may have built some of his tricky Halatian secrets into the structures there, too."

She took another sip. "That wouldn't surprise me, but there are miners out there who might know about it. A few have looked me up over the years when they've come in to Tether Town. They probably know more about what my father did out there than I do."

He went still at that.

Some of the miners had looked her up?

He wondered whether they'd been checking on her, wondered if they'd felt guilt at what they were doing, and then he wondered why none of them had ever raised the matter with him.

He would have to find out who had approached her so he could compensate them if they'd helped her and her sister out, when it should have been him doing it.

He forced himself to speak. "Even if you're right, I still want you with me."

She glanced at Finkle, who pretended to study his screen, then turned to Leo with a sigh. "What am I missing here, Leo?"

He was damned if he would say anything in front of Finkle. "I'll tell you everything when we're on the way to the mine. But right now, I need to organize transportation and supplies for us to take on the journey, and I would appreciate it if you could take

Finkle up to the Under Deck. I'd like someone to watch what's happening up there while we're away."

She studied him, as if assessing his sincerity. Sighed again. "All right."

He raised his cup of jah, tapped it against her own. "Finkle?"

"I should go with you to the mine."

Leo shook his head. "Not while there's a treasure trove of information to be found here, and not while that war ship is sitting in one of the Cores warehouses."

"Then Dee," Finkle said.

"I'll let you figure out who should come. Only two people, plus Sofie and myself."

Finkle tapped at his screen. "I'll get a team together, and then Miss Erdo and I can leave."

Sofie smiled politely at him, and swallowed the last of her jah. "I can hardly wait."

———

The gloves she'd borrowed from Leo were itchy against her back and stomach.

Sofie had put them under her shirt, fixing them in place with a scarf she'd wound around her torso, and she squirmed as the rough edge of a seam rubbed her raw.

"All right?" Finkle asked.

"Fine." She smiled brightly at him over her shoulder.

He'd brought Sam from the team that helped her move the night before along with him, and the two men seemed to be constantly pulling themselves up short, as if they were about to pass her on the stairs, only to remember she was the one who was leading the way.

She faced forward and kept going.

She was climbing as fast as she could, and she'd made the decision not to let them rattle her.

Up ahead she saw the image painted on the side of the wall she and Leo had found last night, the strange, almost naive drawing of a person slitting their wrist, with a pool of blood below.

She said nothing about it as she passed it, and neither did Finkle or Sam.

When she reached the top, she put her hand on the wall and heard the hum of the scan.

From the sound Finkle made at the back of his throat, it seemed he at last grasped the necessity of keeping her around.

"It only works for you?" he asked as she stepped into the secret corridor and held the door for them.

She nodded, and rubbed the gloves under her clothes. "You did pack enough food and water for a while, right? Leo and I will be gone at least five days." In fact, she was worried they'd be longer, and she'd tried to talk Leo and Finkle out of taking someone up here without her around to bring them back out.

"I've got plenty of supplies. I've survived out at the mines in the snow," Sam told her. "Living in climate controlled conditions in the Under Deck will not be an issue."

She had warned them. They were big girls and boys.

She started moving again, but she realized neither man was behind her, breathing down her neck as they had done from the start, so she stopped and looked back.

Both of them were staring through the one-way wall at the foyer, at a small group of Cores execs talking next to the lift.

"How can we hear them?" Finkle's voice was reverent.

"Here." She showed them the dial, and Sam and Finkle fiddled with it for a bit.

"I thought we were in a hurry," she said.

Finkle pushed away from the wall. "We are."

They followed her down the passageway, past the offices, and then up the stairs to the Deck.

Sam whistled. "The boss told us about it, but seeing it . . ."

"You'll need to prop the door open," Sofie told him. "I think only I can get through."

Sam pulled a small, heavy doorstop out of his pack, and Sofie reopened the door that had shut behind them so he could wedge it in. "All good."

Sofie put her hand in her pocket and brought out a thin transparent bag. "In case of emergency," she said, and lifted up her shirt to pull out the gloves. She put them into the bag.

Finkle stared at her.

She shrugged, looked over at Sam. "It might not work, but it's worth a try if you need to get down before I'm back. They should be covered in my DNA."

Sam took the bag with a nod. Gave Finkle a jaunty salute. "I'll be in constant touch." He tapped his ear, and Finkle nodded.

He looked covetously out at the warehouse, and then turned away.

Sofie followed him out, and Sam came behind her, without his pack.

Looked like he was going to make the warehouse his base of operations.

When they left Sam behind and started down the stairs, Finkle went first this time, murmuring into his comm set. Sofie guessed he was testing the connection with Sam while he still had her around to get him back in if there was a problem.

From the back and forth, though, it seemed to be working.

She slowed as she passed the image her father had painted, trying to figure it out.

He'd died when she was eighteen. In all the time she'd had with him, never had she seen anything on this level of strange.

She'd never believed the story told by the med tech about what he'd tried to do on his death bed. Never believed any of it.

Now she did.

There might even be a kill switch, she acknowledged for the first time.

She saw Finkle was far below her, but he'd stopped and was waiting, looking up at her.

She jogged a little faster.

By this afternoon, she and Leo would be off to Phansi.

She'd never left Tether Town, never ventured anywhere close to the escarpment, with its dangers and wonders.

She realized the flutter in her stomach was nerves and anticipation.

She'd wanted to go to the mines for a long time. Had begged her father over and over to take her with him.

Too dangerous, he'd said, which had made her laugh. Tether Town, where you could be grabbed as you walked past an alleyway, or knifed in the street, was dangerous, too.

Especially for two young girls whose father was never around to protect them.

They'd had Zyr, and Fallia, and, she'd thought at the time, Veld. But her father hadn't known that.

She saw, with surprise, that Finkle had stopped at the correct level, even though there was nothing to distinguish this floor from the others.

He was good.

She brushed past him to get to the keypad, and he gripped her upper arm.

"I don't know what to make of you."

She looked into his eyes, a mix of browns, blues and sage green in a face of warm brown. "I don't care."

She saw the briefest smile tug at his lips. "Don't put my boss in danger."

She narrowed her eyes at him. "So far, he seems to be doing quite well on that front all by himself. In fact, I've been the one hauling him out of it."

Fink released her. "I don't know what to make of that, either. But you bother me. The timing of when you caught his eye, and now your secret passageways and your connections to the resistance. It just doesn't sit right."

"Well, you better keep an eye on me, then," she told him.

He grunted. "Be sure I will. And if I'm not there, someone else will be."

She smiled at him, tapped out a random number and pushed the door open. "You a loyal guard, Fink?"

"Count on it."

She shook her head. "Life has taught me not to count on anything."

CHAPTER 22

NIGHT WAS FALLING, and from her hover, Dee signaled to him that they should start looking for a place to stop.

He signaled back his agreement, and they both shifted out of auto drive and lifted the hovers up to get a better vantage point.

Up until now, the hovers had flown three feet above the ground, following the route that had been created by the massive transports that moved the ore from Phansi to Tether Town. Years of using the same route had blasted the soil from the rocks, creating a road lined with high dunes of dust on either side.

There was no way they'd spend the night next to the road, though.

Besides the real possibility of being hit by a transport, the Cores sent people up and down this route weekly.

Leo didn't need a Cores snoop coming upon them and asking questions.

The mountains looked close, but from long experience, Leo knew they were another six or seven hours away at least. They would have to find somewhere to camp out on the plains.

Without the need to discuss it, he took the right hand side of the road, and Dee, with Carver hanging on behind her, took the left, and they both rose even higher.

Behind him, Sofie shifted.

Since they'd left Tether Town four hours ago she'd been tucked up against his back, hanging on with arms around his waist.

It was a feeling he could see himself learning to crave.

As Dee rose up, Carver stood and twisted at the waist, looking back to check if they had anyone coming up on them from behind.

They could have had a scanner fitted, kept better track, but that worked both ways. Scanners were easy to pick up, bright and clear as a hello wave.

Most people took their chances without one, including the Cores.

They'd mostly stamped out the hijackers--the Cores weren't averse to dealing with crime when it affected them directly--but there were always a few mad or desperate enough to try and take a transport for the riches inside it. If they could sell the ore, in most cases it was enough to set them up for life.

That kind of one-off score inspired some to take the risk.

None had managed it for a while, though. Or, not that Leo had heard.

Still, no sane traveler would risk spending the night beside the road.

Dee peeled off with a wave of her arm, and Leo followed her as she led them up a slight rise and down the other side.

It looked like everywhere else at first glance; choppy, uneven ground that was too exposed, but when they got to the bottom of the incline, he saw there was a rock overhang and just around the corner, lush greenery that suggested water.

"Been here before?" he asked as they parked the hovers between two massive bushes tucked close to the hillside.

Dee nodded. "My mom found it back when she worked the

transport crews. She showed me years ago when I worked with her, but it's tricky to find."

"Ever have to run off hijackers when you worked a transport crew?" Sofie asked as she slid to the ground.

Dee glanced at her. "A few times."

"I didn't think the hijackers went for Gaudier transports. At least, that's the rumor."

"And we make sure to keep that rumor alive." Carver winked at her as he pulled off his helmet.

Sofie snorted out a laugh. "It's working. I've never heard anyone brag they've taken one of yours."

There was silence.

"That's because no one who's ever tried has managed to live long enough to brag." Dee stored her helmet in the long, deep storage space at the back of the hover.

Leo winced. His outfit was brutal, but for the first time, that bothered him. He didn't want Sofie to see him as no better than the Cores.

Sofie shrugged. "It's not like they don't know the deal going in."

Dee blinked, and Leo realized she'd deliberately been baiting Sofie, trying to scare her off.

He caught his lieutenant's eye but she stared back blandly.

They thought they were protecting him, which would be hilarious if Sofie wasn't their target.

With her, he was long past saving.

"Well, are we going to stand around, or are we going to set up camp?" Carver asked. "I'm starving."

―――――

"Thanks for dealing with those oppos for me the other day." Sofie glanced over at Carver, then spooned up more stew. "It was you following me, wasn't it?"

He paused a moment, then nodded. "Sorry I scared you down the alley in the first place."

She noticed he kept his words soft and didn't look in Leo's direction, as if he were trying not to attract Leo's notice when it came to this.

Had he been in trouble for it, she wondered?

"Thought you were from the Cores," she explained. "And you thought I was an untrained admin clerk."

He shrugged. "First rule of business; never assume."

Leo looked over at them, and Sofie sent him a bright smile.

He didn't smile back, and she bet he'd worked out the direction of their conversation.

Carver must have thought the same, because his shoulders were hunched.

"Well, I appreciated you taking them down." She patted his arm and stood, walking to the small waterfall pouring down the side of the rock to rinse her bowl.

They weren't drinking the water--they'd brought enough supplies they didn't need to take the chance--but the constant rain of the last few days must have fed the source of this spring, because it was leaping off the rock it was so full.

Leo joined her. He and Dee had been talking in low tones on the other side of the fire and she moved aside so he could rinse his bowl, too.

"Want to take a walk?" she asked.

They hadn't had a chance to talk since Finkle had brought her back from the tower. They'd packed clothes and food, and set off straight away in the two long, sleek hovers, and there had been no way to talk after that.

He nodded, but she read reluctance in the way he put her bowl with his and stacked them with the others.

She'd been wondering what it was he needed to tell her since last night, but whatever it was, he thought she would be unhappy about it.

The thing was, she couldn't think of a thing he could tell her that would make her angry.

She'd known about Leo Gaudier long before she met him. Knew the rumors.

That he was somehow cheating the Cores--that the Cores had sold him old, used-up mines but that he somehow managed to make them viable again, and it had driven the Cores mad trying to work out how he did it.

That he was running transport for the independent prospectors as well as his own operations, and that no one who dealt with him ever went back to using Cores transport services.

That alone made the Cores suspicious of what he was up to, but they'd never managed to pin him down on anything.

Unless he was about to tell her he was actually collaborating with the Cores, she couldn't see a single reason why she would be angry about anything he'd done.

She waited for him at the edge of the fire's glow.

He joined her, flicked on a bright light, and took her hand to lead her through the bushes.

The vegetation thinned, and after five minutes they came to a massive rock, at least three times higher than Leo.

He helped boost her up the face of it, and she clambered to the top, which was almost flat.

She spent the time waiting for him to join her by turning slowly to look around her.

The camp was visible by the muted glow of light, obscured by the bushes. In all other directions, the plain stretched out, undulating and not as flat as it looked from the distance. It wasn't as barren as it appeared from Felicitos, either.

There were small, succulent plants everywhere, growing through cracks in the rock and over the ground.

As Leo pulled himself up, much more smoothly and effortlessly than she had, something lumbered through the undergrowth.

She whipped around to see what it was, but it was too dark.

"Most likely a curban," Leo said, stepping up close and looking over her shoulder.

"What's that?"

He tilted his head to her in surprise. "About this big." He showed her with his hands. "Snub nose, fine scales. They'll bite if cornered, but they'd rather run away."

"You've seen them up close?"

"I grew up on the mines, and they're everywhere there." He drew her in, so her back was to his chest, and hugged her to him.

She settled in, content for the moment, and looked upward.

The lights of Tether Town and Felicitos usually obscured the night sky, but out here, the stars were almost overwhelming in their brightness, the sheer number of them lighting up the galaxy.

"My mother was a prospector." Leo's voice was a rumble in her ear. "She was part of the first wave, when the Core Five were just setting up. They'd claimed the main ore bodies, fighting with each other and eventually settling on a compromise of who got what, carving it up among themselves, but there were still small claims that a few people could work and make a good living on. The trick was picking the right one."

"And did your mother pick the right one?" Sofie tilted her head back but Leo was looking up at the sky.

He nodded. "She found a small seam, worked it herself until I was old enough to help her. But it only lasted six years before we needed special equipment to get whatever was left out."

She didn't say anything, letting him stand quietly for a moment.

"The equipment was available, for rent or for sale, but it was owned by the Cores. They set the price and let's just say it was one we couldn't afford." He rubbed her arm, almost unconsciously. "I'd been working that claim with my mom since I was fourteen, and we were looking at packing it in."

She could hear the bleak fury in his voice.

"What happened?"

"My mom took a Cores job, just a short term, year-long contract, to get us enough to rent the equipment and open the mine again." His hold on her tightened a little, then relaxed. "The seam she was working two months before her contract ended collapsed. She and twenty others died that day."

She turned in his arms, pulled him close to her with her arms around his waist. "I'm so sorry."

"They killed your father, too." His voice was steady.

She let that go, because in many ways her father was her father in name only. Whereas it sounded as if Leo and his mother had been a team.

"When she died, I wanted to kill the Cores."

She heard the depth of feeling in his voice.

They stood there for long minutes and eventually she shifted.

"What about this story has you worried about my reaction, Leo? Nothing you've said so far has done anything but make me admire you more."

"It's what happened next." He turned her around again, drew her in, his arms wrapped around her shoulders as if he couldn't quite face her while he spoke. "They didn't even tell me she'd died. I got worried when I hadn't heard from her and I went up to the mine site. Someone flicked through a screen and gave me the news like they were giving me a weather report."

She gripped his hands where they rested on her collarbone. Squeezed.

"I was so angry. Enraged." He rubbed his chin on the top of her head. "I went back to Phansi and stewed. I watched a transport leave, and then I got together some supplies, went out to the route, and waited for it to come back from Tether Town. And I took it."

She stilled. "And you lived to tell the tale?"

"I forced the driver and the guards out, and they watched me fly away with it. I'd set it all up in advance. I crested a hill, set off a big explosion, and all anyone found were parts of other transports that had been damaged in hijacks over the years. I'd collected them up and scattered them to make it look like most of a transport. Then I rewired the hover I'd taken to emit a new ID."

"And Gaudier Transports was born."

His nod brushed his chin against her cheek.

"I waited out on the plateau for three months, giving the Cores time to forget, then I flew it back into Phansi and told everyone I'd inherited money from my mother's estate, and had bought a beat up transport with it."

"What did you do with the ore?"

He shook his head. "There was no ore. I attacked the transport on the way back to Phansi, not going the other way. They weren't as attentive with no ore to protect, and the Cores weren't as angry about the loss when there was no ore missing."

"What about your partners in the heist?"

He gave a humorless laugh. "There were no partners. It was a solo job. Looking back now, I know the only reason I pulled it off at all is because I did do it solo. The driver would never have stopped if I hadn't been alone, looking like I was hiking back to Phansi. That was how I got the jump on them. They never saw my face, it was winter, bitterly cold, and my face was covered."

"And then they thought you died in the explosion."

He shrugged. "I don't know if I fooled the transport crew, but I didn't hurt them, I left them alive, and it might have been easier just to say the whole thing had gone up in a ball of flames. My guess is they embellished the whole thing, out of embarrassment at being taken by a single person. They probably told the Cores it was a gang and they were overwhelmed. They would have been worried about admitting to anything less."

He was silent, and she had the feeling he was finally coming to the crux of the situation, the thing that had him sure she was going to be unhappy with him.

It made her feel like she'd swallowed rocks. She wanted to get this done. "So now you had a transport."

"I had a transport, but no ore to transport in it." His voice was soft now. "The prospectors in Phansi are a close knit group. They can never compete with the Cores, and early on they made a decision not to do each other down. It works better if they support each other--no one else is going to." He straightened up, dropped his arms, and she turned to look at him, but he faced away from her, eyes on the stars.

"You wanted them to use your transport." That made sense.

"I wanted them to use my transport," he agreed. "Prospectors have to put their ore through a weigh station so the Cores can evaluate how much they've mined. They have to pay a service fee based on the tonnage price, the so-called royalty to the Cores for opening up Garmen and allowing them to come prospect. They can then sell their ore to whichever company they like. The Cores always fill their transports with their own ore first, so only if there's room for extra can the prospectors sell to them, and often, the Cores demand a discount, so the prospectors try to avoid using them."

"So you were in with a good chance." She knew about the weigh station at Phansi. Her father had designed it and supervised its building. He'd even gone back when Felicitos was nearing completion to upgrade it, as it had been running by then for six years.

"The problem was I didn't have the money to pay the prospectors for their ore up front, and I didn't have the contacts to sell the ore even if I got it to Tether Town. And the threshold for getting into the game had been set so high, I was starting to realize I might not get in."

"But you did."

She was starting to realize that whatever he'd done to make himself a player was at the heart of this.

"I did." He paused, and his hands fisted. "I knew all the prospectors, I'd been working with them since I was fourteen, but since our claim was mined out and my mother had gone to work for the Cores, we missed the start of something new, something we weren't included in because of our circumstances.

"When I arrived back in Phansi with my stolen transport, a little feral after my three months in the mountains, I was suddenly the solution to a problem they'd been sitting on for two weeks." He scrubbed a hand over his head. "The next weigh-in was coming up, and they needed a co-conspirator they trusted, because they were all cheating the system."

Sofie frowned. "How were they cheating the system? And all of them?"

He glanced at her, and then away. "All of them, because the way the cheat worked, everyone had to be in on it. The fact that the community was so tight worked in their favor. They knew no one was likely to blab to the Cores. My mother would have been in it, too, if our stake had still been producing ore."

"They decided to trust you."

"I was part of the prospector community. The other transport companies were all outside contractors, coming in to make money off the Cores if they could, and branching out to buy ore from the prospectors when they saw there was a market. There was no way the prospectors were going to tell any of them their secret. They were desperate by the time I showed up. I was familiar to them, and with a transport all ready to go."

"What was the cheat?" Her heart leapt at the notion of the independent miners cheating the Cores. She hoped it was by a lot.

"The weigh station scales had been recalibrated. Made to under-read the weight by twenty percent, although the algorithm was set to decrease slowly over a few months, so it looked like the mines were just getting less viable, which the Cores already thought they would, or they wouldn't have sold the mining rights in the first place."

"But how . . .?" The Cores would surely keep a close watch on the weigh station figures, it was pure profit for them, a way to squeeze the last drop of money out of ore deposits they'd already all but exhausted.

Leo looked at her, face grim. "Your father."

She frowned. "My father?"

"He set the algorithm in place, he sold the scheme to the prospectors. He set up the channel to buy their ore, both the secret twenty percent and the declared amount, and he sold it on to exporters in Tether Town."

She knew her mouth was hanging open.

Her father had been bitter at the Cores for ignoring how the smugglers--the murderers of his people--were hiding from justice by using Garmen as a safe haven. She thought the secret passageways and tunnels of Felicitos had been his revenge. But recalibrating the Phansi weigh station scales seemed such a strange . . .

"Money," she said, on an exhale.

"Money," Leo agreed. "He had a transport. He'd somehow coded it as independent, even though I'm sure he'd requisitioned it from a Cores warehouse, and he was selling twenty percent of all non-Cores ore at full price to off-planet buyers, even though it was royalty free, and splitting the extra profit fifty-fifty with the prospectors."

"It was to finance the secret passageways in the Under Deck." Sofie knew her father had used Cores funds for most of the secret work that had gone into the Lower and Upper Reaches, and the tunnels out of the tower, but the Under Deck had been all his.

"Maybe the Cores started looking at his costings a little too closely," Leo agreed. "He needed a new way to fund what he was doing. And then, he died."

"So the prospectors wanted you to . . . take over from him?"

Oh, she was starting to understand.

He hesitated. "Yes. They were offering me the second transport, the one he'd coopted, and the secret twenty percent of ore."

"So you took over my father's business." Why had her father never said anything about it?

Leo shook his head. "I couldn't do that. I didn't have the codes to get into his accounts, and I could hardly show up and take over whatever office he was using to run the trades, but I took over the transport, and started trading the ore myself. No one ever came to me to demand a piece of the action."

"Because no one knew he was the one running it."

He gave a nod. "In the beginning, I was working so hard, running on nerves, waiting to be called out or caught out, and I was getting a thirty percent split of profits from the prospectors until I could start paying them for their ore upfront. But it didn't take long to work my way up to fifty-fifty." He finally held her gaze. "What I didn't do is look to see if Ronald Fadal had any family. I was young, I was ambitious, and I was making serious money, and sticking it to the Cores at the same time. I didn't try and find out if Fadal had dependents who were suddenly in trouble because of his death."

"You started living the high life. Building warehouses, fancy houses, and renting space in the Upper Reaches, while Rach and I had to scrounge for work and count every penny." She saw the road his mind had gone down.

He rubbed his upper lip. "You said some of the prospectors sought you out, that they told you stories about Phansi. But they never mentioned you to me, I swear, although that's no excuse on my part. After the blur of the first few months, where I negotiated deals without really knowing what I was doing, and ran two transports full of undeclared ore to Tether Town, I should have come looking. I should have asked who had the right to come knocking and ask me what the hell I was doing with Fadal's transport, but if it occurred to me, it didn't stay in my head for long."

"I would never have come knocking, because I didn't know anything about his little side deal." She gave a dry laugh. "I didn't even know if he'd been paid by the Cores. I thought they might be cheating him of his salary before he died, because there was no money, ever. When he died and Rach and I got his final payout, we saw he had been paid, he was just spending it as fast as it came in. I never knew where that money went until I saw those passageways in the Under Deck. But his salary wouldn't have been enough to pay for everything we saw there. It makes sense that he'd organized another income stream. And it would have satisfied him immensely that he was doing it at the Cores' expense."

"Did the prospectors help you?" Leo asked.

She thought back to those days, to the hard-eyed men and women who'd sought her and Rach out in the coffee houses or taverns of Tether Town. "Some." She nodded slowly. "They'd pay for our drinks or our meal. And sometimes I'd find ports in my pocket or under my plate. It confused us." It was coming back to her now. "It didn't last long. It went on for maybe six months, a year, after my father died, then it faded out. They stopped coming around, or we looked more settled, maybe, and they let well enough alone." She shrugged. "Maybe they thought that keeping it up would raise questions they didn't want to answer, what with that fifty-fifty split, and all."

Leo winced. "Maybe."

"So, what would you have done?" Sofie asked. "If your conscience had pricked you enough to find us?"

"I don't know." He slid his hands into the pockets of his jacket. "I honestly don't know, and that bothers me. When I think of you doing it hard, struggling, while I and most of Phansi got rich, I want to punch the younger me in the face."

She crossed her arms over her chest. "Those prospectors who came to see me, the ones you're thinking were so noble? My guess is they didn't tell you about us because they were scared you *would* have done something. That you *would* have insisted on cutting us in."

He went still. Gave a slow nod. "Maybe. I don't know if they were right."

"I do." She stepped up to him, put her arms around his waist again. She liked that he slid his arms around her with no hesitation. "My father never gave us anything, not even food on the table most of the time. He was secretive, obsessive, and driven by his own demons. If he'd meant us to benefit from what he'd set up in Phansi, he had every opportunity to do so. But he didn't. When he died, nothing changed for us because we were forced to look after ourselves long before then. That you're feeling guilty about not helping us when he obviously didn't is more than a little telling about the difference between the two of you."

"I will make it up to you," Leo said, his lips brushing the tip of her ear.

"Oh, I'll make sure you do." She laughed as she tipped her face up. Then went still at the look she saw in his eyes.

"You really don't blame me, do you?" He slid his hands into her hair, twining his fingers through it as if to anchor her in place.

She shook her head and then made a sound of approval as his lips slanted over hers.

"I think this calls for a celebration." His grin was wicked against her lips.

She gave a squeak as he swung her up and then sat down on the rock, holding her in his arms.

It felt right.

She closed her eyes as yet another reason to stay tighten around her, tethering her to Garmen. She had never believed, as Rach had, that there would be consequences for the Cores if the stories of suffering her sister had worked so hard to obtain got out, but she'd spent the last year working towards doing it anyway, as a tribute to Rach.

Now, as Leo's hands worked their way under her shirt and he nuzzled her neck, she found it harder to call up the desire to leave.

CHAPTER 23

"SO." Sofie shifted uncomfortably beside him, and Leo lifted her off the hard, cold rock and draped her over his chest.

She was startled into silence for a moment, and then made a contented hum, threaded her fingers into his hair and tucked her head under his chin.

The warmth he suddenly felt was from far more than just her body heat.

They had dressed again, but the night air was getting colder, and they would soon need to go back to the fire, and the warmth of their sleeping bags.

"Now that you've admitted to living the high life off my legacy, do you want to tell me why we're racing to Phansi?" There was humor in her voice.

It still amazed him that she didn't seem to hold it against him that he'd taken her father's scheme and not given a thought to her and her sister. She thought it was a joke, was already teasing him about it.

He hadn't realized how heavy the burden of guilt he'd been carrying was until she'd cut it away.

"The reason we're going up there is the algorithm has reset."

She lifted her head. "Let me get this straight, you tell me about secret money just as it comes to an end?"

He saw the flash of laughter in her eyes, shook his head at her. "To be fair, I only heard it had come to an end this morning." He tucked her head back under his chin. He liked it there. "This outcome isn't going to ruin me. I'll make less without the royalty free twenty percent obviously, but I've got a fully operational, legitimate business now. I've been selling the other eighty percent this whole time, and I've bought mines of my own. I've gone after the rare mineral sands and ores that the Cores didn't think about until it was too late."

"And earned an extra twenty percent royalty free on those, too?" she asked.

"On those, too." He smiled.

"So someone came running from Phansi to let you know the scheme has come crashing down?"

Leo stroked a hand down her back. "Eight years to the day after your father set it up."

"So, he put in a timer." She wondered what else he'd put a timer in. Was there something in Felicitos that was going to suddenly fall over?

It was not a good thought.

"I wondered if you could take a look at the weigh station. See if there is anything there your father left as a clue. Something on the floor or walls to read that only you'd understand."

She sighed, and he felt her head shake. "Don't hold out any hope. He never intended me to go to Phansi. Said it was too dangerous."

"I understand. If there's nothing, we're no worse off. But if there's even a small chance . . ."

She lifted her head again. "What's the end game here, Leo? Just for you and the prospectors to make money at the Cores expense?"

He held her gaze. "Not that I don't think that's worthwhile in itself, but no. I use some of the money for projects that make a positive impact in Phansi and in Tether Town, but the real danger is the Cores are about to be presented with figures that make no sense. The output of the mines are supposed to be declining, not suddenly jumping twenty percent. If they take a look, they're going to find they've been robbed for years, and they will lay waste to Phansi. At the very least, they'll use it as an excuse to reclaim the mines, something they've been trying to do for months because trade with the VSC has started falling off."

"They've been trying to get the rights back?" She sounded surprised.

"They've sent me three offers in the last three months, all a tenth of what my holdings are worth. Everyone else in Phansi has gotten the same offers. The time is coming soon that we'll have to fight them openly, because things are reaching a tipping point."

"That's why they're trying to kill you?"

"They're trying to kill me because with me gone, they'll get my businesses."

"You really think the VSC is easing away from dealing with them on moral grounds?"

Leo shrugged. "Part of it has to be that whatever Zyr and the resistance has been doing is working, pitting them against each other. They've also made a mistake with their attacks on the Verdant String. The VSC was never thrilled with the Breakaways, and since the attack on Cepi and Parn, they're even less inclined to deal with Garmen and Lassa, because they're sure the Breakaways are responsible. The trade with the VSC is definitely drying up."

"Why do you think they even went there, poked at the VSC in such an obvious way?"

Leo sat up, taking her with him, as the rock got too uncomfortable. "I think the attack on Cepi was a genuine attempt to grab the alien enviro and grav tech, to try to replicate it and sell it. When that went wrong, they tried to create a diversion on Parn. My guess is that the VSC suspected the Breakaways were behind the attack on Cepi from the start. Maybe they were making noises about it. So someone came up with the bright idea of distracting them with trouble on Parn. From what I saw on the interplanetary comms, the person they sent to create the distraction was a Halatian motivated by revenge. I think they gave a madman with an agenda the money and equipment he needed to wreak havoc and sent him off to do his worst, hoping it would take the pressure off them and make the VSC look in another direction."

"Except, the VSC caught them, found out the truth." There was a thoughtful tone in her voice.

Leo dropped lightly off the rock, and held out his arms to her.

She slid down a little way, then pushed off, and he caught her, swung her down beside him.

"And now they're getting in bed with Caruso." Sofie toyed with the charm bracelet on her wrist. "And if that doesn't tell you greed has blinded them, I don't know what will."

Leo agreed. Caruso would chew the Cores up and spit them out. If they continued down this path, Garmen would be a vassal of Caruso within the year.

That was not acceptable to him.

The time really had come to stop the secret games and make a stand.

A shout rang out from the camp, and then they both heard the sound of a hover.

"Stay here." Leo didn't wait to see if Sofie obeyed him. He ran toward the camp.

Someone had found them. Chances were, it wasn't a friend.

———

Sofie watched Leo disappear into the darkness, running toward the faint glow of the fire.

She just caught a glimpse of him pulling out his laz from one of the many pockets of his pants as he went.

She didn't have a laz herself.

In the Verdant String they were banned except for use by the military and the security services, which meant they were rare and expensive.

The same rule didn't apply on Garmen. They were still expensive but they weren't rare. If you had the money, you could have a laz. But not many had the money.

She didn't have a light, either.

Leo had taken it with him, so she was forced to go slower than she'd have liked, making her way to Leo's right, looping around, so she would come at the camp site from a different angle.

She could hear raised voices, and something about one of them was familiar. She sped up a little and stubbed her toe on a rock for her trouble.

She was forced to stop, close her eyes to squeeze back tears of pain, and then limped forward again, teeth gritted.

Someone ran toward her through the bushes, but to her right, and she slowed even more, moving cautiously in the darkness. The shouting had cut off and there was an unnerving silence coming from the camp.

She bent down and felt around for a rock, picking one up that had what felt like a clump of grass attached to it.

She moved forward again, straining to hear where the person who'd run past her was, but the sound of the stream coming over the rock was louder now, and she had the bad feeling she wouldn't hear anyone even if they were right behind her.

The thought stopped her in her tracks, and she looked over her shoulder, but there was no one there.

She shook her head and turned back, edging around the last bush, and stopping just short of the fire's glow.

A hover lay, abandoned, on its side. It wasn't a sleek, silver machine like Leo's or Dee's, there was graffiti scrawled across it and there were dents and scrapes along the side.

One person lay just beyond the fire, a large, slumped figure, and she could just make out someone crouched over them, laz in hand.

It looked like Dee.

The person groaned, and Sofie frowned at the sound of it and took a step closer, coming into the light.

Grass from the rock she was carrying brushed her hand, and she shook it away. When it tickled her again, she looked down and screamed, throwing the rock off to the right, and holding her hand out in panic.

She didn't know what order things happened in next. She didn't much care. Her interest was focused on getting the spider that was almost the size of her palm off her.

Everyone else seemed to have other plans.

Someone grabbed her from behind and jammed a laz against her temple. Leo and Carver stepped toward her into the light on the other side of the fire, and Dee took a step away from the person at her feet, laz raised to point straight at her.

"Get it off!" Sofie tried to flick the spider again, but she felt tiny claws sink into her skin when she tried.

"Don't shake it. If it feels threatened, it'll bite." Leo's voice was steady.

She couldn't form a coherent response, couldn't tell if he was moving closer to her or not, her full focus was on the brown and green spider, with long, frond-like legs and antenna looking at her with shiny black eyes.

"Sofie-girl?" The lump on the ground half rose up, and Dee moved her arm to aim her laz back at her prisoner.

"Zyr?" Leo turned.

As he did, the spider ran over Sofie's wrist and up her arm. She screamed again, flicked her arm back, and spun out of the hold of whoever was behind her.

There was a curse, and wild brushing, and the spider seemed to disappear into the dark.

"Fallia?"

The person who'd held the laz to her head was dressed in black from head to toe and their face was covered, but the curse had given it away.

Fallia pulled her mask up off her face, but her laz was pointed at Sofie again, and she held it steady.

There was no chance she hadn't known it was Sofie before.

Sofie had had the hood of her jacket down, so she could see better as she crept toward the camp fire, and Fallia would have recognized her voice since then.

It hurt to know she had still gone ahead and set a weapon against her temple.

"Fallia, stand down." Zyr's voice was weak.

"Dee." Leo make a gesture, but Dee hesitated a moment before she pointed her laz at the ground.

"Did you do that to him?" Sofie asked Dee, because now she could concentrate on other matters, she saw someone had beaten Zyr. His cheek was swollen and the eye above it was almost swollen shut. His lip had been split, and there was a cut across his forehead.

He'd been her childhood friend; the steady, calm refuge from the storm of her life with her erratic father. When he and Rach had fallen into a relationship, she had pictured them all as a family, had wished for it so hard.

She knew she had been more upset than either of them when they had drifted apart.

But in all the years she'd known him, never once had she seen him like this.

He was tall, strong. Invincible. No one had ever been stupid enough to give him trouble. Not even Veld.

"No." Dee's voice was cool.

"They came down the hill fast, like they didn't know we were here." Carver stepped into the light. "When we jumped up, it gave them a shock, and their hover cut out and hit the ground."

"Except, it's a bit much to think they came on us by accident." Dee kept her voice flat.

"Not by accident. Thought you were further away." Fallia spoke at last.

There was silence for a moment.

Sofie wondered how many had noticed that Sofie had in fact been a bit further away. Out on the rock with Leo, not in the camp.

She had some questions about that for both Zyr and Fallia-- who hadn't lowered her laz, Sofie realized, despite Zyr's order.

She decided to pretend that her old friend had done it anyway.

She turned her back and walked over to Zyr, knelt down, and gently took his face between her hands.

"Sorry for the dramatics. You know how I hate spiders."

He chuckled, and the movement must have split his lip again, because his teeth became coated in blood. "I remember. But that was sure some top flight screaming."

"That was a top flight spider." She shuddered.

"That little thing?" He struggled up to his elbows.

"You can barely see, so how would you know?" She kept her voice light, but now that he'd moved more into the light, she could see how bad it was.

It shocked her.

"What happened?"

Dee, who was still standing just behind Zyr, suddenly lifted her laz and fired, lighting up the night. Sofie had to close her eyes against it.

Someone fell in the darkness just beyond the circle of light, and Fallia, who'd returned fire in Dee's direction, went still and lowered her laz. She held a light in her other hand, and she engaged it and pointed it to where the body had fallen.

"The fucking fucker," she murmured.

Sofie turned back to Dee, but she was unharmed.

"Fallia shot over our heads," Zyr said quietly. "Couldn't hit that guard of Leo's without hitting us."

Dee grinned, a nasty, satisfied grin, but Sofie didn't begrudge her. She'd hit whoever had been sneaking around in the dark, and if she'd positioned herself so that Zyr and Sofie were her shields, that just said she knew her stuff.

"How did he get here, and is he alone?" Leo asked. He walked over to the body, laz still in his hand.

"I'll check." Carver slid past him, and disappeared into the night.

"Might be two of them," Fallia called. "Although not likely."

Carver didn't answer.

"Who is it?" Zyr's voice was a little stronger, and Sofie held out a hand and helped him sit up a bit more.

"Sunny."

Sofie rose up, heart thumping. She walked over to the body, came to a stop between Leo and Fallia.

"That woman does not mess around." Fallia glanced at Dee, then crouched down to feel Sunny's pulse, then stepped back, hands on her hips.

"He's dead?" Sofie knelt to see for herself.

"We don't believe in the niceties out here," Leo said. "It's shoot to kill. No room for prisoners on the hover."

She nodded in acceptance. Garmen was what it was. There

was a better way, but until someone other than the Cores had control, that wasn't going to happen.

She'd long ago accepted reality.

"I see you're not waiting for me back at the rock." Leo's voice was low and deep.

She looked over at him, eyebrows raised. "No. I thought you might need me and my creepy spider to perform a bit of a distraction for you."

He stared at her, grim faced and she smiled back.

His hands curled into fists. "I'll go help Carver," he said, and stalked off into the night.

Dee made a sound, and Sofie looked over at her.

She seemed exasperated.

She'd been left with three potential enemies, in her eyes.

Sofie threw her hands up in annoyance. "Oh, for goodness sake, Dee, we're all harmless. Even Zyr, at the moment." She glanced at Fallia, still unwilling to forgive the laz to the temple. "So, if Dee didn't kick Zyr's ass, who did?"

"Some friends of Sunny's here, I'm guessing." Fallia toed him with her boot.

"And your finding us like this, and overshooting the mark because I was a little way from camp talking to Leo, points to you having some kind of tracker on me." She made it a statement.

Zyr winced, and she didn't know if it was because he hurt or because he heard the sense of betrayal in her voice.

"I've been tracking you since Rach died." He coughed as he sat up, and couldn't speak at all for a minute.

She didn't go help him this time.

"Don't give him shit about this, Sofie." Fallia's voice was hard. "He's watched you like a guardian angel for years. Took out more than one person who was getting too close to figuring out who you were."

She ignored Fallia, looked over at Zyr.

"You have to understand, Sofe. I promised Rach I'd protect you both. But Veld got the jump on me with Rach. I wasn't going to let him get you, too. And he would have, a couple of times, before he got a better offer and left. But I couldn't be sure he hadn't hedged his bets, set someone to keep an eye on you." He shrugged. "You are the only key to Felicitos now."

She drew in a breath. "You know about that?"

"Rach told me, long ago."

Rach had *known*? And never said anything?

Now she really felt like an idiot, only figuring it out so recently. And even then, with Leo's help.

There was a quiet hum in the air, and Dee's focus snapped from them to the darkness behind her and Fallia.

Fallia turned as well, laz out, but it was Leo and Carver, sharing a small, one-person hover.

"Looks like he was following you on his own." Leo jumped down, and Carver carried on, parking the hover with the others.

"So, where's the tracker?" Sofie asked. As the words came out of her mouth, she knew. She lifted the bracelet. "That's really ..." She shook her head. "Which one is it?"

"The cloud."

She spent a moment unclipping the delicate clasp. The cloud was the first charm, and she pulled it off. Threw it at Fallia, as Zyr was in no state to catch it.

"What if she'd taken it off?" Dee asked.

"She never would. It was her sister's." Zyr coughed again, lumbered up to his hands and knees, and then slowly stood.

"What are you doing here, Zyr?" Leo motioned to Carver, and he hauled up the beat-up hover and put it with the others.

They had quite a little collection now.

"After that warning you and Sofie gave me, I was a little forceful in my quest to find out who'd sold Sofie out." Zyr walked gingerly to the fire and lowered himself down in front of it. "I made out I had a suspicion who it was, and while I was walking home from Felicitos, I got jumped by five oppos."

"Real oppos?" Sofie asked.

He paused. Shrugged. "They didn't talk, which isn't like oppos, and they were big, well fed. My guess is Core guards, but it doesn't matter, we know the Cores are behind it, whoever they sent."

That was true.

"So you decided to lead them straight to Sofie?" Leo asked him.

"No, we decided it might be wise to get out of Tether Town for a bit. We saw from the tracker that Sofie was heading off to Phansi at speed, and as no one had said anything to us about it, we decided it made sense to go after her." Fallia walked to the fire as well, and sat, and Sofie saw the strain on her face for the first time.

"We did three loop backs to check for followers," Zyr said. "I guess the transport route really only goes to one place, so Sunny waited long enough to put some serious distance between us at the start, and then spent the day catching us up."

"But how did he know to come over the hill?" Carver asked.

Dee snorted. "If the crash bang these two made when they wrecked their hover didn't do it, Nature Girl here screaming blue murder over a grass spider certainly did."

There was silence for a moment, and then everyone except Sofie started to laugh.

She huffed out a breath. "It dug its claws into my *skin*."

That only made them laugh harder.

CHAPTER 24

THEY STOPPED JUST after midday to stretch and eat something.

Leo never tired of Cloud Falls, the sheer height of them, the icy, crystal pool below, and the misty cloud of spray that gave the waterfall its name.

It lay within view of the route, but they were deep in the mountains now, and there wasn't a good place to rest out of sight. The cliffs on either side of the narrow pass were high and unbroken. There were no gorges branching off them that he had ever found.

And he had looked.

Sofie stood at the edge of the pool with her back to all of them.

The only person she seemed to not be angry with was Carver.

He'd barely spoken to her after he'd returned with Sunny's hover. He and Carver had set up a warning perimeter, so everyone could get some sleep, and they'd set a low frequency fauna repellent as well.

Carver had told her about it when they returned to a camp,

and she had been visibly relieved at the news no spiders would be visiting while she slept.

She had been friendly to Carver before, but now she positively beamed at him.

He'd slept side by side with her, making sure his mattress was next to hers, but she had ignored him, and this morning, she'd taken Sunny's hover as her ride, her look daring anyone to object.

"You've got some making up to do, lover-boy." Zyr said from beside him.

Leo went still, impressed at how quietly he could move. "*I* have some making up to do?"

"Well," Zyr inclined his head. "I do, too. But I've got the advantage of being her brother in everything other than blood. You, on the other hand, are not at that level."

Leo contemplated Zyr's face. He felt an overwhelming urge to add to the bruises that looked worse today than they had yesterday.

As if he could read his mind, Zyr grinned, then winced as the movement hurt his lip. He held up two cups, and Leo caught the scent of jah.

"I'm sure she'd be grateful for a cup." Zyr handed them over. "You owe me, lover-boy."

Leo curled his lip in response, but he picked his way over the rocks to the edge of the pool and came to stand beside Sofie. He handed her a cup without a word.

She took it, glancing at him in surprise. "Thank you."

He sipped his own, gazing into the pool. It was so clear, he could see all the way to the bottom.

A large fish swam lazily through the water.

"You're angry."

She gave a short, bitter laugh. "No, I'm not." She sipped her jah in silence for a while.

"You're going to have to speak to me, Sofie. Spell it out."

She looked at him. "Before I met you, I spent my life in the resistance. I've risked my life many times to get information for the leadership. Information I now know probably went nowhere because I gave it to Veld, but that doesn't take away from the risks I took. And since I met you, I've helped you kill two assassins and I've killed one myself." She drew in an unsteady breath. "And now I find, despite my years of risk, Zyr doesn't trust me enough to let me know he's tracking me, not that it seemed to be of any help to him when Sunny, or whoever else is a traitor in the resistance, sold me out to Flunky and Tapper, and you disrespect me by ordering me to stay back like I'm some helpless ornament, rather than a respected partner and equal." She turned to face him. "I'm not angry. I'm hurt. If this is how it is, I'm done with both of you."

She tipped her head and looked up at Valdos, the uninhabited water planet that hung close to Garmen. He had the sinking feeling she was planning a way to get up there, get free of them all.

"I'm sorry."

She turned to him. Waited.

"I'm sorry I ordered you to stay behind. It's not because I don't respect you. I just want to keep you safe. I should have taken you with me, used your skills. And if I had, you wouldn't have had a grass spider clinging to your hand." He shuddered, and drew her in.

She didn't fight it, but she didn't relax against him, either.

He kissed the top of her head. "Sofie, you're more important to me than getting rid of the Cores, more important than sorting out the problems at the mines. I can see how my ordering you when I have no right to order you, and my subsequent annoyance that you hadn't listened would hurt you, and I will try to make sure it never happens again. The way I spoke to you after Dee killed Sunny was more reaction to seeing that spider on you than anything else. It scared me sick."

She relented a little, resting her head on his chest. "Dee called it a grass spider. I'm assuming it's not poisonous?"

He swallowed. "It's the most poisonous spider on Garmen."

He felt her shiver.

"And you all *laughed*?"

"It was either that," he told her, "or scream myself."

She stood quietly for a moment, then angled a little to one side so she could keep drinking her jah.

"Am I forgiven?"

She sighed. "Yes. But don't do it again."

"I promise to try."

Her eyes were narrowed when she looked up at him. "Try very hard."

He grinned down at her.

"What are you so pleased about?" She sounded grumpy.

"You're talking to me again. That makes me happy."

He saw the hint of a smile on her lips as she turned away and finished her jah.

"I wish I could swim. This looks so good." She crouched down and rinsed her cup, then flicked the water with her fingers.

"I suppose Lake Felicitos was hardly safe." Leo had learned to swim in the deep, swift-flowing streams that were all around Phansi.

Sofie nodded. "A rash was the least of your worries if you dipped your toe in the lake. I certainly never risked it."

"Is it safe to join you?" Zyr was carrying flat bread wraps, picking his way over to them, and Leo put down a hand and pulled Sofie to her feet.

He took two wraps from Zyr, handed one to Sofie, and then stood shoulder to shoulder with her.

"That how it is?" Zyr's lips thinned. "Nice way to thank me, lover-boy."

"This has nothing to do with Leo."

He could hear the hurt in her voice, and Zyr must have, too, because he looked down at his feet.

"Why didn't you just tell me about the tracker? Why not give me the courtesy of asking if I was okay with it?"

"In those first weeks after Rach died, you were barely holding it together. I added the charm, and you didn't even notice. I thought telling you would be an extra burden at a time you had so many, you were staggering under the weight of them. And then, when enough time had passed, I thought it worked better without you knowing, because you didn't behave like someone who knew they were being tracked. You were completely natural."

"Except, it didn't stop the Cores grabbing her and taking her to Under Deck. What was going on with her tracker then?" Leo asked.

"That would have been the evening Sunny was watching." Zyr lowered himself down.

Leo thought he probably had some cracked ribs, because he moved very carefully, but he'd seen Fallia run a regen wand over the big resistance leader's chest and face this morning, so he should be on the mend.

"I went straight to Sunny to ask him about it. He said because you were working for Leo, he thought you were just going about your business for him, taking something up to the Under Deck. I have to admit," he shook his head, "I believed him completely."

"Sounds like he wasn't so sure you did," Leo said. "Were they trying to beat you up, or kill you?"

Zyr rubbed his chest. "Definitely kill me. I was lucky--a couple of resistance members were right behind me, and they jumped in to help. And even luckier that whoever the attackers were, they were trying to make it look like an oppos attack, so no one had a laz."

"Did any get away?" Sofie's voice was still neutral.

"Two." Zyr didn't say what happened to the other three, but

Leo could guess.

"Do you think Sunny decided to follow you on his own, or was he ordered to?" Leo asked.

"No way to tell. We left a couple of hours after they beat me up, so there wasn't much time for either him or the Cores to make a plan."

"There's nothing in the storage hold on his hover," Sofie said. "So that makes it more likely he jumped on and flew after you without a plan. Without anything."

She went still, her gaze fixing on the cliff to their left.

Leo followed her gaze, and took a deep breath in. A shadow prowler stood looking down at them; body still, its focus intense. "We need to go."

Zyr swore softly. "How quickly does that thing move?"

"Very quickly." Leo grabbed Sofie's hand, started moving her toward the hovers.

"I never thought I'd see one," she said, still craning her neck to look at it.

As if in answer, it roared, the spine-chilling sound echoing around them, loud even over the sound of the falls.

Leo could only hope it had eaten recently.

"Carver, you take the single hover." He wanted Sofie right behind him, holding on tight.

Carver shot him a grin and climbed onto it, and within a minute, they were skimming up the transport route.

"I can see why you chose it," Sofie whispered in his ear.

"Chose it?"

"The shadow prowler logo."

He switched the drive function to auto and looked around. "Why would I have anything to do with that?"

She laughed in his ear. "Give up the act, Gaudier. Who else would care enough to mete out justice in T-Town?"

Who else, indeed?

CHAPTER 25

SOFIE CONSIDERED the roar of the shadow prowler even as they approached Phansi. The deep, eerie call seemed to resonate in her head, and set her teeth on edge. But it was the look of it in the flesh--the massive shoulders, the long, almost prehensile tail, and the big, curved fangs, that really made an impression.

Its short, dark fur seemed to suck light in. She'd only noticed it by the waterfall at all because its tail had flicked.

Leo said they didn't come near Phansi often, but that didn't reassure her, and she noticed no one complained when they pushed through the night to make it to Phansi, rather than spend another night out in the open.

The mining town sat on the flat part of the escarpment, above the mountains they'd spent the day ascending, and lightning crackled down, hitting the rocky hills that formed a ring around the northern end of the settlement. It illuminated low buildings, and the massive, boxy ore silos that stood like a line of sentinels on either side of the main road into the town.

Beyond the silos, as they passed between the two closest to the road, was an even bigger structure, fully lit despite the fact it was past midnight, with automaton trucks rolling in and out of the huge entrance.

Leo turned to her. "The weigh station."

She studied it more carefully.

She could see nothing of her father's whimsy in it, but then, he'd been a specialist in designing mines and buildings associated with mining for many years before he was tasked with Felicitos.

Perhaps this *was* his usual style.

They rode through streets that lit up as they approached, on a motion sensor system that seemed to activate lights attached to the sides of buildings.

Like Tether Town, the structures were square and efficient, and in the same state of disrepair.

The tumbledown look of it shouldn't have surprised her, but somehow it did.

Dee took the lead as they turned off the main road, and they followed her as she wove through a few smaller streets to eventually stop at a building in what Sofie guessed was the high end of town.

The discrete sign on the gate said Gaudier Transport, and Dee turned down the drive. When they got to the end, a garage door opened up for them, smooth and silent, and Dee maneuvered the hover without hesitation into the large, well-kept space.

"What's the plan?" she asked Leo in the sudden silence as everyone's hover was switched off.

"We need to speak to Kalo." Leo opened the storage hold and pulled out Sofie's bag and then his own.

"That's handy, because I need to speak to you." A man ducked under the closing garage door. His hair was an equal mix of black and gray, and his face and body looked hard-used and tough.

Dee, Carver and Leo all suddenly had a laz in their hands, all pointed at the newcomer.

Fallia slowly did the same.

Kalo lifted both hands, saying nothing, and after a beat, Leo lowered his weapon.

It took Dee and Carver a little longer to do the same.

"Jim got to you with the message, then?" Kalo dropped his arms.

"He did." Leo bent to pick up the bags he'd dropped, slung them over his shoulder. "You been waiting out there long?"

Kalo laughed, the sound husky and rough. "No, as a matter of fact. We didn't think you'd make it in until tomorrow at the earliest. But you obviously pushed yourself."

"And the Cores?" Leo walked to the door that connected the garage to the rest of the building and ran his finger through a laser lock.

"There's no one new in town asking uncomfortable questions, if that's what you mean." Kalo looked over at Sofie with dark, almost black eyes, then flicked his gaze to Zyr and Fallia. "Yet."

Leo held the door open for everyone.

Sofie held back as they filed through, and took the hand Leo held out to her and stepped over the threshold with him as the door swung shut behind them.

She looked up, and he gently tucked a strand of her hair behind her ear, his fingers lingering on her cheek.

"You think this is a pleasure trip?" Kalo stood to one side, watching them with eyes narrowed. "This is serious business, Leo."

"I guess you've forgotten me." Sofie turned to Kalo, sliding her arm around Leo's waist. "You looked me up a few times eight years ago, but I was a lot younger then."

"What are you talking about?" Kalo's voice didn't lose its belligerence.

"It seems an introduction isn't necessary," Leo said, and she could hear the chill in his voice. "But this is Sofie Erdo. Ronald Fadal's daughter."

———

The wave of fury that crashed over Leo took him by surprise.

It was a direct reaction to the dismissive tone Kalo had taken with Sofie, and it was tempered only by the way she gave back as good as she got.

Kalo had stopped talking after Sofie's challenge, and remained silent as they'd moved through into the big kitchen on the ground floor of the building.

Dee and Carver took control of making jah and hunting up something for everyone to eat, while Zyr sat in one of the comfortable chairs near the window, clearly near his limit. Fallia stood beside him, wary and on guard.

"I was interested to learn you and a few others looked Sofie and her sister up after Fadal died." Leo led Sofie to another chair and then stood behind it, hands braced on the back of it. "Especially as you never mentioned it to me."

Kalo looked away. "We just wanted to make sure they were doing well, is all."

"Wanted to make sure we didn't know anything about our father's scheme and wouldn't make trouble for you about it, more like." Sofie accepted a cup from Carver with a smile.

"Maybe." Kalo leaned back against the wall, arms crossed defensively over his chest. "You didn't know anything, though."

"Now I do," she said, sweetly.

He pursed his lips. "Too late, girlie, the fun ride is over. Only thing in our future is a nasty visit from the Cores. You want your fair share of that, be my guest."

"What are you really doing here?" Leo kept his voice clipped, because he didn't want Kalo to see how furious he was. "You stood outside, waiting for me to come riding in and bail you out of your trouble, although it sounds as if you don't think I'll be able to."

"I wanted to hear if you've got any inside information. Technicians who've been working the weigh station for the last eight years can't work out how to reset the algorithm, so I doubt you can." Kalo straightened up. "I want to know how far behind you do you think the Cores are?"

Leo released his hold on Sofie's chair and stepped out to the side. "Not far. We left yesterday afternoon. If they left this morning, and pushed it, they'll be here tomorrow afternoon."

"Do we stay or do we go?" Kalo asked.

"You volunteered to wait for me tonight, didn't you? So you'd be the first to know if you need to cut and run." Leo shook his head. "If we can't fix it, I say we stay and fight. But I know your thoughts on the matter." He sank down onto the arm of Sofie's chair.

"I only came to Garmen to make money. I never wanted a part in any rebellion." Kalo slid his hands into his pockets. "Sure, I took the deal Fadal offered us, but that was to line the pockets of his revolution, not mine."

"The question is, will you stay neutral, or will you work against us?" Dee was sitting on a high chair beside the counter, both hands wrapped around her mug.

Kalo bared his teeth at her, and flicked his hand, as if batting her away.

Dee had told Leo long ago Kalo would be a problem when the time came to act, because he could only be trusted to look out for himself. She'd been sure if he thought he'd get a benefit from selling them out to the Cores, he'd do it.

The way he was behaving now, Leo agreed with her.

"We'll eat something, catch a few hours sleep, and then get to the weigh station." Leo told him. "You want to smooth our way?"

"What are you doing to do? If Donnie and Ursula can't fix it, what chance have you got?"

"What does it matter?" Carver asked, and Leo could hear the anger in his voice. "You've got nothing to lose, either way."

Carver, and Dee, for that matter, had both grown up in Phansi. Had both come to work for him when he first started out.

They knew Kalo better than he did, especially as their families still lived here and worked the mines.

Kalo inclined his head. "True enough." His gaze snagged on Leo's hand curled around Sofie's. "All I did was give the girl a few ports to help her out. Looks like you've given her a lot more." There was something salacious and deeply disrespectful in his voice. "Why the hell would you bring her here? Trying to guilt us into paying out some of the profits? If so, you've wasted your time."

Leo was suddenly in front of him, right in his face. "I'll remember you said that, Kalo." He forced out a deep breath. "I'll expect our path into the weigh station to be clear."

"And if it's not?" Kalo was all bravado.

Leo simply looked down on him, at the bitter droop of his mouth and the hard, cynical glint in his eye.

"All right, all right." Kalo flapped his hands. "No one will give you any trouble."

He turned and walked out, and they were all silent as they waited for his footsteps to reach the door and then heard the sound of it opening and closing.

"He's lying," Dee said. "He'll give us trouble."

Leo simply nodded.

CHAPTER 26

SOFIE APPROACHED the weigh station by Leo's side, huddled deep in her jacket.

Dawn was just breaking and the lights were still on, throwing shadows on the dusty ground that crunched beneath her boots.

She felt out of sorts, the four hours of sleep almost making her feel worse than she had before she'd curled up next to Leo on the big bed in his quarters.

The guard at the gate gave Leo a welcome salute, and as they exchanged a greeting, Sofie studied the small, well-lit guard booth.

It mirrored the weigh station in its building materials and design, but along the roof she saw the first sign of whimsy--the first indication of her father's eclectic style.

A carved stone bird protruded from the end of the gutter, wings spread, beak pointing in a clear direction.

As she followed Leo through into the main area in front of the weigh station's massive double doors, she scuffed the ground with her feet, looking for any designs that may have been worked into it, but although she caught glimpses of differing colors in whatever had been used in the paving, it was so deeply ingrained with ore dust it was impossible to make out.

"What's that?" she asked Leo as they passed a small building around the same size as the guard house, which also had decorative edging around the gutters.

"The control box for the station's power." Leo glanced at it, then made for the open weigh station doors, skirting around the big, wheeled automaton trucks lined up one behind the other. They seemed about to drive into the massive warehouse, all loaded high with ore, but none had their motors running.

The only sounds were the wind, and the intermittent banging of a loose piece of metal as it hit against the side of the weigh station wall.

Sofie looked up at the lintel of the massive double doors as they approached them, and saw two carved depictions of the wind from Halatian myth, clouds with mouths blowing what looked like wavy lines, protruding from each end of it.

They pointed, not forward, or left and right, but both in the same direction, giving them a strangely off-kilter look.

Sofie didn't need to wonder what they were pointing to.

It was a little obvious for her father, but he had never meant for her or Rach to come here, so perhaps he'd left clues that a surrogate less steeped in Halatian myth and legend could read.

Weigh pads filled the interior space, big enough for the trucks to drive onto and be weighed. Beyond them, big transport hovers waited to accept the ore for sale in T-Town, or the few smelters that Leo told her operated just north of Phansi.

"They stopped weighing when the communications equipment with T-Town went down." Leo led her to a set of stairs built against an interior wall of the warehouse. "One of the prospectors managed to get the onsite Cores staff to think it was their idea. It's all about delaying things, now. For as long as possible."

Sofie could see the miners clearly dreaded what would happen when they could delay no longer.

The tension was palpable.

Men and women stood around near the weigh pads, and those who were looking their way nodded to Leo, their faces grim and their eyes worried.

There was a set of offices at the top of the stairs, cut off from the rest of the weigh station by a transparent wall.

A door slid open as they approached and they stepped inside, with Dee and Carver right on their heels.

As the doors closed, they were enveloped in absolute quiet, and the acrid, musty scent of the ore dust cut off.

Four people turned to look at them.

"I didn't know you were coming up to Phansi." The man who spoke was thin, with sharp eyes and graying hair.

Sofie guessed he was a Cores staffer. One of the ones who bought into the fairy tale they could somehow work their way up.

"Hello, Hendric." Leo nodded his head. "I always come up once a month. Now I'm glad I came up a little early. I understand there's a problem with the comm signal?"

Hendric nodded, tight-lipped. "A direct lightning strike. It's not like we haven't had one before, but this time something went wrong." He didn't sound suspicious, just nervous he'd get the blame despite it not being his fault, Sofie decided.

That was business as usual for the Cores.

"Well, given things aren't moving at the moment, would you mind if I showed my friend around?" Leo slid his arm around her shoulder, and pulled her close.

"Your . . . friend?" Hendric's focus swung to Sofie.

She smiled. "I've never been to Phansi before."

Hendric looked across at the other person Sofie guessed was Cores staff, a woman who wore the heavy site uniform of safety jacket and trousers with a sleek style her colleague wasn't able to pull off.

"What's there to see?" she asked Leo directly.

"Plenty, if you've never seen a weigh station or an ore silo before," Leo said to her. "Don't you remember how strange everything looked when you first came here, Suz?"

The woman tilted her head back, possibly annoyed at Leo's reminder that she was an interloper, unlike he was. Then shrugged, as if she didn't care, either way.

"Excellent. Donnie and Ursula, this is Sofie." Leo had turned to the two other people in the room, and while they probably also took their salaries from the Cores, Sofie remembered their names from last night. These were the two Kalo said had tried and failed to reset the algorithm. Part of the conspiracy.

They each sat at a control panel set along the back two walls, and had spun in their chairs when she and Leo had stepped into the room. Neither of them looked thrilled to see her.

"I'll show Sofie around, Leo." Ursula stood up and stretched as if she'd been hunched over the control panel for too long. "You probably have things to discuss with Suz and Hendric."

Leo hesitated, then gave a nod. "See you later." He kissed her cheek, and Sofie just managed not to grin at the overly solicitous way he did it.

"Was that for show?" Ursula asked as they stepped back out of the room and made their way down the steps.

Sofie glanced back and saw Carver was coming after them. "Mostly," she said, and caught the laughter in Carver's eyes.

The controller grunted, and then stopped at the foot of the stairs. "What kind of specialist are you? I heard from Kalo you're a little busybody from T-Town looking for a piece of our action."

Carver made a sound behind her. "Kalo is an asshole, Ursula, one who'd say anything if he thought he'd get an advantage out of it, and you know it."

Ursula paused for a moment, then gave a tight nod of her head.

Sofie looked over at her, decided the hostility level had abated a little. "I'm a specialist in Ronald Fadal."

Ursula frowned. "Then you might want to see this." She lead the way across the warehouse floor to the far side, where there was another enclosed area.

Unlike the offices, it was on ground level; a long, thin lounge area, with couches and jah machines, and no transparent walls.

Until Ursula opened the door, Sofie had no idea what she'd find inside.

When they'd all stepped into the room, Ursula waved her arm in an expansive gesture.

The space didn't look like something her father would design, but perhaps he'd had to be more practical here. It would have irritated him, though, to take beauty out of the equation he always worked to when he built.

She wondered what Ursula thought she would see here. She already read the signs her father had left behind and knew where to go, and it wasn't here, but she took her time looking over the space.

When she looked down at the floor she saw part of a floor design hidden under a floor covering.

She grabbed the end of it, began rolling it back, and Carver stepped up to help her.

She looked at the design for a long time. Lifted her gaze, and looked at the walls.

Although this room was in a corner of the weigh station, the thick sheet metal that made up the structure wasn't obvious here, the walls were clad in a smooth material. There were no windows looking out, as well as looking in to the interior of the warehouse.

"Why did you bring me in here?" She walked to a wall, ran a hand down it, and then looked over at Ursula.

"My father worked on the construction of this site with Fadal." Ursula shrugged. "He told my father this room was the heart of the site. That if anything ever went wrong, my father should run here."

"What is it?" Carver finished rolling up the carpet for her.

Sofie shook her head, crouched down to look at the floor design more closely. "What happened when the algorithm reset?"

"Well." Ursula pursed her lips. "The whole plant sort of flickered. All the power surged, then almost went out, then settled back to normal. But it had never happened before, so we stopped the trucks coming in and put a test weight on a weigh pad. We do it every few months, to make sure the twenty percent under-reading is still in effect."

"Right under the Cores' noses?" Sofie couldn't keep the surprise out of her voice.

Ursula nodded. "Leo made the test weight. It has the weight stamped on the side."

"And that stamp is twenty percent less than the actual weight of it. And no one in the Cores has ever thought to independently check it." Sofie gave a slow, satisfied smile.

Ursula nodded. "It over-read. Or," she shrugged, "read correctly, I should say. We couldn't risk letting any of the trucks weigh in, because there would be an official record of it, so Donnie put out a theory we'd been hit by lightning, and he wasn't getting a signal. Then a few people went up on the roof to 'check' and made sure we couldn't get one."

"Do not, under any circumstances, let a truck weigh in." Sofie rose to her feet. "I need to get to that power control hut."

She headed for the door, and Carver opened it for her, looked out, and then just as casually closed it. "Ursula, you know who those people are who are walking to the office?"

Ursula stepped up beside him, and he angled the door open again.

She peered out. Hissed. "Cores."

They were out of time.

"I need to get to that power control hut *now*." Sofie didn't hide the urgency in her tone.

"You got a spare uniform?" Carver asked Ursula.

She nodded. "Not here, though, in the sign-in unit near the guard house. There are showers and lockers there."

"Too far, will take too long." If someone switched something on, this was not going to end well.

"What do you think is going to happen?" Ursula's stare was skeptical.

"If a truck drives onto a weigh pad, this whole place will explode. My father has set it to blow, and the trigger is the first weigh-in after the algorithm switches back."

There was silence at her words.

Carver's face told her he not only believed her, he understood the urgency.

Ursula looked less sure.

Sofie crooked her fingers at Ursula in a come-here gesture. "Give me your uniform. Stay in this room, because my father built this to withstand the explosion. It's the bomb shelter. Call everyone you can using your comm set and get them here." Sofie held out her hand impatiently for Ursula's jacket.

The controller's mouth formed a mulish line. She turned to Carver. "You buying this bullshit?"

He nodded. "Give her your uniform, Ursula. If anyone can turn this around, it's her."

"Even if this is bullshit, what do you have to lose?" Sofie asked her quietly. "A few hours at most, and a bit of embarrassment at buying my story." She let that thought settle. "And if I'm right, at best you help save the weigh station, at worse, you save the lives of your friends and colleagues."

Ursula shrugged off the jacket, and it was big enough for Sofie to don it over her own. She slid out of her trousers and swopped them for Ursula's in quick, efficient movements.

"How do I get people in here?" Ursula asked, tugging Sofie's pants up over her hips.

Sofie shook her head. "Any way you can."

She stepped out with Carver, putting her head down and staying on the far side of him.

"You think they'll recognize you?" Carver murmured.

She shrugged. "No sense taking the chance."

If Flunky and Tapper had circulated her image as someone to look out for, that could be a problem. But usually execs or techs coming to inspect a mine or plant wouldn't have access to those notifications.

She hoped.

They made it as far as the doors when they encountered three double hovers, just like Leo's, and four guards ranged across the entrance.

"Where are you going?" One of the men tapped the laz he was holding against his leg.

"There." Sofie pointed at the power control center. She kept going, moving with a purpose, but unhurried. Carver strolled beside her, hands in his jacket pockets, body hunched as if against the cold.

"Wait." One of them snapped out the order.

Sofie turned, but kept walking backward. "What?" She made her tone a little irritated, a little bored.

"Who gave you permission?"

She came to a stop, and Carver did as well, angling himself so he could shield her if he needed to.

Oh, no. None of that. No one was being hurt for her.

"Excuse me?" She kept her tone even, her head angled in confusion. "Permission?"

"Who said you could go there?" The guard took a step closer.

"Why don't you go in there and ask?" Sofie said, gesturing into the weigh station. "We have to be at the panel before they try to reboot the comm signal, but if we're not, and it makes things worse, I'll make sure to let them know who stopped us. What's your name?" A sudden gust of frigid wind tugged at her jacket and icy dust pelted her hands.

The guard had to turn his face away for a moment, and the way he moved told her he was starting to regret his challenge.

Beyond the guards, the two Cores techs had reached the top of the stairs, and were stepping into the offices.

Her heart sped up a little.

Leo was inside there. And the first truck that rode onto a weigh pad would set this place up like a conflagration.

The design on the floor of the rec room couldn't have been more clear.

If these idiots didn't let her and Carver go, they would have to make a run for it.

"For fuck's sake, Dyl, you don't know how this place works. This isn't T-Town. Let them do what they have to do." Another guard shifted his weigh, then pulled the top of his jacket closed and rolled down the face protector from where it had been sitting on the top of his head. It turned him into a faceless thug.

"Why don't I make sure you get where you need to go?" Dyl smiled at her with a show of teeth.

"Suit yourself." Sofie spun back and started walking again, and after a moment, Carver fell into step with her.

He looked like he wanted to say something urgent to her, but Dyl was suddenly on her other side.

"What's the hurry?" Dyl asked.

"You delayed me." Sofie hunched deeper into her jacket.

The door to the control room was facing away from the entrance to the weigh station, something her father had surely done on purpose, to give him cover as he came and went.

She hadn't had time to stop and wonder why he'd done this. Set things to explode. It was probably as simple as he wanted everything the Cores touched to burn, and this was the first step.

Followed to its logical conclusion, Felicitos would be next, or maybe it was burning right now. She shook off the thought. She couldn't do anything about it, even if it was.

There was a keypad on the door, and she hesitated for a moment. Her father never wanted her here, so she couldn't assume a DNA identifier would be in place. This wasn't Felicitos.

She glanced at the guard.

"Thought you were in a hurry." His eyes narrowed in suspicion.

"I'm not supposed to open it in the presence of a non-employee for security reasons." She spoke by rote, as if from a memorized rule book.

Carver stood in front of her, blocking Dyl's view. "That should help," he said, but there was a tension in his stance, and she could hear it in his voice.

He was worried she couldn't open the door.

For the first time, she was, too.

She typed in her special code.

Nothing happened.

She closed her eyes for a moment, then held her breath as she typed in the general resistance code used in Felicitos.

The door clicked open.

"Only authorized personnel allowed," Carver said as she stepped through, and he edged in after her, shuffling so that Dyl had no way to come in.

He pulled the door shut, pulled out the laz he'd been holding in his pocket, and leaned back in relief. He didn't say anything--they both knew Dyl was standing on the other side, listening--but the look of exaggerated relief he gave her was funny enough she had to suppress a giggle.

Then she turned to look at the floor to ceiling panel in front of her.

Time to work out how to stop her father's vengeance lighting up the sky.

CHAPTER 27

LEO CAUGHT a glimpse of Carver making his way out of the doors.

The woman beside him was in the bulky uniform worn by weigh station staff, but that made no sense.

He was supposed to be watching Sofie's back.

Leo stepped closer to the transparent wall, and realized the woman could be Sofie. It wasn't Ursula; her hair was a bright chestnut to Sofie's dark brown.

So why was Sofie wearing her uniform?

His comm set chimed as he turned to the door. Ursula.

"You need to distract the Cores fixers coming up the stairs." The controller's voice was urgent.

As she spoke, he saw them walking up. When he glanced at the entrance, he noticed the hovers and the guards.

He couldn't see where Sofie and Carver were.

"Why?" he asked.

"The weigh station is going to blow up if they try to switch anything on."

Leo tried to keep the surprise off his face. "According to who?"

"Your little Ronald Fadal expert. She says the next truck on the weigh pad will trigger an explosion."

"Is that so?" Leo tried to keep his tone neutral, turning away and walking blindly toward Donnie as Hendric and Suz made a fuss of the Cores fixers as they came through the door.

"It seems like it," Ursula's voice was tinny in his ear. "She says the lounge is a bomb shelter, so everyone needs to get in here, or as far from the weigh station as possible."

"Call a meeting." He kept his voice soft, and bent toward a surprised Donnie, pretending to be talking to him. "The arrival of the Cores will make everyone want to find out what's going on anyway. It's a good opportunity."

"True, but Sofie thinks the arrival of the Cores means we're about to have some idiot demanding we switch the weigh pads on again."

That was true, too.

"Where did she and Carver go?"

"To the power control hut."

From his current angle, bent over Donnie's workstation, he could see the three hovers, and the guards who would have made the journey from T-Town to Phansi.

"Did they get through the guards?"

"Don't know. I've got my own job." The strain was evident in Ursula's voice. "I have to start reaching out to everyone. You stop those Cores touching anything." She cut off, and Leo bunched his fists.

He wanted to check that Sofie was safe, but Carver was with her, and as she'd proved to him many times before, she could more than look after herself.

He bent a little closer to Donnie. "Can you stop them switching anything on? Do something to the controls?"

Donnie glanced behind him and turned back. "For a bit, I suppose."

"Anything you can do will help. Fadal set this place to blow at the first weigh-in after the algorithm shut down."

Donnie's eyes widened. "Are you serious?"

Leo nodded, and Donnie's hands trembled as they danced over the panel.

"Leo Gaudier, I didn't know you were here."

Leo turned, and although he hadn't recognized the Cores fixer earlier, he now realized he looked familiar.

There was a beat of uncomfortable silence.

"Oh? Had you heard something else?" Leo asked politely.

"No, no. Just thought I saw you in Felicitos a day or so ago."

Leo shrugged. "Did you just arrive?"

He nodded, and Leo remembered his name, Servos, a mid-level exec. The woman with him must be the tech he'd brought along. She was looking at Donnie, her dark eyes narrowed.

"What are you doing?"

Donnie didn't seem to realize she was speaking to him, and she walked toward him, irritation in her step.

"What are you doing?" She reached his side, and frowned down at the panel.

Donnie lifted his head, a puzzled expression on his face. "There've been some recent power variances. I'm running a diagnostic on them."

"How long does the diagnostic run?" The woman bent a little to get a closer look at the screen in front of Donnie.

"Half an hour."

She straightened with an explosive sound of disgust. "I can't test anything while a diagnostic is running."

Donnie lifted his shoulders. "I didn't realize you were coming right now." His comm set chimed. "Sorry. Have to attend a meeting."

He stood, nodded politely to the woman, and walked out of the room.

Leo decided he would try to hire Donnie away from the weigh station the first chance he got.

If they managed to survive the next half hour.

———

"You should go back to the lounge." Sofie stared at the panel in front of her, and then glanced at Carver. "There is no sense in us both being blown up if I get this wrong."

He shook his head and she sighed.

Behind the big panel in the power control building, they'd found a spiral staircase going down into a small bunker with a panel covering one wall.

"The problem is, I don't think he made a contingency for the explosion to not go ahead." She'd come to that conclusion pretty fast, but she'd hunted in panic for any suggestion she was wrong.

She was just wasting time now, and she knew it. Knew lives were on the line.

"You mean there's no off switch." Carver had stayed out of her way, keeping back as he leaned against the doorjamb and let her get on with it.

"Oh, there's an off switch, but it's for the whole plant, as far as I can work out. Not the explosion."

Her father had obviously wanted the power to shut everything down at will. Exactly what she'd expect of him.

"How long since the Cores execs arrived?"

Carver glanced at his comm set. "Twenty-five minutes."

Panic gripped her again with sharp claws. "We can't wait much longer. And I don't think it'll help, anyway. We'll need to find the bombs and defuse them at their source."

"That would have been fine if we'd managed to get here way

ahead of the Cores." Carver tapped at his comm set, then looked up in frustration. "Still no signal. Probably blocked down here."

"If I switch it all off, we could look for the bombs under the guise of checking for the fault." It was the only thing she could think of.

Carver nodded. "That will have to work. I know some of the prospectors have explosives sniffers for the mines, to make sure everything has been gathered up after a controlled blast. We'll have to get them to the weigh station."

Sofie nodded. Her hand hovered over the switch that would shut everything off.

She wondered again what was happening in Felicitos.

Whether there was a kill switch just like this hidden somewhere behind a panel there, too.

It was looking increasingly likely.

"No downside," Carver reassured her. "It's either this, or boom." He opened his fingers and fluttered them.

She gave a tight nod and pulled the lever down.

CHAPTER 28

LEO LEANED against Hendric's desk, and out of the corner of his eye, he saw weigh station staff and some of the prospectors who'd been waiting with their ore trucks make their way one by one, or in pairs, to the lounge.

Ursula was getting the word out.

There were ten minutes left until the system rebooted.

Leo wanted to walk down to the lounge himself, more to find out if they'd heard from Sofie than for his own safety, but he didn't want to leave the Cores unsupervised.

If he had to shoot them to stop them fiddling with anything, he would.

"Any reason you're hanging around?" Suz had stepped away from where Servos and Hendric stood beside the jah machine, and she kept her voice low.

Leo grinned. "Just want to see what they're up to, is all."

"Thought so." She flicked a glance at the two men, and then glanced at Haga, the Cores tech, who sat at Donnie's station, scrolling through information on the screen. "Looks like she's keeping an eye on the scan. When it's done, they'll want to start everything up."

That's what he was afraid of.

Leo shrugged. "I've got a deep investment in this place, and I don't trust the Cores."

She made a face. "Those are my bosses you're talking about."

Leo said nothing. Suz had to know what everyone in Phansi thought of her and Hendric, and the other Cores employees who lived and worked here.

Servos couldn't have heard what they said, but Leo saw his head rise.

"You got some pressing orders for ore waiting in Felicitos, Leo, that you're here so early in the morning?"

"I do," Leo smiled. "I was just up for my normal visit, but when I got in last night, I was told the weigh-pads were on hold while the comm signal was down, and I came in early to see what was happening."

"You made good time. I know I saw you two days ago in the Upper Reaches."

Leo crossed his arms over his chest. "Shadow prowlers." He leaned back against the wall. "Don't know about you, but I can't sleep well when I know one is around. It tends to make everyone more eager to stay on the road."

"You saw evidence of one?" Suz looked at him with interest.

"Actually saw one in the flesh at Cloud Falls. Thought we heard one about six hours after that." He accepted a cup of jah from Hendric with a nod of thanks and took a sip. "We weren't particularly interested in sleeping out another night after that."

"We saw evidence of one at Cloud Falls," Servos admitted, his tone a little less aggressive. "Probably the one you spotted. Was it big?"

Leo took another sip. "They all look big to me."

Hendric chuckled. "Tell me about it. I've only ever seen two with my own eyes, and both times, I didn't stop to compare how big they were."

"Well," Servos set his cup aside. "If your business here is concluded, Gaudier, we'll be using this office to test the system."

In other words, get lost.

It was nothing more than a dominance move--he didn't think Servos suspected he was hanging around to interfere.

"I'd like to watch the experts, if you don't mind." He set his own cup down.

The look Servos sent him was venomous. "Actually, I--"

"Done." Haga looked over at Servos and gave him a sharp nod. "I overrode the last three checks, so we can get going right now."

Leo slipped his hand into his jacket pocket, and closed it over the cool, hard surface of his laz.

Haga and Servos were talking to each other, and he used the distraction to walk to the window, look down over the weigh pads, and put in a call to Donnie. When the controller answered, he didn't explain or bother with pleasantries, and he kept his voice low. "They overrode the systems check. Tell whoever has the first truck in line to not drive it onto the pad." He cut off the call, and turned around, leaning back against the wall, with legs crossed at the ankles and both hands in his pockets.

"We need to get the first truck moving." Servos turned to Hendric. "What's the process?"

"Either Donnie or Ursula will call them up." Hendric looked around the room, as if surprised neither was there.

"I'll call them in," Suz said, and picked up her comm.

Like Leo, she walked to the window as she activated her comm. "Can you come back to the control center. The system has finished its reboot." She was silent for a moment. "Then leave the meeting early. You're needed here." She cut off the call, and Leo could see she was irritated.

If they refused to come, she'd look bad in front of the execs, and they most likely had never disobeyed her before.

"I don't need them back here to start the line moving," Haga said. She tapped at the screen, and the first truck started up.

"Where's the miner that truck belongs to?" Leo asked, and he knew his tone was sharp.

"I don't need to know, the trucks are all automatons, and the system can control them while they're in the weigh station."

Leo vaguely remembered the wording of the Cores contract, and she was right.

His grip on his laz tightened.

If he shot Haga and Servos, there would be no going back. No working against them in plain sight. No walking the fine line. This would put him firmly over it. And that meant he would be much less effective.

He straightened up, and curled his fingers more tightly around his laz.

"There's someone standing in front of the truck," Hendric said suddenly. "They're waving their arms."

"If they don't move, I'm fine with running them down." Servos stalked to the window to look at what was happening below.

"What can they see that we can't?" Suz asked. "There must be a problem down there."

"I can't see anything--" Haga turned in her chair, and the lights went out.

They were inside the building, with no outside windows, and the darkness was impenetrable for a moment, until Leo's eyes got used to it and the faint dawn light filtering through the big open doors illuminated the interior.

This had to be Sofie's doing.

He smiled.

She always came through.

"I guess Donnie was right to be worried about the power fluctuations," Suz said.

Leo looked out over the massive warehouse space, and saw the people Ursula must have gathered in the lounge were all standing in front of the truck Haga had started up.

Its engine coughed a few times, and then it fell silent, and everyone began making their way out of the warehouse toward the open doors and the light.

His gaze landed on Ursula, and she flicked her hand in a 'come here' gesture.

"Well, I'll let you get on with your work," Leo said. He nodded to Hendric and Suz and walked toward the door.

"Gaudier." Servos's voice was trembling a little.

Leo turned back, eyebrows raised in question.

"We're in control here, not you."

Leo smiled. "Of course you are. Everyone knows that."

———

Leo was walking toward them as Sofie and Carver rounded the corner of the power control hut.

She quickened her pace, unconcerned about holding back.

With Leo, she'd decided some time ago, she was all in.

But he gave a tiny shake of his head when they got close, and she slowed again, and tried to set her face to neutral.

"Could you tell where the power fluctuations were coming from?" he asked, and she knew it was for the benefit of the guards standing nearby.

She shook her head. "It was all over the place. Then it just went down."

"Ursula and Donnie need a word," he said, and turned back toward the doors.

She fell into step with him, and Carver kept pace on her other side.

"That was not a moment too soon," Leo murmured.

Sofie bit her bottom lip. She should have done it earlier. She'd been too cautious.

Donnie and Ursula were waiting for them in a huddle away from the doors, along with about five men and women who she guessed were prospectors.

"What's the story?" Ursula asked as soon as they joined the group. She kept her voice low.

"There's no way to stop the explosions from the hidden board. The only way to do it is to find them one by one and deactivate them individually. My only solution in the interim was to flip the kill switch for the whole plant."

"Shit." One of the prospectors sent her a startled look. "There's a kill switch?"

"Saw it myself," Carver said quietly.

"Shit." He looked around, as if unsure what to do.

"We need explosives sniffers brought down here." Carver was talking to Leo. "And the cover story can be we're looking for the power fault."

"Well, there *is* a power fault." Donnie was looking at Sofie with interest. "I'd like to see that kill switch, if I may."

She nodded, but she didn't know whether that was a good idea or not. Something to think about later.

She watched from the sidelines as things were organized, her gaze swinging around to the Cores guards. They were yawning as the sun finally broke through clouds and shone down on Phansi, warming the air a little, although the wind still cut through clothes and skin, right to the bone.

Hendric came out, with the two Cores execs trailing behind them, and he looked desperate.

"Don't worry, Hendric, we've got all the prospectors on board to help look for the fault. We're just calling them down now. They'll be crawling all over the place in about half an hour."

"We don't have enough equipment for them all." Hendric was holding a screen in his hand, and he obsessively tipped it end over end.

"They've got their own equipment for their own operations. I've asked them to bring it along, so there's no problem there."

"Well, the sooner the fault is identified, the sooner we can start weighing again. It's in their own interests." The female tech's tone was bored.

"You going to help, Gaudier?" The male exec asked.

Leo had been standing with Carver and Ursula, head bent in deep conversation, but he lifted his head and smiled a slow, lazy smile that made Sofie shiver. "You couldn't keep me away."

The man grunted. "Good." He looked over at the guards. "We've been racing through the night to get here. We'll go catch up on some sleep. I hope there's good news for us when we come back."

It was a less than subtle threat, but no one reacted.

Getting rid of the Cores for a few hours was the best case scenario.

No one waved them goodbye, but as they got on their hovers and left the plant, she could see a few prospectors wanted to dance in relief.

CHAPTER 29

LOUD VOICES WOKE HER.

Sofie kept still, and kept her eyes closed.

She must have fallen asleep in the deep armchair beside the fireplace at the end of the kitchen. She could hear the fire crackling and the clink of cups in the kitchen, but most of all, she could hear the anger and bitterness in the voices of the two men and one woman who were talking to Leo.

They'd brought the smell of cold air and ore dust in with them.

The man who woke her up must have thumped a fist on the table. "He'd surrounded the whole weigh station with explosives. We think we've got all of them, and there were twenty. He hid them in the lids of the access tunnel covers."

"I always thought those lids were too heavy." The woman's voice was slightly hoarse, as if she'd spent time shouting. "I was told they needed to withstand a gas build-up in the tunnel when I asked about it."

"Who told you that?" Leo asked.

She was quite a moment. "Renard. He's gone now. Killed in a hijack on the transports before the raiders were shut down."

"You think he knew about it?" The third man spoke.

"Someone had to set it up. I don't see Fadal knowing much about explosions, do you?"

There was silence again.

Sofie thought about it.

No. She didn't see explosives as being her father's strong suit, either. Although nothing would surprise her anymore.

She opened her eyes, and took in the five people standing around the kitchen counter.

Leo stood with his back to her, as if he'd put himself between her and the newcomers. Carver stood to one side, red-eyed and exhausted, and then the three prospectors were huddled close together, their faces streaked with ore dust and their clothes dusty.

"We need your expert to switch the plant back on." The woman lifted her gaze as she spoke, and caught Sofie's eye.

Sofie pushed herself out of the chair. "You sure you've got all the explosives?"

Her voice was a little rough.

Leo turned when she spoke, and she limped over to him on a foot that had gone to sleep, and let him tuck her under his shoulder.

"We've crawled over that plant from top to bottom. If we haven't found one, we're not going to find it." The first man tugged at his ear, watching her.

"Then I suggest that everyone either gathers in the lounge, which is bomb-proof, or stays away from the weigh station when I flick the switch back on." Sofie rubbed at her face.

"What if we haven't found them all?" Carver asked, and then yawned hugely.

"Then the few that we haven't found blow up." The second man shrugged. "We're pushing the limit of what the Cores will accept already. We've had to sneak live explosives out from under their noses for the last three hours. They're starting to get suspicious. They'll be hunting on their own in an hour or less if we don't 'find' the fault and get things going again."

Carver shrugged. "Let them look. Especially if you've found and removed all the explosives."

"And if they do a deep search through the files and find Fadal's fingerprints all over the algorithms? Or if they really, really put their minds to it and find the switch this friend of yours pulled to shut down the plant?" The first man narrowed his eyes at her.

"They'll do anything to make sure there's no disruption to the bottom line," the woman said.

Sofie drew herself up straight. "As long as everyone realizes that once the power is on again, the moment the first truck drives on a weigh pad, whatever explosives may be left will blow."

"We can't find any more than the twenty. Which were enough to vaporize the place." The first man was still bitter about that.

She nodded. "Then let's go."

Leo helped her into her thick jacket and she climbed behind him on the hover, the prospectors following on small, individual vehicles. She pressed her face against Leo's back to combat the wind as they drove through the deepening dusk, trying to shake off the feeling of not quite being in her body.

The search had taken all day, but Sofie decided it was a good thing she was coming back to the weigh station as the shadows grew and the light faded.

It was easier to slip around unseen this way.

They were forced to park at the gate.

Leo had spent the trip speaking to Ursula on his comm, and as they walked through the entrance, the three miners who'd come to fetch her strode ahead, hailing friends and using their comm sets, too.

"I can't go down into the bunker until I know everyone is

clear." Sofie leaned in close to Leo, keeping her voice low. "There's no comms down there, and I don't have one, anyway." Tapper and Flunky still had hers. She hadn't had a chance to replace it yet.

Leo looked up from his comm set. "I need to get you one. Ursula says it's clear. She even has Hendric and Suz in the lounge, but we'd better hurry because she doesn't think she can hold them there long."

Sofie turned to the power control building and Leo fell in beside her, his shoulder rubbing against hers in a way that she liked a lot.

With the power shut off in the weigh station and the people all in the lounge, there was a strange silence in the air, and perhaps because of it, they didn't speak as they walked to the door.

She typed in the code and pulled it open, and then froze at the sight of the woman inside who whirled to face her.

"Haga," Leo said, voice smooth. "Find anything?"

"No." She narrowed her eyes. "What are you doing here?"

"We came to find you." Leo smiled. "There's some sort of meeting in the lounge. They think they've found the problem."

"Oh?" She lifted up her comm set, and obviously dissatisfied with what she saw, lifted her head. "Why haven't I heard?"

"You're hearing now. Hendric and Suz were just called in."

Her lips thinned. "Well, let's go then."

Leo stepped back, holding the door, and Haga brushed past them. Instead of striding off, though, she turned to wait for them.

"I left my comm set in the hover." Sofie patted her jacket pocket absently. "I'll go get it. I'm not interested in the power fault, anyway." She used the bored tone she'd employed often in the Upper Reaches bars where she went to eavesdrop.

Without waiting for a reply, she strode away into the growing darkness.

"She'll care if you make less money because of it," she heard

Haga say to Leo, and dipped her head to smile into her jacket as Leo gave a shout of laughter.

She walked slowly, as if picking her way uncertainly across the ground in the darkness, and then, when their voices faded, she turned back, keeping the power control building between herself and the entrance to the weigh station.

She had just reached the door again, and was typing in the code, when a hand came down on her shoulder.

She spun, heart thumping, and found herself face to face with Dyl.

"Where's Haga?" he said.

She breathed out, trying to keep it even so he wouldn't realize how much he'd spooked her. "There's a meeting in the weigh station. She just headed there." She cracked the door open a little and angled herself so she could slide through it.

"What's in there?" he asked, grabbing the door and pulling it open.

Sofie stepped inside, blocking the entrance. "Just control panels. I'm afraid no non-employees allowed."

"Why are you not in uniform?" he suddenly asked.

"Because I was off duty when they called me back in. Said it was urgent." She put her hand on the inside handle. "Now if you don't mind--" She shoved the door, trying to close it, but he put a massive, booted foot in the way.

"But I do mind. And I think I need to come in and make sure you're not doing anything you shouldn't be."

She stared him down coldly. "If you think delaying the repair of this plant will endear you to anyone, and that includes Haga and your other boss, you're mistaken."

"I'm not delaying anything." The smile he sent her was taunting. "I'm just going to watch you work."

She shook her head, but in a way that signaled she had given up, but was still disgusted by it.

He relaxed, sure in his win, and she lashed out hard, hitting him on the knee with her booted foot.

He gave a cry of surprise, eyes wide, and his leg gave.

She timed it just right, so as he wavered, she kicked him again, this time in the gut.

He staggered back just enough for her to slam the door in his face.

She heard him hammering as she bent to press the button in the bottom corner of the panel, and then she slipped behind it and closed it quietly.

There was risk to this. If he managed to get in, or got someone else to let him in, there would be legitimate questions about where she'd gone, but the prospectors had not been exaggerating their worry that the Cores would start a top down, thorough hunt through the plant if it didn't switch back on soon.

She ran down the steps and into the hidden control room, her hand hovering for a moment over the switch. Dyl wasn't safely in the lounge, but there was no way to get him there, especially not now. She had to hope her father wouldn't have wanted a place he might be hiding in to be near an explosion, and that Leo was in the lounge by now.

He surely must be.

She flicked the switch.

CHAPTER 30

THE LIGHTS FLICKERED ONCE, twice, and then came on.

Leo watched everyone blink in surprise as they switched off the lights they'd been carrying around.

"Who's responsible for this?" Haga looked around the room. "Who called this meeting?"

Donnie raised his hand. "I thought I saw a problem with one of the underground cables, so I had someone go uncouple then couple it again, and then I set a battery powered diagnostic on the panel upstairs. It must have just finished running."

"Well." Haga stared at him. "That's good." She looked around the room. "Who's truck is first in line?"

Gert, who'd been one of the three who'd come to fetch Sofie this evening, raised his hand. "You want me to start it up?"

Haga nodded, and then she jogged out, with Donnie on her heels.

Leo grabbed his arm as he passed by. "Remember, if they haven't found all the explosives . . ." He didn't elaborate further.

Donnie gave a tight nod. "I need to keep her from looking

too closely at my 'diagnostic'." He pulled free and tried not to look like he was chasing her across the open space toward the stairs.

"She came through." Ursula stood beside him, and lifted a sleeve to her forehead and rubbed. "Twenty explosives, Leo. And I nearly dismissed her out of hand."

Leo nodded, opened his mouth to speak, and then closed it with a snap.

One of the Cores guards was limping across to the lounge from the open doors.

He had a sudden, dry-mouthed feeling of panic. He was standing near the door already, and when the guard stepped in, they faced each other.

"Where's Haga?" The guard almost spat the words.

"She just went up to the office." Leo pointed. "What happened to you?"

He opened his mouth, and then paused, and closed it again.

And Leo knew.

"Come, I'll show you where to find Haga." He opened the door, slung an arm around the guard's shoulders as if to help support him, and propelled him out.

He caught a quick glimpse of Ursula, and she shook her head, making the sign of a geyser with her hands to remind him the place could still explode.

He would take his chances.

"I don't need your help." The guard twisted in his grip, but Leo held on.

He was the same height as the guard, although not as bulky, and he tightened his hold as the door closed behind them. "I don't want to help you. I want to know how you got that limp."

"Why?" The guard finally broke away and stepped back, hands fisted.

"Because there was only one other person out there other than the guard at the gate, and she already had a run-in with you today."

The Cores thug thought about it for a moment.

Too long, as far as Leo was concerned.

He stepped forward, putting his arm across the man's shoulders a second time, and moving in to give him a hard, quick, double punch to the gut.

"What did you do to her?" He bent his head forward as if he was sharing a joke.

"Nothing," the guard hissed. "She kicked my knee and then my stomach. I'll be letting management know."

"You do that, and I'll make sure you're standing beside her at some point, so Servos can see how you were bested by someone half your size."

The guard sucked in a breath. "Then you tell her to make sure she keeps out of my way."

Leo's hand clamped harder on the guard's shoulder. "This is her place, not yours. You keep out of *her* way." He stepped back, slapped the guard's shoulder in what hopefully looked like a friendly fashion, and then felt the ground beneath him rumble.

He shot a look at Gert's truck on the weigh pad, saw it was just driving off.

Ursula was suddenly at his side. "That came from near the gate."

They ran out together, and saw the long, narrow sign-in building was no more.

Parts of its roof had landed on the security hut at the gate, but even as they raced toward it, the guard crawled out of the wreckage.

There was a cut on his forehead, but he otherwise looked unharmed.

The same could not be said for Leo's hover, or any of the other vehicles parked beside the gate. They were buried under debris.

Servos and two of his goons arrived as Leo was helping the gate guard to his feet.

"Haga told me the power was back, but what the hell happened here?" Servos jabbed a finger at Leo.

"This is your plant, not mine. How the hell should I know?" Leo kept his tone short.

He turned away and looked at the power control station. He wanted to go there so badly, his hands were shaking.

"When the power went back on, obviously a badly insulated connection started heating up." Ursula spoke as if she were figuring something out. "There's always been concerns about pockets of gas in the tunnels below the weigh station. Renard had heavy lids built over all the entrances to help contain a blast if one ever happened. Gas must have collected under the sign-in tunnel when the power went out and the systems couldn't filter the air, and when the power came back on, it ignited."

Servos rubbed at his head. "Well, what'll the impact be?"

Ursula shrugged. "We'll have to put a sign-in inside the weigh station until we can rebuild."

Servos stared at her. "That's it?"

She nodded. "The plant itself seems to be untouched."

"Then do what you have to do, as cheaply as you can do it." Servos strode off toward the double doors.

"As easy as that," Ursula murmured.

"Different story if it had been the weigh station," Leo said. He started walking toward the power control building, but as he headed there, Sofie emerged from the darkness.

She stopped when she caught sight of him, seemed to sag a little, and then kept going.

She was in his arms in moments.

"You're all right." She spoke against his chest.

"And so are you." He pulled back to look at her. "I saw your victim limp into the weigh station."

"Dyl." She made a face. "Not sure if he was just being an asshole, or if he was planning to do something to me, but he wanted to come into the power control room, and I couldn't let him." She shrugged.

Leo turned with her, to look at the small area where his hover had been parked. "I'm afraid our ride home has been destroyed."

She stiffened. "Leo, we need to get back to Felicitos. If my father set this place to blow after eight years, what's to say he didn't do the same to the tethered way station?"

Leo stared down at her, mouth open. "You think . . .?"

She shrugged. "He did it here, didn't he?"

"But you've never seen something predicting an explosion like the floor mural here anywhere on Felicitos?"

She shook her head. "I haven't. But I can't believe he'd destroy one part of the Cores' wealth, and not the other. Unless he just couldn't bring himself to, because of what Felicitos meant to him."

"We can't go yet anyway." Leo bent his lips to her ear. "We still have the original problem, of the weight algorithm."

"Oh, no." Sofie turned to look up at him. "I fixed that while I was down below just now."

"What?" He gripped her a little tighter.

"It wasn't hard. But it's a year by year thing now. I can't set it for longer than that." She grinned, and then winked, and he realized she knew exactly what that meant for her and her importance to the ongoing scheme.

He threw back his head, and laughed.

CHAPTER 31

HE WOKE HER WITH KISSES.

Sofie stirred, and then slid her hands up Leo's back, tipping her head on the pillow so he could have better access to her neck.

She shivered as he worked his way down, and then gripped him hard to stop him going lower.

He looked up at her, eyebrows raised.

"We need to leave right away. If Felicitos comes down . . ."

She could see the thought was as horrific for him as it was for her.

He sighed, then kissed his way back up.

She stretched beneath him, feeling sated and happy. She caught his face between her palms. "I think I love you."

He blinked. "Do you, now?"

She gave him a slow smile. "Yes."

"Well. And then you cruelly tell me I can't have my way with you?"

"As you've been having your way with me all night, I don't think you're too hard done by."

He kissed her lightly on the tip of her nose. "Perhaps you need a day to recover, having been awake all night?"

She laughed. "Maybe I do." Then she sobered. "I have too many friends in T-Town to be able to relax today, knowing something my father did could have put them all in danger. If Felicitos comes down, will anything survive?"

He sobered. "No. No, nothing would survive. Certainly not T-Town. And I have friends there, too."

He stood, put a hand down, and pulled her to her feet.

For a moment they stood, naked, in each other's arms. She loved the feel of his skin on hers, warm and vital. She took a deep breath, drawing his scent into her lungs.

"I don't think I love you. I know it." His fingers danced across her cheek and pushed a strand of hair behind her ear.

When she raised her head, she found his eyes were almost painful to look at they were so intense.

Someone knocked on the door, and Leo sighed, then dropped his arms to grab his pants.

Sofie kissed his shoulder and then went into the bathroom, diving through the shower and then coming down to the kitchen.

Dee stood at the counter, glaring at Leo's back while he made two cups of jah. "I don't like it," she said.

"I don't like it either, but now that Sofie's brought up the prospect of a similar trap laid at Felicitos, we can't ignore it." Leo turned, saw her, and gave her a slow smile as he handed her her cup.

Dee shifted, thrusting out a hip in irritation. "Carver and I dragged the hover out of the debris last night, and while it can be repaired, it'll take at least a day. But we have a spare, so that's fine."

"We need to go as soon as we can pack up." Sofie could feel the urgency, the panic, rising up in her at just the thought of what might happen to Tether Town if what her father had tried to do there what he'd done here. It burned away whatever comfort just being around Leo gave her.

"You really think Felicitos is coming down?" Zyr's voice startled her, and she almost spilled her jah as she turned to look at him.

He'd kept away from the weigh station yesterday, and so had Kallia. It wouldn't do for them to be recognized by the Cores guards or execs so far from Felicitos.

A pair of maintenance techs from the TWS had no reason to be in Phansi.

But now, after a day's rest and the use of the medical kit Leo kept at his offices, her friend looked himself again.

Sofie nodded. "I don't know how, but there was no way to cancel the explosion here. He'd made up his mind it was going to blow, and he made no provision for a change of heart. I've had time to think about it, and I realized he set twenty-one charges, the same number as the smuggler ships who took hostages from Halatia. He intended it to be payback for the Cores doing nothing to hand the smugglers over the the Verdant String. If that was his intention here, why would it be different for Felicitos?"

"Because he was more invested in Felicitos than here?" Fallia said. "It'll be much harder to destroy, as well. Your father knew how to build for the long term."

"True." She set down her cup. "I hope I'm wrong, but I can't shake the feeling there's a nasty surprise waiting. If it hasn't happened already."

"I'd prefer to stay here another day. The comms signal will be fixed in four, maybe five hours, and then we can contact Finkle, find out what's happening in T-Town. Carver and I also need the sleep." Dee rubbed at her shoulder, but her stance had softened, and Sofie could see she'd been persuaded.

"Fallia and I can each take a hover," Zyr said. "You and Carver can be our passengers. Rest a bit."

Carver nodded, and after a moment, so did Dee.

"Anyway, no chance the Cores won't be listening in to whatever we say over the comm signal, especially not after the last few days. We might as well not contact Finkle for all we could say to each other." Leo pushed away from the wall he'd been leaning against.

"Don't forget Sam is stuck up in the Under Deck, too. He can't get out without me." Sofie had dreamt disturbing dreams of him wandering the tunnels, trying the doors. He weighed on her mind.

"He'll find a way if he really needs to," Dee said, completely sure of herself.

But Sofie didn't think so.

Like whatever her father had planned for Felicitos, she had a horrible feeling she was the only key to the problem.

———

It was long past midnight the following day when Felicitos came into sight, looking like the towering shaft of light it was, the beacon of high tech achievement and advancement the Cores wanted to portray to the world.

It had been five days since they'd ridden their hovers away from T-Town, and seeing it up ahead again filled Leo with a strange mixture of pride and anger.

The solution to getting rid of the Cores still seemed so unclear, if he wanted Felicitos and Tether Town left standing at the end of it.

Ronald Fadal had obviously not seen a way either, his solution to simply destroy the Cores' assets, with only minimal consideration to the innocent victims that could be caught up in it, like the bomb-proof lounge.

But at least Felicitos was still upright, lit up and glowing against the night.

Leo could tell Sofie was relieved as well. She relaxed her hold on him a little.

He made his first call to Finkle before they even reached the city outskirts, and his lieutenant answered straight away.

"Where are you?" He sounded nervous, like he was expecting Leo to say he was still in Phansi.

"Just under an hour out."

Finkle was silent a moment. "Good. That's good. Sam's been collecting a treasure trove, but I think he's ready for someone to relieve him."

"Anything urgent?"

"Plenty." Finkle hesitated again. "I think it's best we talk when you get in. It's clear."

Which meant there were no Cores operatives watching the house at the moment. Something Leo took as a good sign. Although Servos would have passed on the message he'd seen Leo in Phansi. And as far as the Cores knew, he was still there.

They rode directly to Leo's.

Zyr lifted his helmet, meeting Leo's gaze in silent question, and Leo gestured him into the big garage.

There could be no secrets any more. That time was over.

Too much was happening. From the Cores playing dangerous games with Caruso, allying with them, to the near miss they'd just had in Phansi.

It was time to make a move.

They weren't as organized as Leo would like them to be, but the moment had arrived.

There was no denying it.

Finkle was waiting for them, closing the big doors as they rode through them, and reengaging the locks.

He was so tired of living like this. Worried for his life, worried for the lives of his people.

He watched as Sofie lifted off her helmet, her attention on

something Fallia was saying, and felt a wave of fierce protective-ness rush over him.

He wanted a family with her. He wanted them all to be able to live without looking over their shoulders, or having a group of bodyguards wherever they went.

And the time had come to do something about it.

Sofie stored her helmet, then turned to him, and something of what he was feeling must have been visible on his face, because she held his gaze for a beat, and some of the rage in him settled.

"You're probably hungry," Finkle said. "I've got a meal ready."

They all followed him in, and everyone sat around the big staff table and spooned up stew.

"I see the comm signal is back up." Finkle leaned back, the only one without a bowl in front of him. "The plant shut down, then there was a strange gas explosion, but all the problems are now resolved."

Leo frowned at him. "Since when do we have that sort of intelligence?"

"Since we have Sam more or less sitting in on the Cores board meetings." Finkle smiled, a modest, small smile, that said volumes.

Leo grinned. "Of course."

"Why was there a gas explosion?" Finkle asked.

"There wasn't." Dee shoved her empty bowl away from her. "Ronald Fadal had set the weigh station to be wiped off the planet. We found all the explosives except one."

Finkle looked like he wanted to ask more, but he glanced at Zyr and kept his mouth shut.

"The main thing is the weigh station is back to running exactly as it was before." Leo touched Sofie's hand. "But the explosives raise another issue."

"What?" Finkle's gaze rested on their hands for a moment.

"I worry he organized a similar fate for Felicitos." Sofie hadn't finished her stew, but she pushed it away anyway.

"Surely . . . not." Finkle looked at Leo as if he could somehow have the definitive word on it.

Leo shrugged. "I hope not. But it's not an impossible idea. There were twenty-one explosives set at the weigh station and no way to switch off the trigger. Sofie had to shut down the whole place and we searched for the explosives with sniffers one by one."

Finkle blew out a breath. "So what's the plan."

Sofie shrugged. "I'll have to start looking for some clue to what might be coming. As soon as I get a little sleep, I'll get on it."

Leo curled his fingers around her hand and gave it a gentle squeeze. He knew it was weighing on her, far more heavily than anyone else. "Speaking of Sam, what's been happening up there, other than interesting board meetings?"

Finkle rubbed a hand over his ultra-short hair. "The Caruso are weighing that warship down with every weapon they can fit on it, and adding all kinds of other tech." He sighed. "But the main issue Sam picked up was that the Garmen Cores and the Caruso plan to annex Lassa, on a 50/50 deal. The Caruso get half the mineral rights, Garmen gets the other half."

There was a long moment of silence.

"How can the Cores think that the Caruso won't turn on them afterward?" Dee shoved out of her chair and began to pace.

"Some of the execs brought that up in a very heated exchange in the boardroom that Sam witnessed. There seems to be two groups; one lot obviously only have their eyes on the profits from half of Lassa's income, with no investment in mines or infrastructure necessary because they're already there, and the other group is less trusting of the Caruso. They're worried they're looking to expand their influence."

Leo tapped his fingers on the table. "Which group is winning?"

Finkle shrugged. "Not sure either has come out a clear winner, but no one wants to lose the opportunity to take Lassa, so they're going along with it, with a decision to watch their backs and be ready to turn on the Caruso at the first sign of a double-cross."

Leo's laugh was bitter. "It's almost like they've imposed a inter-planetary comms ban on themselves. Don't they follow what the Caruso have been doing for the last ten years?"

Finkle shook his head. "They believe what they want to believe, because it's going to make them money."

"We need to get word to Lassa." Dee stopped her pacing and spun to face them. "Specifically, Ruanne." She met Leo's gaze when she spoke the name of the woman who was running a similar operation to Leo's on Lassa.

Leo nodded slowly in agreement. "Ruanne usually manages to get me a message when one of her ships stops off at the Deck to pick up ore. Eunice has the schedule a few weeks in advance in case I have a message for her. We'll put something together."

"What if it's intercepted?" Zyr asked.

"I always check out the ship and make sure the person receiving it is someone Ruanne's vouched for." Dee walked back to her seat. "I'm officially Leo's inventory manager. It gives me access to the Deck."

Zyr played with his spoon. "There's a resistance movement in Lassa. I got a message a few months after Veld disappeared. Not sure what he did with the ones that came in before, but as they were still coming, I assume he hadn't told the Cores about it."

"Maybe he did," Sofie said, bitter. "And the Garmen Cores were only too happy to hear that Lassa had a resistance that was hopefully undermining the Cores there."

Zyr paused, looked at her, and gave a nod. "Fair point. But now, they need to be warned, as well. And if the Cores here do know about them, they'll waste no time trying to find them if they do take Lassa with the Caruso."

"If you give me the message and who it should go to, I can ask Ruanne to help," Dee offered.

Zyr shook his head. "I need to use my own channels. It's taken me months to set them up, and they won't trust anything coming from somewhere else. But I'll need to check the schedule, see if I can get a message out as soon as possible. When are they planning the attack?"

Finkle rubbed at his face. "Don't know. Not immediately, given the work they're doing on their warship, but not months from now, either. Weeks, I'd say. A month at most."

"So no time at all." Leo tapped his fingers again. "I need to reach out to that contact from Arkhor who sent that message when I searched for information about Veld."

Zyr looked over at him, head cocked meaningfully. "What's this?"

"It happened . . ." Leo looked down at the date on his comm set . . . "six days ago. Sofie was on her way to tell you about it when she was kidnapped, then you were beaten up, we all raced to Phansi, saved the weigh station, and raced back. I didn't have time to share the information."

"You're sure it *is* someone from Arkhor?" Fallia asked.

Leo lifted one shoulder. "As sure as I can be."

"He's tried to make contact every day since you've been gone," Finkle said.

Leo nodded. "I'll leave him a message now." He stood up. "Everyone, get some sleep. We're going to need it."

CHAPTER 32

LEO WOKE HER AGAIN, only this time, they weren't naked in bed, and there were no kisses involved.

Well, only one. To her forehead.

"I have to go out." His voice was soft in the darkness.

Sofie forced herself out of sleepy half-consciousness, and Leo's hands went to her shoulders to push her back down on the pillows as she tried to sit up.

"Go back to sleep, I just wanted to let you know I was going somewhere with Finkle."

She shook her head, swung her legs over the side. "Where are you going?" Her voice was a croak.

He hesitated. "The Arkhoran contact wants to meet me at a spot outside T-Town."

His words forced her to her feet, where she swayed a little as she got her balance. "What?"

"Shh." He pulled her close. "If the Cores see him come in, because my guess is he's piloting in from nearspace, then the situation could turn nasty, so I'd be happier if you stayed home."

Home.

She tilted her face to look up at him. Leo's house wasn't home yet, but something in her warmed that he saw it that way. "Leo, I'm coming. Who's saved that very nice ass of yours the last few times you went into a dangerous situation?"

"Finkle and another of my team will be there--"

She moved away from him, pulling on her trousers, reaching for a shirt.

She heard him sigh.

"When do you need to leave?" She pulled on her boots.

"Now." He sounded a little guilty, and she guessed he'd waited until the last minute to let her know, so she wouldn't come.

"Nice try, Leo." She knew the hurt in her voice was obvious, and when she stood again, he pulled her into his arms one more time.

"Sorry. I just want you safe."

It was her turn to sigh. "Sure, I want the same for you, but none of this last-minute bullshit."

He nodded.

She took his hand as they walked out the door, and she saw Finkle, waiting in the hallway, frown at the sight of her.

She gritted her teeth, but said nothing.

There was no cure for Fink's suspicions but time.

They moved in silence, going to the garage, climbing onto the hovers, and then navigating the streets slowly to keep the sound down and with no lights.

They reached the road out to Phansi, and then turned right, curving back in a wide arc that took them west and then north of the city, along the shores of Lake Felicitos.

Leo must have been looking at a screen with coordinates, because he made a signal and then cut off the engine, and Fink did the same.

The other guard riding with Fink hadn't been introduced to

her, but she'd heard Leo call her Partia when he'd greeted her quietly in the garage.

She jumped down from Fink's hover and moved silently to a spot a little away from them, hiding between the bushes and then going very still, until she almost completely disappeared.

Fink stood beside Leo in an obvious stance of protection, and Sofie stood beside him, fiddling with her bracelet.

Fink gave her a dirty look when the crystals tinkled and chimed as she played with them, but she ignored him, and looked out over the lake.

She hadn't been here in years.

The stink and the decay were too depressing to endure.

It wasn't as bad as she remembered it.

She'd heard rumors someone was cleaning it up, that it was getting better, but she'd dismissed them.

"Are you the one cleaning up the lake?" She turned to Leo as the thought struck her.

Before he could answer, she heard the strangest sound. It was difficult to tell its direction, but Fink and Leo were looking up, so she did, too.

Something was coming down, an engine of some kind, with a frame below it.

In what little light they had, what looked like some kind of nightmarish monster sat in the frame, on a basic seat.

The contraption landed, and four struts automatically shot out, stabilizing the whole thing, and the monster stood up, and touched the side of its head.

The glistening black of its face retracted, and in the faint glow from the light Fink was pointing at the ground, Sofie looked into gray eyes in a bronze face.

The monstrous shape slowly resolved into a soldier in a bulky suit, probably designed to withstand space to ground maneuvers, and when he stepped a little closer, she saw he was more or less the same height as Leo.

"Leo Gaudier?" The man's Arkhoran accent was clear.

"Yes. And you are?" Leo kept a wary stance.

"Captain Mak Carep, Arkhor Special Forces." The captain gave an Arkhoran salute.

"There's an Arkhoran Special Forces warship nearby?" Sofie didn't know what to think of that. Her mother had been Arkhoran, and her stories of her home planet had made both Rach and Sofie long to go there. But Arkhor had left so many of its people to rot here. They hadn't acted, and she couldn't believe they didn't have spies in T-Town. They had to know what was going on.

After all, it seemed easy enough for Captain Mak Carep to come and go as he pleased.

The captain turned to look at her. "And you are?"

"Sofie Erdo." Sofie watched him without wavering.

Erdo was her mother's name, an Arkhoran name, and his attention sharpened. "I cannot comment on the position of Arkhoran warships."

"Why were you so interested in meeting, and in such a hurry?" Leo drew the captain's attention back to him.

"You're a hard man to get hold of," Carep said.

"I was out of town with no comms." Leo kept his stance and his gaze steady. "You must know interplanetary comms are limited here."

The captain gave a nod. "I wanted to know what you can tell me about Veld and Garde, and anything else you might know about what's going on here."

"And why would we do that?" Leo asked.

The captain was quiet for a moment. "Because you're obviously working against the Cores. We've intercepted a few messages between some of your clients, and they lead us to believe you're not following the rules."

Leo smiled. "Maybe I'm just a greedy, cheating bastard."

Carep barked out a laugh. "Maybe you are. But you're a greedy, cheating bastard who is interested in Garde and Veld, and so are we."

Leo hesitated. "Sofie's the one to tell you about Veld and Garde, I never met them personally."

Once again, she had the captain's full attention. "You knew them?"

"Knew? They're dead?" Sofie heard her own breathlessness.

Carep's eyes widened a little. "I'm sorry, I thought you knew that."

"No interplanetary comms," Leo repeated, his voice dry.

"I--" For the first time, the captain looked flummoxed, as if he'd stepped into something he didn't know how to handle.

"How did they die?" Sofie asked.

"Their allies killed them."

"How did they do that?" She held Carep's gaze.

"Are you sure--?"

"Yes." She felt Leo's hand on her back.

"They were buried in the rubble of the ruins of Cepi, when a warship obliterated it with laser cannons."

"You're sure they're dead?" Buried in ruins probably meant no one had seen the bodies.

"We did a full life-scan afterward. They're dead." Carep sounded more and more uncomfortable.

Sofie took a deep, cleansing breath, and then blew it out. She shrugged her shoulders a few times to loosen them, and then lifted her gaze back to Carep. "Thank you," she said, seriously. "That means a lot to me."

His eyes widened even more.

"Veld used to be the head of the Garmen resistance," she told him. "But then he was involved in sending my sister to her death, and questions were asked by other resistance members, me, most of all, and he was ousted. Once someone else got into his files, it became apparent that he had never been the leader of the resistance, but a Cores stooge from the start, and his side-kick Garde along with him. After they were kicked out, they disappeared, some said to do a big job for the Cores."

"Do you have sources who would be prepared to testify to that?" Carep was trying to keep his voice from sounding too eager.

"Testify where?" Sofie gave him a cold look. "To the VSC, who's abandoned us here, and watches from the sidelines, doing nothing?"

Carep was silent again. "What do you mean, abandoned you?"

She narrowed her eyes. "I was brought here when I was ten. Do you honestly think I should be living under a contract my parents signed that stops me leaving the planet? That restricts my rights and forces me to live in a place with no system of justice, crime prevention, workplace safety or environmental protections? Not to mention education." She waved at the strange, bullet-shaped vehicle he'd come down in. "You can obviously get here unobserved, are you telling me you've never sent someone in to see what the conditions are like for the people here?"

"I can't comment on the operations of Arkhor Special Forces." Carep's voice was stiff.

"Of course." Sofie didn't hide her sarcasm. She glared at him, playing with her bracelet as she did so.

Leo's hand ran down her back, as if she were a child needing soothing, and she sent him a glare, too.

He dropped his hand. "Moving on. We didn't, in fact, agree to this meeting to tell you what you wanted to know about Veld and Garde."

Sofie thought, with some satisfaction, that Carep turned to Leo with alacrity. She obviously made the Arkhoran captain uncomfortable.

"Then why did you?"

"If you've got a warship nearby, you might have noticed the Caruso are coming and going from here, but what you might not know is they are currently fitting a warship that looks a lot like the one I saw on the footage from the Cepi incident with as many of their weapons as can fit on it."

"How sure is this intel?" Carep asked carefully.

"All three of us have seen it with our own eyes." Leo twirled a finger to include them all.

"And how did you do that?" Carep lifted both hands in question. "If they were doing it openly on the Deck, we would know about it."

"We have access to the Cores warehouse on the north end of the Deck." Leo crossed his arms over his chest. "We've been watching them for the last week."

Carep looked like he wanted to take a running jump on his flying machine and race off to share the news.

"There's more." Leo obviously had the same impression.

Carep's hands fisted. "I'm listening."

"The Caruso and the Cores have an agreement to invade Lassa. The Caruso are providing weapons and troops, in return for fifty percent of Lassa's mineral rights."

"When?" Carep breathed it out.

"We haven't managed to find out. We think less than a month."

"And the Cores think the Caruso will be happy with fifty percent at the end of it?" Carep's tone was incredulous.

"Some don't. Some worry where it will all lead, but most can only see the shining prize of Lassa and don't want to think about it too much." Finkle spoke for the first time.

"We can't fight the Caruso." Leo's voice was level, but implacable. "I hoped we could fight the Cores, one day, but we can't fight the Caruso. The only way we can win is if the VSC, or at least Arkhor, help us."

"Any other revelations?" Carep took a step toward his stealth flyer.

"What's going to happen now?" Sofie took a step closer to him.

"Happen?" The captain tilted his head.

"If the Caruso and the Cores are getting into bed, threatening Lassa, what's going to happen? What will the VSC do?" Because if they did nothing, it was over. She agreed with Leo, the outcome was clear. They could not fight head to head with the Cores and the Caruso. They would be obliterated.

"Damned if I know." Carep looked straight at her. "You sound like you think they should have done something before now."

"My father was Halatian," she said, and saw him start at that. "I know the VSC has a bad reputation for ignoring their own, but haven't they learned their lessons from before? There are children down here right now, as well as people like me who never chose to come but are trapped. The VSC doesn't seem to have asked after them, or checked that they're all right, but they are VSC citizens."

Carep was quiet for a long time. "I happen to love someone who's Halatian, so I have very strong views when it comes to these things. Probably the VSC should have done what you say. As the closest planet to Garmen, probably Arkhor should have done more--they like to interfere, so I don't know why they haven't here."

"The thing that turned the Halatian Incident around was the images and footage taken by Darline Xan." She hesitated, looked down at her bracelet.

"That's what did it," Carep agreed.

"If I had something like that, I wouldn't want it to go to the Arkhor Special Forces." She looked up at him. "No offense, but I don't trust the leaders. They have to know what's going on here, and they've done nothing."

Carep sighed. "Maybe they do know, and they want to do something, and the politics of the VSC is stopping them."

"Maybe. But that still means their hands are tied." She looked him in the eye. "Captain Carep--"

She hesitated.

"Call me Mak." For the first time, his voice was gentle.

She nodded. "Mak. If I handed you something like that, would you be able to pass it on to someone else? Like the Halatian that you love? So he or she can share it, like Darline Xan did?"

He went still. Then held out his hand. "I would."

She unclipped Rach's bracelet, and placed it in the palm of his glove.

He looked at it thoughtfully, then put it away in one of the many little pockets that seemed to be built into his suit.

Carep swung himself into his chair and turned to Leo. "If there's a change in what's happening with that warship and the Caruso's plans, can you send me another message? I'll keep our channel clear. And if you can't get a message out, I'll be here anyway in two days' time."

"Two days?" Leo asked. "We might not have anything to give you that soon."

"Maybe not." Carep raised a hand, gripping what looked like a lever. "But I might have something to give you."

He pulled the lever down, and it seemed like he was sucked up into the sky.

"What did you give him?" Leo asked in the silence that followed.

Sofie closed her eyes, almost wishing she could take it back. "My sister's life's work."

CHAPTER 33

LEO WAS grateful for the length of time it took to ride home.

He was still feeling the little reverberations of shock at Sofie's confrontation with the Arkhoran captain. And the negotiation she'd made with him.

Far more than the information that was given and received between the Arkhoran captain and himself, what Sofie had brought to the meeting was on another level altogether.

If he guessed correctly, she'd given him a bracelet full of crystal data stores, and it sounded as if what was on them was footage similar to what Darline Xan had risked her life to get fifteen years ago during the Halatian Incident.

Xan's images of the Halatians' desperate straights had spurred the VSC into action, where before they'd simply been arguing amongst themselves and wringing their hands.

If her sister's secrets were what he thought they were, it was exactly what they needed. A solid reason for the VSC to swoop in and, as Captain Mak Carep had put it, interfere.

They could use a little interference, because while he had the money, he didn't have access to the weapons or the staff to launch an offensive against a military state like the Caruso.

And that's where this current path was leading. The Cores had taken the first step toward their own demise, and they would take the people of Garmen with them.

But Sofie's conversation with Mak Carep had thrown up a brand new problem.

Because it sounded like his lover wanted to leave Garmen.

And Leo had always planned to stay and fight.

The idea of her wanting to escape made his stomach sink and his heart heavy.

When they reached the garage, dawn was only moments away, and neither of them spoke as they put the hovers away and made their way back to the bedroom.

Sofie undressed with her back to him, carefully setting each item of clothing over the chair beside what had quickly become her side of the bed.

He heard her climb in, and when he turned from tossing his own clothes in a pile, she was watching him, her big, gray eyes serious.

"Where would you go if you could get away?" he forced himself to ask. "Arkhor?"

She frowned at him. "Leaving used to be my goal," she said. She looked down at her now bare wrist, and circled it with her forefinger and thumb. "I went along with Rach's plans to sneak off Garmen while she was alive, and after she was killed, I wanted to leave because I didn't think there was anything here for me. But it used to weigh on me."

"It did?" He cleared his throat.

"I knew I had an advantage. If anyone could find a way off Garmen, it was me, with my access to secret places. But I never believed anyone in the VSC would care about the interviews Rach had done. I didn't think seeing them would change anything. So I would just be leaving because my life would be better, and to hell with everyone else left behind." She wriggled lower under the covers. Gave a wry laugh. "Then when I made the decision to stay, not getting out the information Rach had risked her life for started weighing on me almost as much."

"And now you've given it to Arkhor Special Forces?" He was at last able to move. He got into bed, and she snuggled close.

"The captain seemed to be telling the truth. I think he will pass it on. And whoever the Halatian in his life is, when they see the interviews Rach did with people on the streets of Tether Town they might recognize parallels with what happened to them. And do something about it." She was silent for a while. "It's not certain, but I think it's the best I could ever have done. Even if I had left Garmen."

He kissed the top of her head. "When did you decide to stay?"

She nuzzled him, and he felt a smile curve on her lips. "After I met you, of course."

He was suddenly above her, arms on either side of her head. "Is that so?"

"Well," she grinned up at him. "Not entirely so, but certainly, twenty percent or more of the decision was as a result of meeting you."

He laughed before he dived in, tickling her mercilessly. He suddenly realized, since he'd been around her, he'd been doing that a lot.

———

Morning came too quickly. The round trip out to the lake had taken two hours, and they'd had a hard day's ride before that as it was.

But Sofie forced herself into the shower, and then down to the kitchen, bumping delightfully into Leo in various states of wake-fulness and undress as they got ready together.

She could get used to it.

Zyr was sitting at the counter, still slightly puffy-eyed, but she put that down to tiredness, not so much the last fading proof of the beating he'd fought off.

Fallia paced beside the massive window that looked out over the plain beyond, fiddling with her comm set.

Dee and Carver were also standing by the window, Dee with a cup of jah, which she sipped calmly, Carver with his hands behind his back.

Finkle leaned back against the wall, arms folded, and watched them all.

"I assume Sam's ready to go off duty?" Sofie looked over at him.

"He is. Carver will replace him."

"I want to come, too." Zyr tossed a tiny crystal bead in the air, and caught it. "I'd like to see if I can pass this on. Fallia checked the logs, and there's a Lassian ship coming in that has someone onboard who's passed a few messages back and forth to us before."

"How did they do that?" Carver asked.

"They requested maintenance on a Deck power supply. We've got a few members who work the Deck, although we've been careful with them, because Veld used to work up there, and we worried they'd been exposed by him to the execs."

"How did they go from requesting tech support to exchanging messages?" Dee's eyes were narrowed suspiciously.

"They didn't right away. It took about four visits, where the questions got more and more pointed, before both sides acknowl-edged there was nothing wrong with the power supply, and we opened a dialogue."

"What Lassian ship is coming in?" Finkle had his screen out.

"The Verden." Fallia paused in her pacing.

"That's a pleasure cruiser." Finkle frowned. "What's its business on the Deck?"

Sofie looked at him in surprise. "Has to be false trade."

She was shocked when Dee, Carver, Fink and Leo stared at her.

"What's false trade?" Leo asked.

"You haven't heard of it?" Zyr leaned back on the counter with both elbows. "It's when two ships want to trade something illegal, but they don't have the inter-ship connection capabilities of a bigger craft, so they have to land somewhere with a grav and enviro system. The Felicitos Deck is a good place for that. They trade something they're bringing in, not something coming from Garmen. They'll stock up with food or something small from Garmen as a pretext for their arrival, but their real acquisition is with another ship."

"How come I don't know about this?" Leo looked at his security people.

Finkle looked a little sick as he shook his head.

"I know because I worked for the Cores," Sofie said. "The Cores know what's going on with false trade. They let it happen, because it sometimes leads to legitimate business, and they try to record what goes down as much as possible. They've got a library of feed that can be used to blackmail certain individuals."

"The maintenance crews up on the Deck see it happening right in front of them." Zyr shrugged. "If you're dealing with legitimate customers, I don't suppose you'd know about it."

"Huh." Leo slid his hands in his pockets. "Well, it looks like word has gotten out to our customers about the problems at Phansi, so I'll be spending the day on the comm set giving them the good news its already fixed."

"I'll be up on the Deck, too." Dee finished her jah. "The schedule Eunice sent me shows one of Ruanne's big carriers is coming in in a couple of hours' time, so I'll go up and inspect the inventory, and find someone to pass along our warning that Lassa is about to be attacked."

"What are you going to do?" Sofie asked Fallia.

Fallia snorted out a laugh. "Believe it or not, I actually have a job, one I've been missing from for the last six days."

Sofie gave a nod of acknowledgment. "Will there be trouble?"

Fallia sighed. "Probably not. The others have been covering for us. And now that Sunny's out of the picture . . ."

Sofie blinked. She'd completely forgotten about Sunny. About how his body was still lying out of sight on the road to Phansi.

"How will you explain him not turning up to work?"

Zyr shrugged, but there was no regret or sadness on his face. "T-Town is a dangerous place," he said, his voice a rumble. "People disappear all the time."

CHAPTER 34

BY THE TIME she reached the final stretch of stairs to the Under Deck for the second time in an hour, Sofie was dragging her feet. She hadn't gotten enough sleep.

She'd brought Carver and Zyr up here first, and when they'd seen the strange image her father had painted on the wall near the top step, they had stopped talking abruptly.

She said nothing about it, and neither had they, but being confronted with it again had made her decide to do some looking around while she was up here.

Sam had happily handed over watch duty to Carver and she'd taken him back to the Upper Reaches, and then turned around and come all the way back up.

She'd returned mainly to fetch Zyr, although the Lassian pleasure cruiser, the Verden, was only due in an hour, but she thought she could use the time while she waited for him to search for a clue as to why slitting wrists was so much on her father's mind toward the end.

She put her hand on the wall and stepped into the hidden passageway, and made her way to her father's office.

She stood, watching the empty room for a long time before she risked stepping inside.

She went straight to the door and saw a laser lock that secured it from the inside. She wouldn't have expected anything less from her father.

She activated it, and then looked carefully around the room.

There was the chair and the couch she'd noticed when she'd been in here before but the only truly interesting things were the desk, and the murals on the walls.

She hadn't had a chance to really look at them before.

She tried the desk first, though.

It had just three drawers on one side. They were secured with a laser lock and she had no expectation that it would open for her--she didn't think it was part of her father's original furniture--but she ran her finger through it anyway, and froze in astonishment when it did open.

She pulled out the top drawer, and found it was empty. The second was, too, but the third held a small, three-dimensional model, small enough to fit on her palm. It took her a moment to realize it was a model of the reservoir at the bottom of the way station.

Inside the cylinder, with its pumps and pipes along and down the sides, were stylized images of water droplets, stacked in diagonals on top of each other, all in the same white material the model itself was made out of. Except one. It was red, and it sat right in the middle of the tank.

She frowned at it, then went still when she heard someone outside in the corridor.

She carefully closed the drawer, but she kept the model to take with her.

She could hear voices more clearly now, but whoever was talking seemed to have paused. They weren't coming closer yet.

She looked at the murals, frowning at the representations of the old Halatian myths. Her father had told her and Rach over and over about the ancient stories of sacrifice, which the Verdant String Coalition now interpreted as the original travelers' struggles when their spaceships landed on the planets that now made up the Verdant String.

Somehow the stories from Halatia seemed to be heavy on the heroic men and women who sacrificed their lives for the greater good.

One caught her eye, the story of Abetal, injured in a confrontation with a ugon, one of the fierce, predatory species on Halatia, choosing to lead the beast away from the others in his group using a blood trail.

She connected it with what looked like a drop of blood in the water of the reservoir. The blood spilled in the murals on the walls. And then the strange, strange picture near the stairs.

She was disturbed to her core.

There was a muffled tap from the secret wall, and it startled her out of her thoughts.

She moved to the secret door and opened it, to find Carver and Zyr standing there.

"What are you doing?" Carver hissed, his eyes passing over her and into the room.

"I locked the door from the inside." She moved back across the room, and listened at the outside door, but couldn't hear anyone any more.

She waved the two men back into the passageway, unlocked the door and then ran to the passageway herself, and closed the door behind her.

"What have you got there?" Zyr was looking at the model in her hand.

"My father's model for the design of the reservoir." She looked down at it, at the red drop again, but if either of them noticed it, they said nothing.

"The pleasure cruiser's here. We just watched it land. It's early." Zyr turned down the passage, and Sofie followed him, with Carver behind her.

They walked up the stairs to the Deck. On one side of the passage was the floor to ceiling window into the interior of the warehouse, and a little further down, on the right, was a large window on the opposite wall with a view of the deck itself.

Zyr was wearing a maintenance uniform, and he pointed to the sleek, silver cruiser, the Verden, which had Deck crew approaching it, wearing the same uniform.

A door opened and a ramp extended down.

Sofie looked around, but she couldn't see anyone looking their way, so she opened the door to the outside, and Zyr stepped through.

She and Carver stood shoulder to shoulder, watching him as he moved briskly toward the craft, and disappeared around the back of it.

"What's the red drop supposed to mean?" Carver asked.

Sofie followed his gaze to the model she still clutched in one hand. "That the filtration system can deal with a small amount of blood?" she suggested.

"Or it needs a drop of blood to function?" he said, a hint of humor in his voice. "Aren't you Halatians into blood sacrifice?"

It wasn't far from what she'd been thinking herself when she'd studied the murals, but something in what he said struck her, something so big and crazy, she actually stumbled back and hit the far wall.

"Looks like Zyr's found his man." Carver wasn't watching her, his gaze was on Zyr, standing close to a man in a light gray uniform, their heads together. "Oh, and there's Dee."

Sofie pulled herself together and stepped back up beside him, watching Dee as she rode a small hover past Zyr without even looking in his direction as she made her way toward a massive transport on the other side of the Deck.

"Bad timing for the pleasure cruiser. It's from Lassa and so's Ruanne's transport ship," Carver said. "If this is a false trade, they'd have preferred no home witnesses, surely?"

"Yes." Sofie wondered why they'd risked it.

She saw something big move from the corner of her eye, and she turned to look at the interior of the warehouse.

She had to stare for a few moments before she could understand what she was seeing.

Two long hovers had come out of the black warship.

A Caruson driver was at the controls of each one, and the strange hovers were built so that passengers could stand and hold a central bar, four on each side of the vehicle.

She was looking at eight Carusons on each hover. All holding the bar with one hand, a massive, alien weapon held in the other.

She hadn't realized there was that many of them here.

"Carver."

The hovers nosed past the warship, and someone working in the maintenance area noticed them.

Called out a question.

One of the Caruso lifted his weapon and shot them.

Sofie heard Carver's breath catch as the tech went down, his face caught in a death grimace of pain.

"They're not taking Lassa. They're taking Garmen," Carver whispered.

"And then they're taking Lassa." She just managed to get the words out.

"Or, there's a group on Lassa right now, doing the same thing to the Cores there. Maybe the Caruso have been playing the game simultaneously."

His guess was as horrifying as it was logical.

As the hovers waited for the warehouse doors to open, she forced herself to focus. "Zyr."

"And Dee." Carver had his comm set in his hand, and Sofie heard Dee's voice come through faintly as she answered. "Heads up, the Caruso are taking the Deck. Unit of eighteen coming from the warehouse--fully armed."

"Now Zyr," she demanded, gripping hard on his arm.

Carver nodded, tapped at the screen.

Before he got through, Sofie turned and saw the doors of the warehouse had opened, and the hovers shot out onto the Deck.

They split up, one going right, the other left, and then they opened fire, the two at the back of each hover pointing their weapons back in the direction they'd come from, the middle four on either side shooting sideways, and the two at the front shooting forward.

It had a devastating impact.

People--either Deck workers or the crew of the hundreds of ships docked to either load or unload goods--were taken completely by surprise. She saw them fall, and her hand was on the door, pulling it open before she thought about it.

"Sofie, no!" Carver's hand closed over her wrist. "Wait for Zyr. He's coming."

She paused, saw Zyr was running toward them, zigzagging away from the pleasure cruiser. He was close, about twenty meters away, when a shot glanced off his shoulder and spun him around.

He went down and she cried out and hauled the door open, and this time Carver didn't stop her. He was beside her as she ran to where Zyr was lying.

He was gray, the pallor beneath the dark brown of his skin alarming to her, but he was breathing.

Without discussion, Carver hooked a hand under one arm,

Sofie the other, and they started dragging him back to safety. It took so long, Sofie expected a hit in the back at any more.

She hit the door with her palm, pulled it open, and then heard a change in the sound of the shots fired.

She turned as Carver heaved Zyr into the passageway, saw the Cores had started fighting back, the bulky black uniforms of the Cores guards breaking like a wave from the hover that had come up through the hoverway.

The Caruso had jumped down from their hovers now, and were spreading out through the Deck, their heavy armor shrugging off the return fire they were getting from some of the transport ships crew.

She caught sight of Dee, pinned down by the crossfire right beside the pleasure cruiser that Zyr had visited.

"Get in." Carver was staring at her as if she were mad.

"This can't end well." It was nothing but the truth. She looked up and there, just above the dome created by the grav and enviro generator, was a prickly, ugly looking Caruson warship.

"Sofie!" Carver's voice rose to a shout.

"I can stop it. I think." She took a step away from the door. Looked at him with her heart in her mouth, sick to her stomach, and yet, she knew there was only one chance here. She had to take it. "Tell Leo I'm riding the roofs." She slammed the door closed, knowing Carver would follow her otherwise, try to stop her.

She spun on her heel and ran.

Behind her she heard a body slam into the door.

But no one could open it except her.

And no one else could flip the kill switch, either.

CHAPTER 35

SHE RACED TOWARD THE HOVERWAY.

She glanced left as she ran, saw Dee had scrambled up the ramp of the pleasure cruiser, and as she watched, rolled through the open door to safety.

It lightened the weight on her.

Dee was safe for now. And Zyr and Carver were even safer, behind the hidden wall of the warehouse.

Carver would have a med kit in his pack, which meant Zyr would have some help.

A Cores guard spun her way as she accelerated toward the hoverway, saw she was from Garmen, and angled a little further to the right, and shot at the Caruson walking toward them both. She didn't paused as they engaged, she weaved a little, making her path a little more difficult to predict, and then she was at the hoverway.

A big gen-pop hover was lumbering down--it was probably the one that had brought up the guards--and she leaped over the edge and dropped three meters onto its roof.

Another hover passed them on its way up, and Sofie looked at it as it came by, saw the surprise on the faces of the guards inside at the sight of her.

The descent was slow, but when they reached the first stop, at the Under Deck, she saw why.

It was stopping to pick up more guards, and it'd be going straight back up.

She looked to the upward side, saw an exec hover filling with slick, well-dressed execs, and guessed they were not going up, even if they were on the wrong side.

She ran to the edge of her hover, close to the loading ramp, and heard a few calls of surprise from the guards below at the sight of her. She turned around and used the distance across the roof to wind up for a running jump.

She threw herself across the narrow space between the two hovers, and landed hard on the roof, rolling a few times before she managed to stop.

It dropped, almost as if it had been waiting for her, and fell so fast, the wind it generated buffeted her, forcing her to crouch into a tight ball in the middle.

She would need a knife.

The reality of that slammed into her, because she wouldn't find one on the roof of a hover.

She lifted her head, her eyes watering as she looked around for some sharp edge instead.

She could see nothing.

The hover suddenly decelerated, and she risked standing and taking a few steps to the edge to look over and see what was happening.

They were approaching the Upper Reaches, and there were other hovers in the way.

"Sofie!"

She saw Leo fighting through a crowd of people all queuing for a place in the hover docked at the Upper Reaches loading bay.

Before she could respond, the hover she was on jerked sideways, taking a gap in the traffic on the upward lane, and passing the hover blocking the way.

She fell, rolled, and then lay flat as it moved across the hoverway. By the time she got her hands beneath her, she just managed to catch a glimpse of Leo's face, stark and determined, before the hover dropped, down, down toward the bottom, still tens of thou below.

She didn't know how long they dodged and wove between the hovers, but they came to a stop on the Lower Reaches, and she realized with a start the execs were going to grab their more precious possessions from their apartments before they abandoned Felicitos.

The hover docked, and she risked standing up again and walking to the edge.

A guard pointed a laz at her from the loading bay, and she backed away, out of his range.

There seemed to be a few guards keeping the area free of the gen-pop. Because heaven forbid the execs would have to deal with frightened T-Towners while they loaded up their riches.

She turned to the other side, looking up and down to see what was coming her way.

There was nothing docked on the opposite side, but she could see hovers above her making their way down. Nothing was coming up.

The word must be well and truly out on what was happening above.

She kept her head tipped up, waiting for something to come down that was headed right to the bottom, and she saw a hover going faster than the usual slow, steady pace.

It passed other, slower hovers in a fast path downward and she expected it to race past her.

She braced, ready to jump as it came by.

But it slowed as it reached the dock on the opposite side of the hoverway, and she hesitated.

If the execs in the new hover were also going to grab their stuff, the one she was on now would likely leave sooner.

"Sofie. Jump on."

She stared in shock as Leo leaned out of the window and pointed to the roof.

Then his hover drifted even closer to hers and bumped into it, rattling it in its harness where it was docked to the loading bay.

She jumped.

"Are you all right?" Leo's voice was a little frantic.

"Yes. Can you go down to the bottom?"

He was silent for a moment. "Yes."

The hover began to move, at a far slower pace than it had before.

"You can go faster. You need to go faster."

It sped up a little, but not as much as she would like.

"Do you have a knife in there?" she called.

"A knife?" He sounded strained. "Why do you need one?"

"To cut myself."

He was quiet, and their descent slowed.

"Leo, go faster and give me a knife!"

She wondered what was happening above. What carnage was being wrought.

She looked up, and saw her original hover was coming back down again, catching them as it sped to the bottom.

"Leo, please get word to the crew and techs of the Deck that the enviro and the grav is about to go. Get them to sound the alarm."

"About to go?" His voice rose.

"I'm about to flip the kill switch," she shouted, bending her knees, getting ready for the jump.

"You found it?"

"I am it," she said, and then she leapt.

———

Leo watched Sofie drop past him, her face grim and set, crouched low on the roof of a high-end exec hover.

She had wanted a knife. To cut herself.

He had honestly not known what to make of that.

"It's like that little picture on the stairs, isn't it?" Sam's voice was quiet. He'd been giving Leo an update on his time prowling the secret corridors of the Under Deck when Carver had sent him a desperate message that Sofie was riding the hover roofs again.

Leo nodded. "She must have figured out what it means." He could think of no other explanation.

"Do we warn about the enviro and grav going?" Sam asked.

Leo walked to the tiny serving hatch set into the luxury hover he'd commandeered. "Yes. If she's going to flip the kill switch, everything on the Deck will be sucked up into space." Including the Caruso. It was brilliant. And it seemed she was prepared to sacrifice herself to do it.

The thought slid ice through his veins as his hand closed around a small, sharp fruit knife.

Sam lifted his comm set, and Leo put in a call as well.

"Dee?" He'd already heard from Carver, had barely been able to understand from the shouting that Sofie had simply jumped into the hoverway, but he gathered Carver and Zyr were safe.

Dee was still up there, though.

And she had to be all right.

"Yes." Her answered was so quiet, he had the sense she was trying not to attract attention.

That was fine, he'd do the talking.

"Are you somewhere safe if the enviro and grav fail on the Deck? If not, get yourself there, because Sofie's about to flick the kill switch."

"That's . . . good." Her whisper was approving. "I'm in Zyr's pleasure cruiser. Look for me afterward."

She cut off the link, and Leo slid his set in his pocket. He stood at the window and looked down on Sofie as she rode to the bottom.

He didn't understand how she was the kill switch, but it involved her blood. He fisted his hands in frustration that he hadn't asked her when he had the chance, and he hadn't done as she asked. If he had, she might still be riding the roof of his hover.

It meant he was chasing her again, instead of helping her.

It would only take minutes to the bottom at this speed, although it felt like they were moving slowly through thick, viscous air.

The hover Sofie was riding slowed as it reached the bottom bay, and he kept close watch, expecting her to clamber down the side and make for the exit gate.

Instead she walked to the opposite side, looked down into the big water reservoir, and then jumped.

He punched the speed on the hover as the water closed over her head.

What had she said at Cloud Falls. She wished she'd learned to swim.

Panic held him by the throat.

"Hold it steady when we get to the water," he managed to choke out to Sam, and they slid past the final bay, down another level until they were above the water, the hover churning up the surface.

He couldn't see Sofie, but he climbed onto the sill of the

window he'd had to break, because it wasn't made to be opened, and then lowered himself, hanging onto the sill with one hand.

He searched the water, frantic, knowing just jumping in without an idea of where she might be would be a waste of time.

A dark head rose up, and he heard Sofie choke out a breath before she went under again.

He pushed off the side, into water that was warm on the surface, but he felt the chill deeper down.

He swam to the point he thought she'd surfaced and then let himself go under.

She was a little further away than he'd thought, and he kicked himself in her direction, managing to grab her arm.

He hauled her up and she thrashed, coughing, until he got her in a headlock, head tipped back so they were both looking up the hoverway.

"I tried to bite my tongue." She heaved in deep breaths while she spoke, turning her head to cough up more water. "I don't think I got any blood, though."

She lifted a hand and while he was pulling them toward the side, he saw her try to scratch at her wrist.

"Stop, Sofie." He shook her a little.

"I have to." The face she turned toward him was all eyes and determination. "There needs to be some of my blood in this reservoir."

He was holding her with both arms, but he let go with one, fought the water and his clothing, and drew out the small, sharp knife.

She saw it and relaxed against him.

"Thank you."

"Do it carefully." They had reached the side, and he hooked an arm around the curved metal bar he'd been making for and held her with both hands.

She ran the tip of the knife along a vein on her wrist, and then dipped her arm into the water.

Nothing happened immediately.

"Do you think it needs more blood?" Her voice was a whisper, although above them people were shouting, and Sam had brought the hover almost directly above them.

"I don't know." If Fadal was alive, he'd kill him, Leo thought grimly. He would happily feed *his* blood to the reservoir.

"On the model it looked like it only needed a little, but then, this is a huge amount of water. I don't know how much is enough."

She had her arm in the water, and Leo lifted it, saw she was still bleeding.

Sofie lifted her uncut arm, swopped the knife into her other hand, and cut again.

Leo tightened his hold and then loosened it a little when he saw her wince.

She thrust both arms into the water, and then tipped her head back so it rested on his shoulder.

"Thank you."

"I think your father is a shit."

She laughed. It was weak, and ended on a cough that alarmed him.

"I thought so, too. What a stupid kill switch. He was a little too into Halatian blood sacrifice myths."

"You aren't going to die." He would make sure of it.

She opened her eyes, tilting her head to look at him. "If I don't, it's thanks to you."

He didn't care if there wasn't enough blood in the water. He was about to pull her out and haul her up onto the bar, which he realized was one of several, set as rough steps up to the bottom loading bay, when all the lights in Felicitos went out.

CHAPTER 36

THEY CLIMBED out of the reservoir by the faint light coming from above, pouring through the open doors at the entrance.

As Leo helped pull her up the last bit, a body fell from above, hit the hover Sam had parked at the upward dock of the hoverway and slid so that its feet poked over the edge.

It was a Caruson.

She got her feet under her and looked up as she stood, and saw a muddle of hovers all coming down as fast as they could. Some would have to stop on the higher levels and the passengers would have to take the stairs out. They were already stacked three hovers high.

Another body smashed into a hover with the terrible sound of flesh meeting metal, and she felt the burn of nausea in her throat.

She was responsible.

She shivered as her clothes clung to her skin and the air chilled her, and tried to tell herself shutting Felicitos down had surely saved T-Town--maybe even the whole of Garmen--from the Caruso.

"Let's go." Leo put an arm around her and Sam was suddenly on her other side.

The main platform was full of people, jostling and fighting to get out, and whatever possessions the execs had stopped off to retrieve from their apartments, they were having a hard time keeping hold of them in the push and shove of the crowd.

Leo shielded her as best he could as they were swept up in it, moving through the crush to the big doors that led outside.

They stepped out into rain--the fine, relentless downpour that defined T-Town--and onto ground that was churned-up mud, slippery and treacherous.

In the chaos, people went down, falling beneath trampling feet, although Sofie was pleased to see them being hauled back up by those around them.

She felt Leo's hand on her arm tighten and she looked over and followed his gaze.

Captain Mak Carep of the Arkhor Special Forces stood to one side, and men and women in the same uniforms were spread out beside him.

She looked back across the stampede, and through the crowd she could see more Arkhor troops.

"What do you know," Leo murmured in her ear. "Looks like the real invasion was happening on the ground."

Mak gestured to them, and they angled through the crowd to meet him.

High, high above them, hidden from sight by the thick cloud, something exploded, and she hunched her shoulders.

"Do you know who shut the way station down?" Mak asked.

Sofie shivered. She was cold, and although she'd been wet before she'd stepped out into the rain, the wind outside chilled her to the bone. "I did."

Mak gaped at her. "By yourself?"

"By myself." If there was any blame for this, she would take full responsibility.

"And can you turn it back on?"

She hesitated. "Why?"

"The danger is over now. It would be better if the Deck is usable."

Another boom echoed from above, and she looked up, skeptical.

"Better for whom?" Leo asked. His gaze flicked over the special forces teams who were herding the crowds to one side.

"There is still a bit of fighting going on in nearspace, but it's just the last bit of Caruso resistance. We'd like to land on the Deck, if the enviro and grav can be restored."

"Why would you like to land on the Deck?" Leo kept his gaze on Mak steady.

"This is a takeover," Mak admitted. "Garmen will get full vassal status until you're stable, then full-fledged membership of the VSC. And we'll want locals working for us from the start."

"Why now? Because the Cores made a devil's bargain with Caruso?" Sofie asked.

"Because of that," Mak agreed. "And then they obliged us by attacking Felicitos. On top of that, your sister's interviews didn't hurt." Mak rubbed the back of his neck.

"Surely no one's had time to see them?" Sofie didn't bother to keep the suspicion out of her voice.

"I sent the information to my . . . friend, Dr. Nyha Bartoli, straight after I met you last night, and she watched them right away. She put a few up almost immediately after that, and it has made things a great deal easier for the VSC to intervene here--they got full council support."

So, Rach had been right. Watching real people talk about their lives was the key.

"So." Mak watched her with a frown. "Can you switch it back on?"

She hugged herself. "I think it will switch on by itself. After my blood works its way through the filtration system."

Mak stared at her, and she held out her wrists. "My father was very into the Halatian sacrifice myths," she explained.

"You stopped it with a . . . blood sacrifice?" Carep's voice rose at the end. "Who was your father?"

Sofie winced. "Ronald Fadal, the architect of Felicitos."

Leo must have given the captain a look or gesture, because his voice softened. "However you did it, it was inspired. It meant the VSC could engage the Caruso warship in Garmen nearspace without worrying about them taking hostages, or controlling Felicitos."

"How many innocent people died up there?" Sofie asked quietly. "There had to be some."

And she would have to live with that.

"There were Core guards who died while they were fighting the Caruso," Mak said. "But someone got a warning out to the crews and the maintenance techs that the enviro field was coming down. We had some spies amongst the crew on the Deck, and they're all safe. I think the Caruso and the Cores were the only big losers."

"What now?" Leo asked, pulling Sofie to his side. She curled her arm around his waist to get closer and share some body heat.

"Now we wait for the power to come back on so we can check what's left on the Deck, and we deal with what's left of the Cores." Mak grimaced.

"Will you be dealing with them personally?" Sofie asked, and his lips twitched.

"No."

He seemed approachable again, his blank, stern face had softened a little.

"Tell me, why did the council react so strongly to my sister's interviews? There couldn't be anything in them the VSC didn't already know."

"True." Mak pulled something out of a pocket and shook it out, handed it to her. It was a thin blanket, and she draped it over herself and Leo and felt the instant warmth. "But there was nothing about what was happening to the Halatians they didn't know either, fifteen years ago. It took Darline Xan's images and visual feed to bring the reality home. And it took your sister's thoughtful questions and gritty filming to teach us a lesson in empathy again."

"What are you going to do to about it? About those stories?" A flash of light came from above, strong enough to pierce the heavy cloud, and Sofie clutched her blanket tighter.

"It's not up to his discretion." Leo tore his gaze from the clouds. "We're working under the VSC rules now."

Mak hesitated, then gave a nod. "VSC rules apply."

That was all she and Rach had ever wanted. Fairness. Equality for everyone. Freedom.

They had won.

CHAPTER 37

THE POWER DID COME on by itself.

Sofie went almost weak with relief when the way station hummed to life. She realized in that moment that she'd never noticed the sound of it before, but it was a sweet, sweet melody to her ears.

She was warm and dry, having gone back to Leo's to shower and change.

Leo was edgy and restless, wanting to get to the Deck as quickly as he could, and he seemed to be taken by surprise when she led him and Sam through the backways and to the underground tunnel again.

"We can take the lift to the Lower Reaches. More likely to get a hover from there."

He gave a grateful nod, but there were no hovers on that level when they got there. They were all still down below.

They took the stairs, and then the secret staircase back up to the Under Deck.

She stepped from the stairwell to the hidden passageway and

then stumbled to a halt.

Through the one way wall she saw Cores execs lying dead, strangely positioned up against walls or on the floor.

"When the grav and air went, they're close enough to the top, they would have floated. Been pulled upward." Sam leaned against the wall and looked at the scene calmly.

"I didn't even think of that." Sofie couldn't believe she'd forgotten what would happen this high up.

"Are you feeling bad, Sofie-girl?" Zyr asked, and Sofie gave a cry of relief and spun around, leapt into his arms.

He grunted a little, and she eased back, remembering he'd been hit in the arm.

"How are you okay, when they're not?" Sam asked.

"Seems like your father made sure this floor was completely insulated. We didn't lose air." Carver patted Sofie's shoulder. "They were open to the hoverway on their side, don't forget, and fortunately for us, your father knew how to build a solid door."

Sofie remembered the sound of him throwing himself against a door her father had built, trying to stop her from running toward the hoverway, and she winced.

"Sorry about shutting you in earlier. I worked out how to flip the kill switch. I had to go."

He nodded, his gaze going to Leo a little nervously.

"What did she do?" he asked.

Carver sighed. "She held the door while I dragged Zyr into the passageway, then she slammed it shut in my face and I couldn't open it. I had to stand and watch her run straight for the hoverway and jump in."

"How did you flip the switch?" Zyr asked, his hand going to his upper arm, rubbing it as he spoke.

"I rode the roofs all the way down, jumped into the reservoir, and cut myself so I would bleed into it."

There was an uncomfortable silence for a moment.

"That is fucked up." Carver shook his head. "Your father could build a door, but he was nuts."

"That's what he was trying to do when they poisoned him." Zyr's words were soft. "He knew he was dying, and he tried to shut it down."

Sofie nodded. "What's the damage up there?"

"Everything that wasn't tied down is gone, and even some things that were tied down are gone." Carver looked over at Leo. "I don't know what happened to Dee."

"She managed to get into the pleasure cruiser from Lassa that Zyr was interested in. She said she was all right, that we must look for her when it was all over."

"Well then," Sofie turned away from the death in front of her. "Let's look for her."

———

Dee wasn't there.

Leo had hoped they'd secured the pleasure cruiser to the Deck, but he knew few did. The enviro and grav meant it wasn't required, but he'd held out a tiny bit of hope.

But that just meant the ship had floated off into nearspace.

Either Dee would start it up, if she could, or if she was onboard with other crew, ask for a lift home.

A hint of unease settled over him. Because if she was stuck onboard with others, she would be vulnerable.

They stepped out onto the Deck, which was more or less deserted.

Whatever maintenance and loading crew had been here, they were still below, and most of the goods and ships that had been here were now space junk.

A big transporter came in to land on one of the pads painted onto the deck. Leo stopped to watch the doors open, and more Arkhorans jump out.

It would be useful to use the hidden passageways to spy on the Arkhoran officials and whoever else the VSC sent.

He smiled a little at the thought, but he didn't have serious concerns about the fairness of things.

If the VSC was tempted to circumvent their own rules by the mineral wealth of Garmen, it seemed the interviews Sofie had given Mak had turned the tide in sympathy for the plight of the Garmen inhabitants.

His comm set buzzed.

"Looking for something specific?" Mak asked.

So, their presence had been reported.

"One of my close associates took cover inside a Lassian pleasure cruiser. I want to find it and get her out."

Mak put him on hold, then came back. "The warships have just started sending out tows to bring the transports and the cruisers back in. Have you tried reaching her comm set?"

"Yes. No response. Too far away in nearspace, probably." He hoped. "What about Lassa? Have you warned them they're next on the Carusons' list?"

"We contacted Lassa." Mak paused, as if thinking through whether or not to share the information. "The Lassian Cores claim they're still in control. Maybe they are, but Bodivas is the closest Verdant String planet to Lassa and they'll send a few warships that way immediately. Find out what's going on."

Leo caught something massive moving out of the corner of his eye and turned to see an Arkhoran warship slide over the Deck.

It couldn't land, it was too big, but smaller craft fell from below it, like a shoal of fish beneath a leviathan.

"Looks like your friends are here," he said to Mak.

"Your friends, too, Leo," Mak answered.

Leo hoped he was right, but from the smile on Sofie's face, she believed it.

"You look happy." He pulled her close.

She rose up and kissed him, and he found himself pulling her in closer, deepening the kiss until he felt almost dizzy.

When he lifted his head, she was watching him with eyes that made him catch his breath.

"This can be home," she said.

"Actually," he kept an arm around her, stepped to the side and looked out at the curve of the planet far below them, "it already is."

COMING NEXT ...

As I was getting to the end of Breakaway, I realised that the story couldn't finish with the end of Sofie and Leo's story. Even though I'd already planned to dive into a different Verdant String story, I knew I had to follow Dee on her adventure.

If you'd like to get notification of when the second Breakaway book is coming out, please subscribe to my new release notification list. I'll let you know when I have a new release, and occasionally inform you of giveaways and special offers. Sign up to my new release notification list at my website: michellediener.com.

Best wishes

Michelle Diener

ALSO BY MICHELLE DIENER

SCIENCE FICTION NOVELS

Sky Raiders series:

Sky Raiders

Calling the Change

Shadow Warrior

Class 5 series:

Dark Horse

Dark Deeds

Dark Minds

Verdant String series:

Interference & Insurgency Box Set

(Interference also appears in the anthology Orphans in the Black but Insurgency is a new, 45,000 word short novel.)

———

HISTORICAL FICTION NOVELS

Susanna Horenbout and John Parker series:

In a Treacherous Court

Keeper of the King's Secrets

In Defense of the Queen

Regency London series:

The Emperor's Conspiracy

Banquet of Lies

A Dangerous Madness

Other historical novels:

Daughter of the Sky

———

FANTASY NOVELS BY MICHELLE DIENER

Mistress of the Wind

The Dark Forest series:

The Golden Apple

The Silver Pear

———

SHORT PARANORMAL FICTION

Breaking Out: Part I (Short story)

Breaking Out: Part II (Novella)

ABOUT THE AUTHOR

Michelle Diener is an award winning author of historical fiction, science fiction and fantasy.

Michelle was born in London, grew up in South Africa and currently lives in Australia with her husband and children.

You can contact Michelle through her website or sign up to receive notification when she has a new book out on her New Release Notification page.

Connect with Michelle
www.michellediener.com

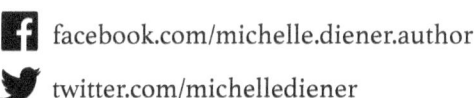

 facebook.com/michelle.diener.author
 twitter.com/michellediener

ACKNOWLEDGMENTS

Thank you so much to Edie, Justin and Jo for your eagle eyes and great suggestions as always, as well as to my awesome reader team! Thanks as always to EJR Digital Art for the truly beautiful cover!

www.ingramcontent.com/pod-product-compliance
Lightning Source LLC
Chambersburg PA
CBHW030633110726
47901CB00002B/434